THE LAST REFUGE

Recent Titles by Clive Egleton from Severn House

A DYING FALL

NEVER SURRENDER

THE RENEGADES

A SPY'S RANSOM

THE SKORZENY PROJECT

THE SLEEPER

THE LAST REFUGE

Clive Egleton

This title first published in Great Britain 2006 by
SEVERN HOUSE PUBLISHERS LTD of
9–15 High Street, Sutton, Surrey SM1 1DF.
First published in Great Britain in 1972 under
the title *The Judas Mandate* by Hodder and Stoughton.
This title first published in the USA 2006 by
SEVERN HOUSE PUBLISHERS INC of
595 Madison Avenue, New York, N.Y. 10022.

British Library Cataloguing in Publication Data

Egleton, Clive
    The last refuge
    1.   Garnett, David (Fictitious character) - Fiction
    2.   Military occupation - Great Britain - Fiction
    3.   Alternative histories
    I.   Title
    823.9'14 [F]

    ISBN-10: 0-7278-6182-4

Printed and bound in Great Britain by
MPG Books Ltd., Bodmin, Cornwall.

Author's Foreword

When I started to write *The Last Refuge*, my publisher was already talking about commissioning another three novels on the Resistance theme. *Never Surrender* was the story of ten days in the life and death of a resistance cell, when everything that could go wrong did go wrong. *The Sleeper* dealt with a split in the Resistance movement and the ambivalent attitude of the population towards the Resistance and what the Russians called terrorist crimes.

Since I had only one more theme left, I felt the plots would become more and more repetitive with each book. *The Last Refuge* was therefore written in such a way that the theme could not be resurrected.

'Patriotism is the last refuge of a scoundrel'

Boswell's *Life of Johnson*

1

THICK FROST SPARKLED ON the roofs, traced fern-like patterns on the window panes and carpeted the quiet streets.

At the dead hour of three o'clock in the morning, a black Austin Westminster turned into South Hill Avenue and purred up the steep incline towards Harrow on the Hill. Just two kilometres away, on the Roxeth Road, another car pulled into the kerbside and dropped off three men who climbed over the wooden fence surrounding the school playing fields. As they crossed the flat ground and approached the forward slope of the hill below St. Mary's Church, they fanned out and advanced in extended line like a row of beaters. On the other side of the Hill, directly opposite but out of sight of the advancing trio, a line of eight plain-clothes policemen were picketing the open ground forward of the main road to Wembley. Every road, lane or alley which led up to the Hill had been sealed off with a road block. The Hill was now cut off from the surrounding town by a cordon which had moved into position without being detected.

The Austin Westminster went through the road block at the top of South Hill Avenue, turned left, and still climbing, passed the turn-off to the hospital. There were four men inside the car. They were Chief Superintendent Hulf

7

and three hand-picked sergeants from Special Branch—Parker, Stratton and O'Dwyer. O'Dwyer was driving with Parker sitting alongside him. In the back, beside an impassive Hulf, Stratton was screwing a bulbous silencer on to the barrel of the specially modified Webley .38. He was the only one so armed; each of the others carried a Browning 9mm twelve-shot automatic. They had spent some hours studying photographs and a scaled model of the building which was to be raided, and each man knew to the split second exactly what he had to do.

The road levelled off and then narrowed as they approached the King's Head Hotel. Just before they reached North Street, O'Dwyer reduced their speed appreciably and then, as they passed the intersection, he flicked off the headlights, swung into the kerb and pulled up outside a shop with twin bow-fronted mullioned windows. The gilt lettering on the white signboard above the door said, 'Hawes—established 1869.'

The four men got out of the car and, leaving the doors partially open, crept across the pavement and took station on either side of the entrance. On a hand signal from Hulf, Stratton fired twice into the lock. The Webley made a faint plopping sound and then the door burst open as Hulf put his shoulder to the broken lock. They catapulted into the shop and started to scatter to the left and right, anxious not to be trapped in the narrow entrance.

They were fast, but the gunman inside was faster. A shotgun blasted a spread of pellets which hit Parker in both thighs, abdomen, stomach, chest and face and shattered a display cabinet of Dresden porcelain. O'Dwyer, who was behind Parker, jumped back into the street and threw himself sideways. As he did so, the sawn-off twelve bore spoke again and the pellets thudded harmlessly into the bodywork of the Austin Westminster. Lying on his side, and protected by the low brickwork beneath the mullioned windows, O'Dwyer was able to reach up and shatter one of the thick panes of glass with the butt of his automatic. Twisting on to his back, he pulled the heavy duty flashlight out of his overcoat pocket, and then, rolling on to his right side again, he poked the flashlight through the broken pane and trained the beam against the ceiling in the far corner

8

of the room roughly above the spot where he thought the gunman was concealed.

The reflected light from the ceiling picked out a grand-father clock to the left of the back door, an oval-shaped dining table and a large mahogany writing desk on the top of which stood an oil lamp. The desk was at the back of the shop and facing lengthways on to the front door.

Although the light was playing tricks with his eyes, Hulf felt sure that someone was crouching behind the desk, and, keeping his back against the wall, he began to inch his way cautiously down the right-hand side of the shop so that he would be in a position to get an oblique shot at the target. He noted with satisfaction that Stratton was adopting the same tactics on the opposite side of the room.

Hulf covered some three metres in this fashion, and then squatted down on his heels listening for the slightest sound which would indicate more accurately where the gunman was hiding, but all he could hear was a faint bubbling sound which puzzled him at first, until he realised that the noise was coming from the entrance where Parker was lying. Hulf moistened his dry lips, opened his mouth, and in a loud voice told O'Dwyer to train the light directly on to the desk.

The ruse worked like a charm. The gunman came up like a jack-in-the-box and, holding the sawn-off shotgun at the hip, let go with one barrel in Hulf's direction, and then swivelling, fired the other barrel at the mullioned window before making a dash for the back door.

Hulf gripped his right wrist with his left hand to steady the aim, and unlike Stratton, who immediately opened fire, waited until the target was in the centre of the pool of light. Hulf pumped a total of seven rounds in a little over three seconds and missed only once.

As each round went home, the gunman jerked backwards and forwards like an animated puppet until one leg became entangled with the other and threw him off balance. He toppled over on to his left side, tried to raise himself up, and then collapsed face downwards on to the carpet, still clutching the sawn-off shotgun in his right hand.

Hulf opened the back door and ran through the small sitting room with Stratton close on his heels. Despite the

9

room being in darkness, he was able to find the hall door without any difficulty. He took the stairs two at a time and then stopped on the landing facing the bedroom where a crack of light was showing under the door. He flung the door open and stepped aside just in case the unexpected should happen. Nothing did.

The woman was already wearing a pair of black ski pants and calf-length boots, and was in the process of slipping her head into a white polo-necked sweater as Hulf walked into the room. Ignoring Hulf, she finished dressing and then ran a comb through her ruffled hair.

Laconically, Hulf said, 'You had better check the other rooms on the landing, Sergeant Stratton. I don't think Miss Seagrave is going to give us any trouble.' Stratton started to back out of the room. 'When you've done that,' Hulf continued, 'go outside and tell O'Dwyer to let Control know we've got the Pink Panda.'

Stratton said, 'What about Parker, sir, shall I ask for an ambulance?'

Hulf sighed audibly, 'It's either that or a hearse, and it's going to be the latter if you hang around here much longer, Sergeant.'

Seagrave walked across the room, opened the wardrobe and took out a fleece-lined suède jacket. She smiled and said, 'There's no point in catching cold, is there?'

Hulf eyed the rumpled bed. 'Do you normally sleep in the buff?' he said.

'What?'

'I don't see a nightdress anywhere.'

'It's under the pillow.'

Hulf turned the pillow over, picked up a white nylon nightdress and tossed it on to the floor. 'This has to look right, Miss Seagrave. If you were forced to get dressed in a hurry you wouldn't have time to fold up your nightdress and tuck it away neatly under the pillow.'

She smiled in acknowledgment. 'I should have thought of that,' she said.

'You should,' he agreed. 'Now turn round and put your hands behind your back.'

She hesitated before complying. The steel handcuffs bit into her flesh as her wrists were manacled together. 'Is this another piece of window dressing?' she asked.

Hulf picked up a pillow and removed the case. 'We'll go downstairs now,' he said. 'The gunfire must have attracted a lot of attention, and when you walk out into the street people may be watching. They would expect to see you handcuffed and naturally your face would be concealed. Just before we step outside the shop, I'll put this pillowcase over your head.'

'You're very thorough,' she said.

Hulf grunted. 'I have to be.' He picked up her handbag from the chair and ushered Seagrave out of the room.

The lights were burning downstairs now and a Westminster clock was chiming the quarter hour. The gunman was still lying pretty much in the same position as they had left him, with his face buried into the carpet and his knees drawn up to his stomach. He was wearing an old army greatcoat which had been dyed navy blue.

Hulf glanced at the body and then said, 'He looks pretty tatty to be a bodyguard. Do we know anything about him, Sergeant Stratton?'

Stratton said, 'No sir, he wasn't carrying any papers. I'd say he was aged between twenty-two and twenty-five, may have been a labourer if the callouses on his hands are anything to go by, but judging by his appearance, I would say he has been unemployed for some time.'

Hulf smiled thinly. 'How far is he off the mark, Miss Seagrave?'

'His name was Kemp, Martin Kemp, and he was twenty years old. Apart from that, Sergeant Stratton was commendably accurate.'

Stratton said, 'Sergeant Parker's in a very bad way, sir. I've sent for an ambulance.'

'Is he still unconscious?'

Stratton nodded. 'We dragged him inside the shop and made him as comfortable as we could. Inspector Cook is outside, sir, with two additional cars.'

'Who told him to poke his nose in?' Hulf said sharply.

'Control did, sir, after Sergeant O'Dwyer told them we had picked up the Pink Panda.'

Hulf grimaced. 'All right, Sergeant, you go ahead and make sure everything is ready. There's no reason for us to hang around here any longer.' He turned to Seagrave and said, 'It's time we put you into your mask.' He placed the pillowcase over her head, and taking her by the arm, led her outside.

The uniformed police were formed up in two lines between the shop and the car. They had their arms linked as if prepared to hold back a surging crowd of spectators. It was unnecessary—there were no onlookers, only a handful of people watching from the windows in the houses opposite. Hulf pushed Seagrave into the car and then looked around for Inspector Cook.

'Have you got a megaphone, Tom?' he asked him.

Cook said, 'Yes, sir.'

'Good,' said Hulf waving a hand in the direction of the houses across the street, 'then you can tell those bloody people to go back to bed. The show's over.' He got into the car and told O'Dwyer to move off.

They went down the Hill, turned right at the traffic lights, and ran parallel with the railway line until they turned right again and headed towards Wembley. Five minutes later Hulf removed the pillowcase from Seagrave's head. His concern for her well-being did not however extend to removing the handcuffs from her wrists.

Stratton said, 'The Russians are going to be very pleased with this night's work, sir. I mean, it isn't every day that someone in the Resistance as big as the Head of Security decides to defect to us, is it?'

Hulf sighed yet again. 'There are times, Sergeant Stratton,' he said heavily, 'when you talk too much. The only people who knew Miss Seagrave was going to defect were myself, yourself, Sergeants O'Dwyer and Parker, and of course, the Controller of Special Branch. The Russians, Sergeant Stratton, are not going to know a damn thing about it.'

2

THE WALLS WERE DISTEMPERED in that peculiar combination of pea-green up to the level of the radiators and off-white from there to the ceiling. The carpet was olive-green Wilton, the steel desk functional and the swivel chair too low for comfort in relation to the height of the desk. Two ladder-backed wooden chairs with green plastic seats were available for visitors. The room was like any other government office except that in this case it belonged to Anthony Warner, the Controller of Special Branch.

The green check Irish tweed suit was in keeping with the heavily built frame of the man. The square-shaped face with narrow brown eyes, carefully trimmed moustache, bushy eyebrows and dark hair parted neatly on the left side, coupled with the affected accent, matched the accepted caricature of the retired army officer. The image was false. Warner, who was fifty-two, had never served in the armed forces, for he was an ex-colonial policeman who had spent the greater part of his service in Hong Kong.

He glanced briefly at the woman sitting in front of him massaging her sore wrists, and then opened the file on the desk. The top page concerned Seagrave. Dropping his eyes, he read: 'Seagrave, Charlotte. General description:— Age 48? Single. Height—approx. 5ft. 6ins. (1.6 metres). Weight —estimated 154 pounds (70 kilos). Matronly appearance, eyes blue, hair grey.'

Warner looked up. 'Grey hair?' he mused. 'I see you've

had a blue rinse. It doesn't suit you.'

'Surely we have more important matters to discuss?' she said coldly.

Warner drummed his finger-tips on the desk. 'You are referring to your proposition, of course.'

'I am not alone—there are others who are in favour of the idea.'

Warner said, 'I'm aware of that. If you lacked support you would be inside a cell, not sitting here talking to me.'

'That is a matter of opinion.'

Warner said, 'Suppose we get on with the business in hand?'

Seagrave glanced at the short, burly figure of Hulf sitting beside her, impassively chewing on a mint lump. 'It's all right,' said Warner, 'you can speak freely in front of Charlie Hulf, Miss Seagrave.'

Seagrave said, 'Our proposal is very simple. We are offering co-operation in exchange for a covert voice in public affairs.'

Warner lit a cigarette. 'Spell it out for me,' he said.

'There are certain people we would like to see in the Cabinet. If our wishes are met, we in return, will stop mounting attacks against the Russians and you people.'

Warner laughed. 'Why should we buy that?'

'The Russians are withdrawing...'

'And we have the Chinese to thank for that. If they hadn't marched into Siberia, the Russians would still be here in force.'

Seagrave ignored the interruption. 'The Russian Occupation Army has been reduced to three divisions. If they were sure of our loyalty to Moscow, they might consider further withdrawals.'

'And when the Bear ate the Dragon, they would be back.'

'Do you want them to return?'

'No,' said Warner.

'Nor do we, but we have to get rid of them first.'

Warner said, 'And we are going to achieve that objective by playing it cool, is that the idea?'

'Yes.'

'If there is an armistice of sorts, can you guarantee your people will toe the line?'

14

'Apart from a few extremists, I think the majority will go along with the leadership.'

'It's the extremists who worry me.'

'We propose to deliver them into your hands.' Seagrave smiled thinly. 'Such a move would do much to restore your credit with the Russian authorities.'

Warner stubbed out his cigarette in an ashtray. 'You could be selling us a pig in a poke,' he said. 'With the way things are between Russia and China, we don't have to make a deal with you. We can sit back and wait for the pickings to fall into our laps.'

'There's no harm in taking out a piece of insurance, is there?'

Warner opened a sliding drawer in the desk and brought out an Aldis projector and a magazine of slides which he placed on the desk. He swung round in the chair and plugged the Aldis into the power point behind him. 'All right, Miss Seagrave,' he said quietly, 'let's see what you have to offer.'

'I can give you the Head of Intelligence and the Director of Propaganda Warfare.'

'Their names probably wouldn't mean anything to me.' Warner looked at Hulf and said, 'Move your chair to one side, Charlie, and put the lights out. We'll use the wall as a screen.'

In his usual unhurried fashion, Hulf placed his chair next to Seagrave, put the lights out and then sat down again. He felt inside his jacket pockets, found another mint lump, unwrapped it and popped it into his mouth. Rolling the sweet paper into a ball, he casually flipped it into the wastepaper bin by the side of Warner's desk. It was a good example of dumb insolence, but Warner, who was loading the slide magazine into the Aldis, didn't notice.

The first slide was an Identikit portrait. The face resembled a sad bloodhound and the hair was silver.

'Vickers,' said Seagrave, 'Major-General Austin Vickers, Director of Resistance Operations—a ruthless man, who could never be persuaded to co-operate with the puppet regime or the Russians!'

'Good,' said Warner. 'Now where do we find him?'

'I don't know. Vickers makes it a rule never to spend

more than one night under the same roof.'

Hulf snorted. 'I might have known it. We're about to be sold a pup.'

Warner ignored the interruption. 'How do you make contact with Vickers?'

'We use a D.L.B. system, or a telephone number if it's really urgent. The number is 89140625.'

Warner made a note of the number and then changed the slide.

'This was taken about six months ago outside an employment agency in Salisbury. Subject is described as being just over six foot and weighing about one seventy to one eighty pounds; believed to be aged between thirty-six and thirty-eight; has dark hair greying at the temples and blue-grey eyes. He took out a resident's permit under the name of George Abel.'

Seagrave said, 'That is David Seymour, alias David Garnett. He prefers to be known as Garnett. He was a regular officer in the Army pre-war. His wife and son were killed in the ten-megaton strike on Bristol. He was taken prisoner when the armistice was signed, escaped from the Lichfield Detention Centre, was recaptured and taken to Parkhurst, and escaped again. Three months later he assassinated Willie Vosper, the Political Commissar of Wiltshire. After a series of bank raids, he graduated to Security, where he worked directly under the late Hugh Coleman. He organised and led the raid on Parkhurst to bring out Pollard, and last August he destroyed the Teroshkova cell. He dropped out of the Resistance some five months ago.'

Hulf said, 'Isn't it bloody marvellous, either she doesn't know where to find them, or else they're no longer working for the firm.'

Warner rubbed his chin thoughtfully. 'If we did co-operate as you suggest, would this man cause trouble?'

'I think he would. He broke with the Resistance because he didn't like the way Vickers used people. It doesn't follow that he has stopped hating. Anyway, Vickers believes it is only a matter of time before he rejoins the fold. That's why we kept track of their movements.'

'Their movements?'

16

'There is a girl with him.'

Warner said, 'Would she be Valerie Dane?'

'Yes. In fact, Valerie Dane is the reason why Garnett broke away from us. He's in love with her, and Vickers risked her life once too often for Garnett to tolerate. They're living together in Appleby under the name of Simpson. They have a flat above a grocer's shop opposite the Tufton Arms Hotel.'

The telephone started ringing. Warner answered it curtly, listened in silence and then hung up. 'That was the Royal Masonic, Charlie,' he said, 'Sergeant Parker's just died.' He walked across the room and put on the lights.

Hulf said, 'Sergeant Parker was a good man, maybe the best I had.'

'Yes?'

'Someone's going to pay for that.'

Warner lit another cigarette. 'Do you think you can handle Garnett and Dane, Charlie?'

Hulf looked up quickly, 'I know I can.'

'I want them alive, Charlie. Do you understand?'

'Oh, I understand all right.'

'Good. We'll make it look like a routine cordon and search operation. There's a militia battalion stationed at Barnard Castle which could throw a cordon around Appleby. We'll airlift the prisoners back to London in a helicopter.' He glanced briefly at Seagrave. 'It won't be long before word gets around that Miss Seagrave is missing, so the sooner you get started, Charlie, the better.'

Hulf stood up. 'Do you want this job done later this morning?'

Warner said, 'Oh no, Charlie, that would never do. We don't want to telegraph the fact that we've got inside information. Make it look as if they were picked up in a screening job. We want the Resistance to think that Miss Seagrave is holding up under interrogation.'

Hulf walked towards the door.

'One more thing,' said Warner, 'call me when you have them in the bag.'

'Yes, sir,' said Hulf. He walked out of the room and closed the door behind him.

Warner perched himself on the edge of the desk with one

foot planted firmly on the door while the other swung gently back and forth. He smiled at Seagrave. 'And now,' he said smoothly, 'I'd like to talk about those other people in Intelligence and Propaganda you were about to mention earlier. We'll have to pick them up before they go to ground.'

Seagrave looked away and her gaze fell on the clock above the door, and with a start, she saw that the hands were pointing to five forty. In another hour or so it would be getting light, and her disappearance would be common knowledge, and, for the first time, the enormity of her action sank in, and she began to wonder if she had made a terrible mistake.

'I'm waiting,' Warner said patiently.

Seagrave turned to face him. 'I'm not a traitor,' she said quietly.

Warner stubbed out his cigarette in the ashtray. 'I never said you were.'

'In case you have the wrong impression, I think you should know that we have had you under surveillance for a very long time.'

'Really?'

'Oh, yes. We know a great deal about you—where you live, where your daughter goes to school, who her friends are, what time she normally arrives home—and we know why you are late getting home on Tuesdays. Your wife thinks you're attending a Joint Services Intelligence meeting. Paul finds that very amusing.'

The smile disappeared from Warner's face. 'Paul?' he said softly.

'Paul Ashton, a very pretty young man with a basement flat in Hans Crescent. We've got some very interesting letters you wrote to him. Of course, that in itself doesn't amount to much, but I really do think you should have curbed your desire to be photographed together.'

'Are you threatening me?' Warner said harshly.

'No. I'm merely pointing out that you do not hold all the cards, and that I came here voluntarily because I thought we could work together. You would be making a very bad mistake if you ever forgot that.'

'And if I did forget?'

18

'The photographs would be delivered to the appropriate quarter. I need hardly remind you that the regime detests perverts.'

'Wouldn't it be simpler to have me shot?' Warner said sarcastically.

'We could arrange that too if necessary.'

Warner stood up, walked round the desk, opened a filing cabinet and brought out a bottle of Haig Whisky, two tumblers and a syphon of soda-water. He placed the glasses on the desk and poured a generous measure into each glass.

'Soda all right for you, or would you prefer water?'

'Soda.'

'Just a splash or right up?'

'Right up.'

He filled Seagrave's glass and handed it to her, added a splash of soda to his own and then sat down behind the desk. He sipped the whisky thoughtfully. 'You know, Charlotte,' he said slowly, 'I appreciate your frankness. I think it's best to make one's position clear, don't you?' Seagrave didn't answer. 'You've been quite open with me, and now I shall return the compliment. For some years you people had a very good source who worked in the central information room. His name was Richard Endicott, and I knew all about his little game long before he was turned and forced to become a double agent. I knew you were going to kill him, yet I did nothing to prevent it. Do you know why?'

'A cynic would say that Endicott was no longer of any use to you once we were on to him.'

Warner smiled. 'My dear Charlotte, if I had lifted a finger to save his life, he would have told me everything he knew about the Resistance out of sheer gratitude. I didn't raise a finger because I wanted, and still want, the Resistance to remain alive. Once the Russians have gone, it will take more than a militia to overthrow this puppet government. That's why I want the Resistance to be waiting in the wings. Do you believe me?'

'I think so.'

Warner drained his glass. 'All right then,' he said briskly, 'let's talk about Intelligence and Propaganda.'

3

THE FAINT WHINE OF a truck grinding away in low gear brought him out of a restless sleep. Garnett sat up in bed, switched on the bedside lamp, and listened intently. Beside him Dane stirred and turned over on to her back, but did not wake up.

He listened to the low murmur of the wind and shivered in the cold night air. Carefully folding back the blankets, he swung his legs out of the warm bed, shoved his feet into his slippers and then padded across the room and unhooked his dressing gown from the door. He slipped his arms into the woollen robe, tied the cord loosely about his waist and crept over to the window. Drawing the curtain aside, Garnett breathed on to the frosted window-pane, and using the sleeve of his dressing gown, rubbed off the ice on the inside.

Below him the Square was lifeless and deserted. He tried peering up the hill to his left, but the moonlight shining on the trees cast long dark shadows across the road. Several times Garnett thought he saw a movement in the shadows, but in the end, he put it down to imagination. He let the curtain fall back into place, walked across the room and helped himself to a cigarette from the packet on the dressing table. As he flicked the lighter and held the flame to the cigarette, he caught sight of his reflection in the mirror. His face had lost the tired and drawn look and the lines beneath the eyes were fainter. He had put on weight, not a significant amount, but the cheeks were no longer hollow. He looked younger than thirty-seven, despite the occasional grey in his dark hair, and he felt fitter than he had for years—and he had Dane to thank for that.

He was aware of a grating noise, like chalk squeaking on a blackboard, and turning, he saw that Dane was grinding her teeth in her sleep. He walked over to the bed, touched her cheek gently, and the grinding stopped. Her long, silky blonde hair was spread out over the pillow and wisps of it lay across her prominent cheekbones. Even now, when she was asleep and relaxed, Garnett was struck again by the near-flawless perfection of her features.

Garnett stubbed out the cigarette in an ashtray, untied the cord and was just removing the dressing gown, when he heard the whine of a propshaft again. This time there was more than one truck and they sounded closer than before; and he had the impression that the noise was coming from the direction of the A66 which ran through the centre of the town on the far side of the River Eden.

He snapped off the light and sat there in the dark listening. Presently, his sharp ears picked up the distinctive sound of a tailboard slowly being lowered. Instinct told him that a cordon and search operation was in the process of being mounted, and if it followed the normal pattern, the road leading to Warcop in one direction and Penrith in the other would already be blocked. He was prepared to bet that the truck which had woken him up moved in a party to seal off the minor road leading to Orton on the south side of the river.

Garnett grabbed Dane by the shoulder. In a sleepy voice she said, 'What's the matter?'

'Wake up,' he snapped, 'we've got to make a run for it.'

She turned over and raised her head. 'What are you talking about?' she said huskily.

'We're due for a house to house search. It's odds on they're looking for us.'

Dane kicked the blankets aside, scrambled out of bed and stripped off her pyjamas. Naked, teeth chattering with cold, she rushed across the room, grabbed her underclothes from the chair and started dressing.

Garnett pulled on a pair of slacks over his pyjamas, found a roll-neck sweater and a pair of socks in the chest of drawers and then, groping under the bed, pulled out a pair of elastic-sided shoes. Still tugging the sweater over his head, he ran across the room and drew back the curtains. Kneeling down under the window, he flipped back the carpet and pried one of the floorboards loose with his finger nails. Reaching into the cavity, he brought out two oilskin packets and unwrapped them. The smaller packet of the two contained a bundle of used notes and two identity cards. He arranged the money in two piles, placing their respective I.D. cards on the top of each pile.

The larger packet contained a 9mm. Luger, spare magazine and twenty rounds of ammunition. Pressing the release catch, Garnett removed the magazine from the butt of the automatic and then loaded each magazine with seven rounds. He pushed a loaded magazine into the butt, snapped the action back and put the change lever to safe. He scooped up the spare magazine and loose rounds and shoved them into his pocket. Garnett then replaced the floorboard and re-laid the carpet. He tucked the Luger into the waistband of his slacks, picked up both piles of money and stood up.

In an anxious voice Dane said, 'How did they know where to find us, David?'

'God knows, Valerie—does it matter?' Garnett walked across the room and dropped a wad of money on to the bed. 'Put that in your handbag,' he said, 'you're going to need it.'

'Aren't you coming with me?' she asked quietly.

Garnett walked round to his side of the bed and sat down. He pulled on the socks and slipped his feet into the shoes. 'You'll stand a better chance if we separate,' he said.

'Can't we find somewhere to hide?'

'Listen,' he said patiently, 'we've got to assume that they know where we are living and that they will have a pretty good description of us. Our only hope is to make them think we have flown the coop.'

He reached for the telephone on the bedside table, lifted the receiver and started dialling.

'Who are you calling, David?'

'Harry Lake.'

'Harry Lake?'

'Yes, Harry Lake,' he said irritably. 'Remember? He has the chemist's shop just around the corner—our yards back on to one another. I'm going to ask him for help.' Garnett hung on to the phone listening to the ringing tone. It seemed an age before someone answered it.

An angry voice said, 'Yes, who is it?'

Garnett said, 'Harry, this is David Simpson. I need your help.'

'At this time of night?'

'It's urgent. Go and unlock your back door; we're coming in over the wall.'

'Are you mad or something? What are you talking about?'

'I haven't time to explain. We're about to be arrested. Are you willing to help us or not?'

There was a longish pause, and then Lake cleared his throat and said, 'Yes, of course I will. I'll go and unlock the door now.' There was a distinct click as Lake hung up.

Garnett placed the receiver carefully on the bedside table. He hoped that by leaving the phone off the hook the police might think someone had tipped them off. He got up, walked over to the wardrobe and took out a jacket.

Glancing at Dane, Garnett said, 'Come on, love, it's time we were going.'

They went downstairs into the small back room which served as a storeroom and, while Dane waited, Garnett made a detour into the shop, unlocked the front door and left it ajar. He then took two tins of luncheon meat off the shelves, slipped them into the pockets of his jacket and rejoined Dane. He opened the back door quietly, paused to listen, and then beckoning Dane to follow him, stepped out into the yard. Locking the door behind him and pocketing the key, he stooped and, with his back braced against the wall, placed both hands palm uppermost on his left leg to form a stepping block. Dane put her left foot into his hands, and as Garnett straightened up, wriggled over the top of the wall and landed softly on the other side. Seconds later, Garnett followed her.

Harry Lake opened the back door of his shop and let them in.

Garnett said, 'For God's sake, whatever you do, don't put on the light.'

'What is all this?'

'Have you ever taken a good look at the Wanted List, Harry?'

'I think so.'

'I'm on it—my name's Garnett.'

'Jesus,' Lake said slowly.

'Do you still want to help us?'

'I would never have recognised you.'

'Do you still want to help us, Harry?'

Lake swallowed. 'Yes,' he said throatily.

'Thank you,' Garnett said simply. He pinched the bridge of his nose. 'Is there anywhere you can hide Valerie?'

'There's a cupboard under the stairs.'

'That's no good, it's too obvious.'

'How about the loft?'

'No. They are bound to search the house from top to bottom.' Garnett snapped his fingers. 'Listen,' he said, 'there is still three or four hours before daylight and that should be enough. You could lift the floorboards up under the staircase and Valerie could squeeze herself down between the joists. There should be at least fifty centimetres of headroom under the floorboards which is about right. You'll have to get the nails out with a pair of pincers, but take care that you don't mark the woodwork. It could be damned cold down there and the air may be pretty foul, but it's the best hiding place we've got.'

Dane said, 'What do you mean by "we"? It's me!'

As though Dane had not spoken, Garnett continued, 'Normally, as soon as it is light enough, they order everyone out of the houses and put them into a pen where they are screened. They will then allow one person from each household to return with the search party. Do you think your mother can stand up to it, because she is the one who's going to be present when the search takes place?'

Lake said, 'I think so.'

Garnett said, 'All right. They'll send a loudspeaker van round when they want you to come out, and that's when

24

Valerie takes to her funk hole and you will nail her up.'

Lake moistened his lips. 'How long will the search last?'

Garnett shrugged his shoulders. 'Who knows? A day, maybe longer, it depends on how thoroughly they search the town.'

'Valerie could suffocate in that time.'

'I think that's unlikely. There are airbricks set into the foundations for sub-floor ventilation. She should be all right. Anyway, I hope the search is going to be pretty perfunctory because I'm going to try to draw them off.'

'How?'

Garnett said, 'Look, Harry, we don't have all that much time. Shouldn't you let your mother know what's happening?'

Lake turned away and went upstairs, moving slowly like a man with a great weight on his back. Garnett waited until he was well out of earshot, and then said, 'I'll have to leave now.'

'Why?'

'Don't ask me why, just trust me.'

'Haven't I always?'

'Yes, of course you have. I want you to lie low until things quieten down, and then make your way to London. Appleby was all right until they got on to us, but now we've no choice but to move on. I'm going to contact Vickers because he still owes us a favour or two. Do you know anyone in London who'll shelter you?'

She shook her head. 'No,' she said.

'Find a lodging house in the Paddington or Notting Hill Gate area. You've got money and a new identity card. You'd better do something about your hair, change your appearance, all right?'

Dane swallowed. 'How do I get in touch with you again?'

'We'll use a fail safe rendezvous.'

'Where?'

'What day is it?'

'Wednesday.'

'Every Tuesday then, outside W. H. Smith on Charing Cross Station during the rush hour between a quarter to nine and nine o'clock in the morning. If we don't connect first time out, give it one more try and then use the contact number. Do you remember it?'

'No.'

'It's 89140625. Repeat it.'

She repeated it twice, and then said anxiously, 'We've not been in touch with our people for over five months. How do we know the number hasn't been changed?'

'We don't, we can only hope that it hasn't.' He drew her close and kissed her. 'Love,' he said softly, 'it's time I started.'

Her arms went round his neck. 'Let me come with you.'

'Nothing is going to happen to me.'

Gently he removed her arms and stepped back a pace, and before she had a chance to say anything more, turned and walked quickly away. He let himself out into the yard, climbed over the wall and unlocked the door to the storeroom. He locked it again behind him, left the key in the door, and went through to the shop. Garnett paused at the street door, and holding the Luger in his right hand, listened intently. Somewhere in the distance a dog was barking.

Jerking the door wide open, Garnett ran diagonally across the empty square and made for the open ground behind the Council Offices. He circled the town, keeping to the back streets and alleyways until he reached the swimming pool, and then struck out in the direction of the river.

The river was dark and bottomless in the pale moonlight. From where he crouched behind one of the trees lining the tow path, Garnett could see the bridge one hundred and fifty metres away on his right. Two figures were standing there leaning against the parapet. The trees and shrubs on the far bank of the river limited his view, and he wondered if a picket line was concealed behind them.

Garnett thumbed the safety catch to fire and aimed at the sentries on the bridge. He had no hope of hitting them at that range, but it would be enough if he attracted their attention. Coolly and deliberately he emptied the magazine, squeezing off one shot after another. In the stillness, the sound of each shot was magnified.

The sentries ducked out of sight behind the parapet, and for a few seconds there was no other reaction, and

26

then a Kalashnikov stuttered as one of the sentries let go with a speculative burst. The bullets whipped the branches of a tree some twenty metres to the right and rear of Garnett's position. In a chain reaction, the fire was also taken up by someone on the far bank. It was equally wild.

Garnett reloaded with the spare magazine and started running in a westerly direction. Behind him there was a confused babble of voices. A Very light soared up into the air and burst high above the trees, bathing the area in a ghostly white light, and immediately an R.P.K. cut loose and sprayed a bush fifty metres in front of him, forcing Garnett to jink sideways towards the river. A mortar opened up, and Garnett went to ground just before three parachute flares opened directly above him. He lay perfectly still as the R.P.K. traversed the illuminated area engaging anything which remotely looked like a target. As the flares died, another spread went up farther away, and as the R.P.K. gunner switched his arc of fire Garnett jumped to his feet and raced forward.

His tactics were simple but dangerous. He followed up in rear of the mortar illumination, going to ground before the flares died, and waiting to see where the next spread would come before moving forward again. They were canny enough to vary the search pattern. Sometimes the flares would be ahead, and then the next batch would burst behind him. On one occasion, they repeated the same shoot and Garnett was very nearly caught out. Slowly but surely, he slipped the probing mortar and came to the outskirts of the town, where he knew that at any moment he would run into the outer cordon. It happened sooner than Garnett expected. He vaulted over a low stone wall and landed almost within touching distance of a sentry.

The man had been watching the flares in the distance instead of the ground immediately in front of him, and had failed to see Garnett approaching his position. By the time he realised what was happening and had reached for his rifle, which had been carelessly propped against the wall, it was too late. Garnett shot him in the ribs and neck. The sound of gunfire alerted the thinly spread cordon but, fortunately, none of the sentries within the immediate vicinity of the dead man was armed with a Very pistol.

Head down, legs pumping, Garnett raced across the open field, jinking continuously to put the sentries off their aim. The bullets kicked up the ground around him and buzzed over his head like angry wasps. Another stone hedge loomed up, and he threw himself over it head first in a diving somersault. Garnett hit the ground hard, scrambled to his feet and kept on running. A flare went up from the right flank to his rear but the stone wall was between him and the nearest marksman, and he knew they would have to chase after him if they were to get a clear field of fire. Heart bursting, and with a gagging sensation in the back of his throat, he forced himself to put one foot in front of the other. He vaulted a third wall, stumbled, fell down and hastily picked himself up again.

It was a bitterly cold night, but the sweat was pouring off him. Reduced to a jog trot, he kept on going, driven on by the knowledge that, even though he had broken through the cordon, he had to find shelter before long. The open moorland offered no cover, and the helicopters would be up there looking for him as soon as it got light enough. Even if bad weather grounded the helicopters, he still had to worry about the tracker dogs. However, they weren't an insoluble problem.

Garnett hit the river and entered it without hesitation. It came up to his chest, and he sucked in his breath sharply as the icy water lowered his blood temperature. Struggling against the current and taking a ducking every time he stepped into a pothole, he made his way upstream for about a thousand metres before he climbed out on the far bank just outside the village of Bolton. He staggered past a driveway and stopped to rest against a lamp-post. The sound of a police car bleeping in the distance set him on the run again before he had a chance to catch his breath. It seemed to his sensitive ears that the police car was moving in his direction, and almost without thinking, he opened the front gate of the first house he came to, tiptoed along the path, opened another gate, and went into the back garden. At the far end of the lawn there was a garden shed, which looked hopeful. He squelched across the grass, found the door was on the latch, and opened it.

The shed was about three metres long by two wide, and as his eyes became accustomed to the gloom, he saw that it contained a mower, garden tools, a hosepipe and three deck chairs which were propped up against one side of the shed. With some difficulty he erected one of the chairs, and positioned it so that it was facing the entrance. He lowered himself down into the canvas and, despite his wet clothes and the numbing cold and every effort to stay awake, drifted off into a restless sleep.

4

THERE WAS A MISTY quality about the scene. Two policemen were standing in their bedroom, one of whom was holding an Alsatian on a short leash. They had found Dane's pyjamas, and the dog, getting the scent, started tracking eagerly. With unerring instinct, it led them down the staircase, through the storeroom and out into the back yard. It went straight to the wall and started barking. The handler dragged the dog away, took it out through the shop, went round the corner and entered Lake's yard. The dog picked up the scent on the other side of the wall, followed it into the chemist's and ran it to ground where it stopped above the hiding place under the staircase. The Alsatian pawed the floorboards and started barking again.

Garnett came out of the nightmare feeling stiff, cold and frightened. In their haste to get out he had overlooked the dogs. He told himself he should have done something about their scent—pepper would have been the answer, pepper sprinkled thickly on the staircase and inside the storeroom would have irritated the animal's nostrils and temporarily destroyed its sense of smell. He closed his eyes and tried to figure a way out of the mess. Perhaps if he walked into Appleby and let them take him, he might be able to convince the police that Dane had got away?—it was, he knew, a very slim chance.

Aching in every limb, he struggled to his feet and

opened the door of the shed. The snow, which was still falling, had turned the lawn into a virgin white blanket. Garnett closed the door and sank back into the deck chair. No dog on earth was going to sniff its way through a thick mantle of snow, but on the other hand, he couldn't leave the hut without making an obvious set of tracks.

Perversely, because he now faced a period of inactivity, Garnett began to feel hungry. He took one of the tins of luncheon meat out of his jacket pocket and opened it. Lacking a penknife, he used the lid for a spoon. He tried not to look at the pink fat-speckled meat, but the taste alone was enough to make him feel queasy, and he had had all he wanted before he was halfway through. Garnett put the unfinished tin in the grass box of the lawn mower, where he didn't have to look at it, and then put his mind to thinking out the next move.

As a matter of routine, the police or the army would have put out longstops once they knew he had broken through the cordon, and then, if experience counted for anything, a number of search parties would start working inwards. He had no idea when it had begun to snow, but it wouldn't take much to put the road over Shap Fell out of action, and that left Penrith, the Lake District and vast stretches of open moorland. The village of Bolton began to stand out like a sore thumb. A lot was going to depend on how many men were available to search thoroughly the outlying villages and farms.

He decided it was about time he had another look outside. The garden was enclosed by tall hedges, but it was still overlooked by the adjoining house. The kitchen and scullery jutted out at a right angle to a lounge with double french windows, and a coal bunker and smaller shed faced the back door. There was no garage space. As he watched, a light came on in the room above the lounge and Garnett hurriedly closed the shed door.

He was shivering, and his body from the waist downwards felt like a block of ice. The damp trousers clung to his legs, but the material was beginning to stiffen, and he knew that, unless he found somewhere to thaw out, he was going to freeze to death before the day was out. Garnett cupped his hands together and blew into them, but there was no warmth in his breath and he thought that being arrested would have its advantages—at least a cell would be warmer.

Whatever temporary advantage a cell had over the garden shed died the instant he heard, in the distance, the distorted voice of the Tannoy. The voice drew nearer but the quality of speech didn't improve. Not that it mattered —long familiar with police methods, Garnett knew that the villagers were being warned to stay indoors until a search of the area had been completed.

One look around the shed convinced Garnett that there was nowhere to hide. To run was out of the question, yet to stay meant certain discovery, for he had seen enough of the house to know that it wouldn't take the police long to go through it from top to bottom, and once they came into the garden, they were bound to look inside the shed. He took the Luger out of his jacket pocket and stripped it down. Then, with a piece of rag he found on the work bench at the back of the shed, he carefully rubbed the working parts dry. He counted out the loose rounds and methodically dried them and the spare magazine. With fingers made clumsy by the numbing cold, he finally managed to reassemble the automatic. He pushed the magazine back into the butt, fed a round up into the breech and put the change lever on safe. As Garnett filled the spare magazine with the remaining four rounds, a feverish voice inside his head whispered, 'Eleven rounds—ten for them, one for you.'

Waiting was, as always, the worst part. Garnett sat in the deck chair nursing the Luger on his lap and stared fixedly at the shed door. He knew that, even if he survived the initial contact and was taken prisoner, he would eventually be hauled before a military tribunal and sentenced to death.

Time passed slowly—an hour, then two, then three. There was no feeling left in his limbs, he was sick with cold and the memory of the fatty luncheon meat made him retch. Then, suddenly, he heard footsteps crunching in the snow, and Garnett held his breath as he listened to the muffled voices outside. There seemed little point in stepping to one side of the door, because that would only prolong the affair and his field of fire would be restricted. Garnett thumbed the safety off and gently took up the first pressure on the trigger. Eyes riveted on the door, he watched the latch begin to raise.

A voice shouted, 'Hey, Joe.'

And just outside the door, another voice said, 'What now?'

'He's been spotted in Temple Sowerby. I've just had the news on the car radio. They want us there right away.'

The hand on the latch hovered uncertainly. Then the voice shouted again, 'Come on Joe, what are you waiting for? We haven't got all day.'

Joe sounded bad-tempered. 'Keep your hair on then, I'm coming,' he said.

The door was still off the latch, and as the police withdrew, it slowly began to swing open. Garnett came out of the deck chair with all the speed he could muster, grabbed the door and closed it softly. Beads of sweat stood out on his forehead, his hands were shaking, and unable to contain the feeling of nausea any longer, he vomited on to the floor. He fell awkwardly into the chair and passed out.

When he regained consciousness some time later, Garnett didn't at first notice the scrap of paper that had been pushed under the door. As his head cleared, he gazed speculatively at it for a few moments before scrambling out of the chair to pick it up. Scrawled in pencil was a short message—'Please go away.' It seemed like a good idea.

Garnett opened the door and looked out. It was still snowing, and the maze of footprints which led from the kitchen up to the hut and back again were beginning to blur. He stepped outside and, keeping to the existing tracks, staggered across the lawn and made his way to the back door. Leaning against the wall, he rang the door bell. No one answered it. He kept on ringing in the firm conviction that someone must be at home.

Someone was. The woman on the other side of the door said, 'Go away.'

Garnett said, 'I need help, please help me.'

'I'll call the police if you don't leave me alone.'

'You do that, love,' he said, 'and I'll show them the note

you pushed under the door of the shed.'

A key turned in the lock and the door opened reluctantly. Garnett quickly stepped inside the house.

The woman was about thirty, and could have been Spanish if the black glossy hair combed tightly back into a bun on the nape of her neck and her olive skin were anything to go by. She was, in fact, Leeds born and bred and still spoke with a marked Yorkshire accent. She barely came up to Garnett's shoulder, and her name was Anne James.

Garnett said, 'Sorry about that.'

'What?'

'Blackmailing you to let me in. I didn't like doing it.'

Anne James compressed her lips. 'It's a bit late to be sorry, isn't it?'

Garnett ignored the comment. 'Do you live alone?' he said.

'No, I'm married, but my husband is at work. There's no one else in the house.'

'What time will he be back?'

'About twelve-thirty. He's on the staff of Eden Grove and comes home to lunch.' She hesitated, then said, 'Why are the police after you?'

'I'm on the Wanted List.'

'They said you're a dangerous criminal.'

'According to them, anyone in the Resistance is a criminal. What do you think?'

'I have no views. It's safer that way.'

'How did you know I was inside the shed?'

'I saw you close the door.'

'If you knew I was hiding there, why didn't you tell the police?'

'I didn't want any trouble,' she said quietly.

'I'm going to stay here until I know how things are. Any objection?'

She eyed the Luger tucked in the waistband of his slacks. 'I can't stop you.'

Garnett said, 'I want to get out of these clothes and dry off. Maybe I can borrow some of your husband's clothes?'

'Fred's smaller than you.'

34

'How about a clean shirt? Perhaps we take the same size in collars.'

'He's a sixteen and a half.'

'That'll be a perfect fit.' Garnett removed his jacket, pulled the sweater off over his head and unzipped his flies. 'I hope you're not easily embarrassed,' he said cheerfully.

Hulf slammed down the phone and walked across the room to join Stratton at the window. The police station had a commanding view of the terraced town, and from the window they could see the interrogation pen on the snow-covered sports field. Hulf picked up Stratton's field glasses and trained them on to the pen. The screening of detainees had been going on for nearly four hours and had yielded nothing. The snow was easing off, but that didn't make any difference to the townspeople inside the pen. They were still the sullen, the angry, the miserable, the apathetic bunch who had been dragged out of their comfortable, warm houses some two hundred and forty odd minutes previously. The attitude of the militia soldiers didn't please Hulf either. The way they lounged around, the fact that they were smoking on duty told him that they had completely lost interest in the search.

Hulf grunted. 'Look at them,' he said disgustedly, 'all they can think about is their centrally heated barrack rooms waiting for them back in Barnard Castle.'

Stratton cleared his throat. 'They seem pretty certain that the people we are after are no longer inside the cordon, sir.'

'According to the local police, they are not in Bolton either, and that business in Temple Sowerby turned out to be a false alarm.'

'When are we going to call off the search?'

Hulf put down the glasses and rounded on Stratton. 'When I'm good and ready, Sergeant,' he said coldly. 'Listen, we know they were here and that these people sheltered them.'

'Sheltered them?'

'Both of them are on the Wanted List, aren't they? Did any of those good people out there bother to tell us they were living in Appleby? Of course they bloody didn't. So, in my book, they sheltered them, and they can stay out in the cold, and we'll take our time over screening them, and then the army can turn the place over, and I don't care how much damage they do. Maybe it will teach this town a lesson.'

'Yes, sir.'

'And when it's over, Sergeant Stratton, you and O'Dwyer are going to stay on for a few days, because I'm curious to know what happens after the army pulls out.'

'Isn't that a job for the local police, sir?'

Hulf searched through his coat pockets, found a mint lump and popped it into his mouth. 'I have a hunch that only Garnett slipped through the cordon, Sergeant. He made sure we knew he had got out. He didn't creep away like a thief in the night, oh no, he opened fire on the cordon. I think the woman is still inside the town.'

Stratton said, 'Well then, let's take the place apart until we find her.'

Hulf sighed. 'I want Garnett, Sergeant Stratton, and I'm going to get him. You know why?'

'No, sir.'

'Because sooner or later the girl is going to come out into the open and rejoin him, and when that happens you are going to be sitting on her tail.'

5

GARNETT SAT IN FRONT of the kitchen fire in a vest, under-
pants and shirt belonging to James, while his own slacks,
sweater and jacket were drying off on a clothes-horse. The
hot tea laced with whisky had warmed his blood and made
him feel drowsy. Staying awake required a major effort of
willpower.

There was no newspaper to read because nobody could
get in or out to make a delivery, and the B.B.C. hadn't
given much away. The eleven-thirty morning news broad-
cast headlined a big round-up in London, but oddly, the
only person listed by name amongst those arrested was
Charlotte Seagrave. The police were claiming that she was
the Head of Security, which was news to Garnett. When
he had last been in touch with Vickers the post had been
vacant. He thought it likely that the police were trying to
make a very big production out of a non-event.

The warmth of the fire had a seductive effect. Garnett
yawned, stretched his arms above his head and fought to
stay awake, but inevitably his eyelids drooped and his head
nodded as he succumbed to sleep.

Anne James closed the oven door with a bang, and the
sudden noise sent the adrenalin rate up and in an instant
he was wide awake.

She said, 'Fred will be home soon.'

'Yes?'

She eyed the Luger resting on the arm of his chair. 'He does not approve of guns,' he said.

Garnett shivered. One moment the room was like a furnace, the next it was like the inside of an icebox.

'If there weren't any guns,' she said, warming to her theme, 'wars would be impossible.'

'They did all right in the Middle Ages.'

'Fred abhors violence. His parents were Quakers.'

'What's that make Fred?'

'A good man.'

'Recipe for a good man—hate violence and have Quaker parents!'

'I don't think that's very funny,' she said coldly. Her eyes strayed to the clock on the mantelpiece and she frowned. 'I wonder what is keeping him?' she said.

'Maybe they are short-handed.'

'What?'

'Perhaps some of the staff are being held in Appleby.'

'I hadn't thought of that.' She stared at Garnett. 'You look very flushed,' she said.

'It must be the heat from the fire.'

'Are you sure you're not running a temperature?'

Garnett touched his forehead. It felt as if it was on fire.

'I might have,' he said, 'I don't suppose wading in the river did me much good.'

Anne James opened the small cabinet above the kitchen sink and brought out a bottle of Aspirins. She filled a glass with water, shook two tablets into the palm of her left hand and held them out to Garnett. 'Swallow these,' she said firmly.

'You don't want a sick person on your hands, is that it?'

'Don't make an issue out of it, just do as I ask,' she said.

Garnett swallowed the tablets and handed back the glass. 'Satisfied?' he said.

Both of them heard the front door open. Anne James looked anxious. Perhaps, thought Garnett, she's wondering what Fred is going to say when he finds he has an unexpected guest.

A cheerful voice said, 'It's me, Anne.'

The door to the kitchen opened inwards, and James didn't see Garnett until he was well into the room. Although

38

he was a good half-head shorter than Garnett there wasn't much difference in weight between them. Thin sandy hair crowned a round good-natured face. The friendly smile slowly died when he laid eyes on Garnett. He wasn't angry or surprised or even curious.

He said, 'I suppose you're the man they are looking for.'

In an anxious voice, Anne James said, 'I had to let him in, Fred. Believe me, I had no choice.'

James ignored the interruption, concentrating his gaze on Garnett. 'They say you killed a man last night.'

Garnett eyed the large hands hanging loosely at James's sides and took his time in answering. 'He was a soldier.'

'And that makes it all right, does it?'

'It was him or me. When you bump into an armed enemy in the dark, you don't wait to see if his attitude is friendly or not, not if you want to go on living that is.'

'I hate violence.'

'So your wife said.'

'So why should you expect me to help you?'

'Because I am being hunted like an animal. Look, I lived peacefully in Appleby for nearly six months. I had no intention of going back into the Resistance.'

'You had renounced violence?' James said, almost eagerly.

Garnett said cautiously, 'I'd had enough.'

James rubbed his large hands together as if pleased with the answer he'd got. Essentially a straightforward man, he was incapable of recognising deviousness in others. As far as he was concerned, Garnett was a victim of circumstances and needed his help. His conscience quietly at rest, he turned a smiling face on Anne and said, 'I think we're all ready for lunch, dear.'

James removed one of the chairs grouped round the kitchen table, placed it opposite Garnett and sat down. Anne James began to lay the table; clearly, he didn't believe in helping her with the domestic chores.

'Well, now,' he said cheerfully, 'what are we going to do with you?'

Garnett didn't reply because he had no need to. James had a habit of throwing questions at his audience and then answering them for himself.

'Obviously,' he said, marshalling his thoughts, 'you must

39

get well away from this area. The problem is how?'

'And when,' said Garnett.

'And when,' James muttered. He shook his head as if perplexed. 'Nearly half of our staff are trapped inside Appleby—we were very short-handed this morning.'

'Yes?'

'There is a road block just outside Penrith too, which is causing long delays.' He swivelled in his chair to face his wife. 'George Pemberton was held up for two hours, dear.'

'Really?' she said vaguely.

Garnett said, 'Who's George Pemberton?'

'Our woodwork master. It's quite clear to me that you can't move out of here until the search is called off.' He winked and said brightly, 'I'm just thinking aloud.'

'Of course,' Garnett said drily.

'I'm the careers master—I'm supposed to take seven of our school leavers in a mini-bus over to Kendal this afternoon for an interview with the Youth Employment Officer. I could postpone it until the search is over. How long do you think it will be before the army clears out of the area?'

Garnett shrugged his shoulders. 'A day, maybe two, or could be as much as a week. Even then, they may leave a few road blocks out; and that could be awkward, because if your school leavers hadn't met me before they got on the mini-bus, they might say the wrong thing at the wrong moment.'

James said, 'They will have to get used to your presence. Perhaps if I spoke to the headmaster, we could pass you off as a school inspector, and you could sit in with them during the morning before we set off for Kendal. They wouldn't think anything of it then—I mean you'd be accepted.' He was visibly pleased that he had solved the problem, but then his face fell as he began to appreciate some of the difficulties involved. 'Of course there's the question of papers,' he said slowly.

'I've got a spare identity card—it may be wet but we can dry it out.'

'I was thinking of things like travel documents and School Efficiency Reports which an inspector is bound to have. I can get hold of some blank *pro formas* from the school, but franking them? Well, that's going to be quite a problem.'

40

Garnett said, 'You get hold of the papers and I'll make you a franking stamp to order.'

'How?'

'I cut a potato in half and carve the details of the stamp into the smooth surface, just like making a woodcut.'

'Will it work?'

'Oh yes,' said Garnett, 'you ask any Post Office official. Some years before the war they lost no end on that dodge. You got hold of a Post Office Savings Book which belonged to somebody else, entered a load of false deposits and franked the entries with various date and address stamps, and then you took the book along to any Post Office other than the one which originally issued it, and drew out money which had never been deposited. The people who worked that fraud used up a lot of potatoes but they got a pretty fair return.'

Anne James banged the plates down on the table. 'Lunch is ready,' she said testily.

James stood up. 'Is anything wrong, dear?' he said mildly.

'Is anything wrong?' she echoed. 'Don't you realise what you are taking on? Didn't the police tell you that the man they are after is David Garnett? He's on their Wanted List, and yet here you are talking of involving your headmaster and the boys in your class. Don't you ever stop to think of the consequences? Of what might happen to them if you're caught? Isn't it enough that we have sheltered him?'

'I think we ought to do more than just offer him a meal.' He glanced at Garnett and a worried frown appeared on his face. 'I say,' he said anxiously, 'are you feeling all right? You don't look very well to me.'

Garnett stood up and started to move towards the table. 'I've got a slight temperature,' he mumbled, 'nothing to get alarmed about.'

He felt light-headed, and he had difficulty in focusing his eyes. He looked down at his feet and the floor rose up to meet him. As Garnett toppled forward, he reached out to grab a chair for support. He took the chair with him as he hit the floor.

Garnett could feel the warm autumn sun on his back,

and he felt singularly light-headed, because he hadn't eaten since going over the wall of the Lichfield Detention Centre some three days previously. He had been heading in a south-westerly direction, and to begin with he had adopted a policy of hiding up during the day and moving only when it was dark, but now that he was drawing near to Bristol, he had abandoned all caution.

He passed through what had once been a small wood. The trees, mere blackened stumps in a bed of grey ash, were a sign that he had reached the outer limit of the fire storm which the SCRAGG H-bomb had created. He calculated that he was thirty kilometres from Ground Zero and a stinking crater.

And now, with each passing hour, the evidence of widespread destruction mounted. The burnt skeletons of outlying villages gave way to partially standing buildings marking the line where the blast wave had finally spent its energy. And then ultimately, in the distance, he could see a vast area of rubble radiating out from Ground Zero. There was not a familiar landmark in sight.

He had no idea in which direction Keynsham lay, but it scarcely mattered now. There was not the slightest chance that Liz and his son had survived the holocaust, and yet he felt compelled to go on. The monstrous odour of burnt flesh and decaying bodies wafted in the air, and he found it necessary to tie a handkerchief over his nose and mouth. In that dead, disgusting world the only sound to reach his ears was the faint throb of bulldozers. Instinctively, he began to walk towards them, stopping every now and then to confirm that he was moving in the right direction. And now he noticed the silhouettes of the dead burnt into the road by a fireball many times more powerful than the sun, which had acted like a camera recording their presence before totally obliterating them. Perhaps, he thought sickeningly, Liz too was just a shadow on a wall somewhere.

Eventually, Garnett came to an open space which might have been either a park or mere wasteland. Stretching as far as the eye could see were a large number of evenly spaced signboards. He went up to one and read the notice. Block capital letters in white on a black background stated:

DANGER
NUCLEAR RADIATION HAZARD
KEEP OUT!
THIS MEANS YOU!

It didn't make sense because he could still hear the bull-dozers, and they were well inside the nuclear boundary fence. Garnett ignored the warning signs, and some four hundred metres beyond the signboards, he chose to ignore the little yellow triangles which were strung out across the landscape like washing hanging on a line. If he had looked up when he ducked beneath the strand of wire, he might have noticed that the yellow triangles sported a death's-head in black.

Someone was shouting, and glancing to his right, Garnett saw a figure in a brown smock, breeches and peaked hat. And as he stood there puzzled, wondering what the man had said, he saw the rifle come up into the Rus-sian's shoulder and he didn't know whether to put up his hands or make a run for it. And then it was just as though someone had slammed him in the chest with a sledge-hammer, and unable to stop himself, he cartwheeled over and over down a bank into a steep drainage ditch, and found himself lying on his back staring up at the pale blue sky, powerless to move because of the pain in his chest and back. And he heard someone running, their footsteps muffled in the ashy soil, and then the Russian appeared above him and he found himself looking into the mouth of the Kalashnikov A.K.M., and he thought, 'I suppose this is where it all ends, and it's funny but I don't really give a damn.' And as he watched the finger tighten on the trigger, he heard another voice shouting, 'Niet, niet,' and the Russian lowered the A.K.M., and that was the last thing he remembered.

Garnett came out of the nightmare and found himself staring at a rose-patterned wallpaper. For a minute or so he didn't know where he was, and then he realised that James must have put him to bed in one of the spare rooms. He was still groggy and his body felt as if it was on fire. He was tempted to kick off the bedclothes, but even that needed

43

more energy than he could summon. The door opened quietly and, turning his head, he saw James standing there.

James said, 'I thought I would look in to see how you are.'

'How long have I been here?' His voice sounded like a croaking bullfrog.

'About three-quarters of an hour. I'm just on my way back to school.' James shoved his hands into both jacket pockets and looked down at the floor. 'I think we shall have to forget the idea of taking you into Kendal. I mean, you won't be fit enough.'

With an effort, Garnett raised himself up on one elbow.

'Listen,' he said, 'don't you worry about me. If they've pulled out, I'll be strong enough to go tomorrow.'

James smiled disbelievingly.

'I mean it.'

'All right, you mean it. Would you like something to eat? A cup of soup maybe?'

Garnett sank back on the pillows. 'Later,' he muttered, 'much later.' He was asleep by the time James had reached the hall downstairs.

The soldiers pulled out just before dark. They had gone through every house like a plague of locusts, smashing radios and television sets, breaking furniture and windows, slashing clothing and bedding, and wrenching doors off their hinges. They stole money, food, drink, cigarettes and anything else that took their fancy. They came from the 281st Battalion, and they had a bad reputation in the militia before they came to Appleby. Now they would be remembered and hated as Cromwell's men had been after Drogheda and Wexford.

Lake's house was dark and cold—dark because every light-bulb and candle had been removed; cold because every window had been smashed. Lake knelt under the staircase and by touch sought out and removed the nails securing the trapdoor to the hide. It took him over two hours to release Dane.

6

THE MORE GARNETT LIVED with it, the more clearly he saw
the risks and flaws in the escape plan. There had been no
difficulty in securing the headmaster's co-operation, and
James had provided him with a plausible enough cover
story, but even so, if they were stopped by a road block,
explaining his presence in Bolton could still be tricky.

The school was almost midway between two road blocks
which had been established on the A66, one outside
Penrith, the other on the western edge of Appleby. To
reach the school Garnett would have had to have gone
through one of these two road blocks. The other worrying
thing was that the quickest way to Kendal was through
Appleby and Orton, and since Garnett had lived in Appleby
there was a chance that someone in the local police might
know him by sight. Yet, if the road to Orton wasn't blocked
by snow drifts, and they went via Penrith, it might be
awkward if they were asked to explain why they had
chosen to go the long way round to Kendal. Garnett also
had to consider the possibility that the guards at the road
blocks might be listing everyone they had checked through.
Eventually, Garnett came to the conclusion that anyone
coming out of Appleby would be subjected to a more
rigorous check than someone trying to enter the town.

The army called off its search on the Wednesday night,

45

but they delayed making a move until the Friday to give Garnett more time to recover. The fact that the snow ploughs were still working to clear the drifts on the Orton Road, gave James an excuse to postpone the visit to the Youth Employment Officer in Kendal for twenty-four hours. It also gave him a day in which to observe the road blocks in action. And on Thursday, at Garnett's suggestion, he collected those members on the staff who lived in Appleby and took them home again in the evening.

Between eight o'clock in the morning and four-thirty that afternoon James passed through the road block on four occasions noting what he saw and, at the same time establishing a pattern of behaviour. During the final trip he noticed that the road block guard had been changed and, learning that the new lot had come on duty at two o'clock, he casually mentioned that although the school was being inspected on the following day, he would still have to fit in a visit to Kendal somehow. As Garnett had foreseen, the police displayed very little interest, but the whole idea was to prepare them in advance for what was to happen on the following day. Garnett believed that their curiosity would be dulled if they were half expecting to see James and a crowd of schoolboys on their way to Kendal, and knowing that the school was being inspected would go a long way to explain his presence on the bus.

Garnett had made it sound so easy, but now, sitting there in the staff room with him while they waited for the boys to get ready, James could feel his confidence ebbing. They had done their best to change Garnett's appearance, but James couldn't help feeling that it took more than a neatly pressed suit, a Gannex mac, briefcase, trilby hat and glasses to change a man.

He leaned forward and tapped Garnett on the knee. 'Are you all right?' he said hoarsely.

Garnett said, 'Stop worrying.'

'I'm not worried.'

'Oh, no?'

'No, really—I was just wondering if you still had a temperature.'

'If I have, the M. and B. tablets are doing a good job of disguising it.'

46

James glanced at his wristwatch. 'I think we ought to be going,' he said reluctantly.

Garnett cleared his throat. 'I don't know what I would have done without your help.'

James looked down at the carpet and turned a delicate shade of pink. 'It was nothing,' he muttered.

'I won't minimise the risks—if they recognise me, you and Anne will be in serious trouble.'

'Yes, I know.'

'You could end up in a Forced Labour Camp. Naturally, I'll understand if you want to back out.'

In a quiet voice, James said, 'I think we've gone too far to think of opting out now.'

'All right. If it's any comfort, we've got two things going for us—you've prepared the ground, and the day before yesterday the police had a report that I was seen in Temple Sowerby. We've got at least an even chance of pulling it off.' James got up and walked towards the door. 'We'll know soon enough,' he said wryly.

James started the mini-bus, reversed out of the parking slot and headed off down the drive. There was a sudden howl of laughter as Garnett made some remark to the boys which he didn't catch. He envied Garnett's apparent lack of concern.

Rain falling from a grey sky turned the snow to slush. A Ford pick-up overtook them and as it pulled in sharply, its rear wheels flicked up a fine spray of muck which covered the windscreen of the mini-bus. The wipers smeared the dirt, leaving James with just a narrow visor of clear glass to peer through. He tried flushing the screen but, when nothing happened, he guessed that the feed lines were frozen up, and he could have kicked himself for not adding anti-freeze to the reservoir. He nearly rammed the Ford when it halted at the road block.

Heart thumping against his ribs, he watched the police sergeant slowly approaching the mini-bus. James opened the side window and stuck his head out.

The sergeant said, 'Afternoon, Mr. James.'

James swallowed. He managed a sickly smile and said, 'Good afternoon, Sergeant Shaw. I'm on my way to Kendal

47

with the boys to see the Youth Employment Officer. I'm a bit late.'

Shaw said, 'Who's the stranger, Mr. James?'

'Mr. Ingersoll, the school inspector—he's been finding out how efficient we are. I offered him a lift into Kendal.'

James was surprised to find that he had managed to speak with such calm assurance.

The sergeant said, 'Let's see his identity card.'

Garnett tapped James on the shoulder and gave him an identity card. Somewhat apprehensively, James, in turn, handed it to Shaw. Sergeant Shaw was by no means an imaginative man, but he was very thorough. Carefully, he studied the photograph on the card and then looked up at Garnett. Seconds seemed like minutes to James and, unable to bear the suspense any longer, he found a piece of rag and climbed out of the mini-bus.

Smiling apologetically at Shaw, he said, 'I can hardly see through the windscreen—the washers are frozen up.'

Shaw said, 'You should have put a drop of anti-freeze in the reservoir, Mr. James.'

'Yes, I should have thought of that.'

James rubbed away at the windscreen with more energy than effectiveness, and from his vantage point, was able to watch Garnett. He saw him yawn and cup his hand over his mouth—the man looked absolutely at ease and, not for the first time, James found himself envying Garnett. Whether or not he had distracted Shaw's concentration, he was nonetheless relieved to see the police sergeant hand back the identity card to Garnett without a word being spoken.

As James climbed back into the mini-bus, Sergeant Shaw said, 'Going via Orton, Mr. James?'

'Yes.'

'Okay, I'll tell our other road block to wave you through.'

James smiled gratefully, shifted into first gear and followed the Ford pick-up through the road block. He let out an audible sigh of relief.

Stratton had established a look-out above the newsagent's from where he could observe both the A66 and the bridge over the River Eden. O'Dwyer, occupying the station master's office was covering Appleby Station. After forty-eight hours of almost continuous duty, with only a reticent police constable for company, Stratton was beginning to lose interest. He was sick of smoking, sick of drinking endless cups of stewed tea, and was fast coming to the conclusion that Hulf must be losing his marbles if he seriously believed that Dane was still hiding inside the town.

He picked up the binoculars and went through the motions of a check search, logging everything he saw, because that was what Hulf wanted. The log sheet made dull reading to date. The fifty-third entry didn't lift it out of the rut either—it said: '1545 hours, two elderly women carrying shopping baskets entered the Co-op.'

Stratton checked the bridge again and whistled softly as he focused in on the girl. She was tall, and the fawn-coloured trench mac she was wearing did nothing to disguise her slim figure. A silk headscarf concealed her hair, black leather boots reached up to her knees but didn't alter the fact that her legs were worth a second glance. She was looking down at the pavement to prevent the rain driving into her face, and so Stratton really couldn't see her features, but he was pretty certain it was Dane, for the simple reason that it was the first time he had laid eyes on this girl since coming on duty, and she was the sort of dish he was unlikely to forget. He called up O'Dwyer on the Mitre radio set.

He said, 'Could be suspect is coming your way. Confirm and report.'

Fifteen minutes later O'Dwyer reported, 'Suspect booked return ticket to Leeds, will follow.'

Stratton said, 'All right. Keep in touch and stay out of trouble.'

'You must be joking.'

Stratton laughed. 'I saw her first, you sexy Irish berk.'

Garnett thought it wise to part company with James before they reached County Hall. He had two ideas in mind, the most important of which was to change his appearance yet again, and having done that, he planned to hitch a lift on a truck going south.

Changing his appearance meant changing his clothes. It sounded simple enough, but Garnett had to walk round the best part of the town before he found a shop which specialised in selling off surplus government stores. On the pretext that he was planning to spend Easter walking through the Lake District, he bought a pair of boots, a checked shirt, whipcord slacks and a dark blue reefer jacket. After the assistant had wrapped his purchases, he left the shop carrying the parcel under one arm and made his way to the public lavatories.

At three o'clock in the afternoon the lavatories were deserted. There was no attendant on duty and the urinals stank. Pornographic drawings and cryptic sexual suggestions covered the distempered walls, and most of the light-bulbs were either smashed or missing. Garnett found a cubicle which still had a latch, locked himself in and changed his clothing. He opened the briefcase, removed the Luger and spare magazine and slipped them into his hip pocket. He shoved the pair of shoes inside the briefcase and then, after carefully folding the discarded mac, shirt, jacket and trousers, he placed them on top of the briefcase and wrapped the whole lot up in the brown paper. Using a biro, he addressed the parcel to E. J. Rivers, 39, Tavistock Gardens, Ealing, London W.13. He left the lavatories without regret and went straight to the Post Office to mail the parcel. Garnett didn't know whether there was such a person as E. J. Rivers or if Tavistock Gardens even existed—it was simply an easy way of getting rid of some unwanted clothes.

Leaving the Post Office, he walked towards the outskirts of town looking for a transport café. He found one lying back from the road which had a fair-sized parking area. The choice was limited because trade was slack. There were just four trucks—two articulated E.R.F., a Commer belonging to Watkiss & Son, Haulage Contractors, and a shabby-looking Bedford low loader. Of these four, the low loader seemed the most promising. Garnett walked over to the Bedford and looked around to see if anyone was watching him before raising the tarpaulin at one corner. Waxed card-board boxes were stacked six deep one on top of the other, and stencilled on the side of each box were the words, 'Canford's Tinned Apples—The Best in Britain'. He let the tarpaulin fall back into place, walked down the side of the truck, got into the cab and waited for the driver to appear.

Footsteps crunched on the gravel, the door opened and a burly figure climbed into the cab. He caught sight of Garnett and his jaw dropped. 'What are yo doing here?' he said. He had a Staffordshire accent that was a credit to the Black Country.

Garnett fished the roll of banknotes out of his jacket and peeled off twenty pounds in fives. 'I want to go where you're going.'

The man eyed the notes. 'Where's that then?'

Garnett said, 'I checked the number plates. I figure it could be Wolverhampton.'

The driver pocketed the money. 'Yo'd be right,' he said. He cranked the engine into life, shifted into gear and pulled away. 'Who yo runnin from?'

'The police.'

The man shook his head and laughed. 'Jus like our kid, he always comes straight out with it. What are yo going to do if we're stopped by the police?'

'We'll worry about that when it happens.'

'We?'

'I don't think you'd like it much if they were to take a close look at your load.'

'Why?'

'You're a one-man haulage business—no trade name anywhere on your truck. I think you're carrying something more than tinned apples.'

'Jus medicinal comforts.'

'Such as?'

'Whisky.'

They turned into the slip road for the M6, ran down the filter lane and eased out into the traffic. The driver said, 'M' name's Cas, short for Caswell. What's yourn?'

'Dave.'

Caswell winked and said, 'Be a bit embarrassing if we did get stopped though—might have to tip them off about yo, to save me own skin like.'

Garnett slid the Luger out of his hip pocket and showed it to Caswell. 'You do that,' he said pleasantly, 'and I'll blow your bloody head off.'

Caswell didn't blink so much as an eyelash. 'That really would be a bit of hard luck.'

51

'Wouldn't it.'

'Jus like Enoch and Eli.'

'Who?'

'Enoch and Eli—they both werked in the pits, see, only Eli, he had brains and so he went away to better hisself, and comes back a lawyer. And one day, on his way home from werk, our Enoch sees this sign up in Cannock saying—"Eli—Solicitor", and Eli says to Enoch, "If ever yo'm in trouble yo come and see me." About three weeks later, Enoch calls on Eli and says, "I'm in trouble." Eli says, "Oh yes?" "Yes," says Enoch, "yo know we'm got a lodger." And Eli says, "Go on." "Well," says Enoch, "the other night I come home from werk and the lodger was in the alleyway by our house with the wife, and he had his hand on it, and I don't like it." "Did he?" says Eli, reaching for his law book and searching through it. After a bit, he says, "Are yo sure it was his hand, Enoch?" And Enoch says, "Yes." "Well," says Eli, "I reckon yo've had a bit of bad luck." "Bad luck?" echoes Enoch. "Yes," says Eli, "if it was his foot, we'm could have had the bugger for trespass."'

Measured on a map, Kendal is 227 kilometres from Wolverhampton. At an average speed of eighty kilometres an hour, the journey took them a shade under three hours. Caswell talked non-stop—his fund of dirty stories was bottomless.

7

GARNETT STAYED WITH CASWELL in his back to back house near the Molineux Sports Ground, because he didn't want to arrive in London late at night when the railway police were at their most vigilant. He thought there was less risk of being stopped for a snap search in daylight when there were more people about. Staying the night in Wolverhampton also gave him the opportunity to acquire a fresh change of clothes. Inevitably, Caswell knew a tailor who wasn't too fussed about clothing coupons as long as he was paid over the odds. Luck, too, was favouring Garnett. It so happened that Wolves were away to Arsenal, and he figured it would be safer to travel with the Wolverhampton supporters. He caught the nine thirty-six out of Wolverhampton and arrived at Euston at eleven fifty-four. He had to stand all the way.

Garnett came into the open concourse at Euston and stayed with the crowd as they moved in a solid block towards the Underground. A couple of policemen standing outside Menzies' bookstall gave him a nasty moment when they looked his way, and he was glad that he had ditched the Luger before he set off. There was always the chance that he could bluff his way through a snap check, but if they found a gun on him, he would be finished. The policemen, however, merely eyed the noisy crowd disdainfully and decided to stay aloof.

Garnett took the Victoria Line as far as Oxford Circus,

changed on to the Bakerloo and got out at Baker Street. He thought it unlikely that anyone would be following him, but where security was concerned he made it a rule never to assume anything. He walked along Baker Street until he found an empty call box.

He went inside, closed the door behind him, rang 89140625 and waited. An enterprising call girl had wedged a pink card in the slot where it said, 'In an Emergency ring 999', and now it read, 'In an Emergency ring Miss Lash 95968946—French and Deportment lessons taught under strict supervision'.

A male voice said, 'Hullo.'

Garnett said, 'This is Tim. I've been out of touch for some months. I'd like to make an appointment with the man.'

Someone at the other end cleared his throat and then said, 'Okay Tim, hang on.'

Garnett hung on counting off the seconds. He got up to one minute forty and began to sweat.

The same deep voice said, 'Baron's Court Station, three-thirty.'

'I'll be there,' said Garnett. He hung up and left the call box in a hurry.

Everything was wrong. He should have hung up and left before the minute was up, but he wanted to confirm his doubts. Well, all right, he thought, so now you know the contact number is blown, because no one in the Resistance would be stupid enough to fix an R.V. without running a check on the caller. Last time he had used that number, Control had sent him on a grand tour of the Underground and had made him call back half a dozen times before they were satisfied enough to give him the R.V.

He hopped a number 74 bus to Marble Arch and took to the Underground again. If they had a computer memory bank on the circuit, it was possible they had traced his call, and he was determined to leave a confusing trail behind him. He spent an hour switching trains before alighting at Fulham Broadway, where he joined the crowd moving towards Stamford Bridge Stadium. He went through the turnstiles, bought a programme and positioned himself in the middle of the crowd behind the far goal post. He opened the programme—Chelsea were at home to West Bromwich.

He spent just over two hours in the tightly packed arena on an open terrace watching a goal-less draw. It wasn't Garnett's idea of how to pass the time on a cold, raw, February afternoon, but at least it gave him time to think.

He had to find another way of contacting Vickers, and that entailed visiting some or all of their previous meeting places in the hope of picking up a lead. Some, like the Antique Shop at Harrow on the Hill and Bloom's house in Hampstead were no longer safe because they were known to Seagrave, and it was possible that under interrogation she had told Special Branch about them. In any case, as far as Bloom was concerned, Garnett had met him only once, and that at a cocktail party given ostensibly to celebrate the publication of a bestseller by one of Bloom's authors. Bloom hadn't impressed Garnett then, and even supposing he was still in circulation, Garnett didn't feel disposed to trust him.

Garnett was left with the choice of a disused G.P.O. tunnel in Kilburn, a call girl's flat in Havelock Gardens and a grocer's shop on Paradise Street. He crossed the tunnel off the list because no one was likely to be there. He decided to try Havelock Gardens first because it was the nearer of the two from Stamford Bridge. It took him some minutes to recall that the girl's name was Jean Inglis.

When the stadium emptied, Garnett stayed with the crowd until he reached Fulham Broadway, where he stopped to buy an *Evening Standard* before entering a snack bar. He sat up at the counter, ordered a cheeseburger and coffee and read the paper from cover to cover. The news was as bad as it could be.

Splashed on the front page were the photographs of two men. In one, taken in a cellar as far as Garnett could judge, a man was lying on his stomach with his head turned over to one side. A pool of blood had formed around his open mouth. The caption above said, 'Steven Cripps, Head of Intelligence'. The other photograph was a police mug shot. The man, round-faced, double-chinned, with thick, dark unruly hair, was staring pop-eyed into the camera. He was listed as Mervyn Donnelly, Director of Propaganda.

With Seagrave, Donnelly and Cripps accounted for, only Vickers and the Co-ordinator of Political Strategy were left. Garnett found he had lost his appetite. He finished the coffee and left the snack bar.

Havelock Gardens was still the same seedy-looking square it had been when last he saw it eleven months ago, except there seemed to be a few more Pakistanis and West Indians about. The park, which was encircled by terraced houses with slate roofs and shabby colour-washed walls, had accumulated a collection of worn-out tyres, rusting bicycles and a battered pram. The few remaining evergreen bushes were fighting a losing battle against the encroaching rubbish.

Number 165, Havelock Gardens was no different. The house still reeked of boiled cabbage, curry and sour sweat and, like the last time, the staircase creaked under his weight. Garnett stopped outside Flat 3, rapped on the door and waited. A voice said, 'Come in, the door's open.' He went inside. The girl was wearing a pink satin trouser suit and open-toed sandals. A silver-coloured plastic belt hugged her narrow waist and toned with the silver lipstick on her mouth and the glitter dust on her eyelids. She was a Nigerian and she felt the cold. Two electric fires were burning in the room, the heat full on.

In a soft voice, she said, 'Well now, you look as surprised as what I am. I'm Josephine Appiah. Who are you? —the new rent collector?'

Garnett said, 'How long have you been living here?'

Her eyes narrowed. 'No, I guess you're not the rent collector after all.'

'I'm looking for a friend.'

'Aren't we all.'

'Jean Inglis, you know of her?'

'A prostitute used to live here.'

'That's right.'

'And she was Jean Inglis?'

'Yes.'

A harsh note crept into her voice. 'All right, white trash,' she said coldly, 'get out of here. I'm no call girl, I sing for my bread.'

Garnett said, 'Do you know where I can find Inglis?'

'Man, you really must be aching for it.' Her voice was a spiteful hiss. The long slim fingers plucked at the belt around her waist. 'What makes you think I know where your whore is? Do you think all my friends are whores?'

'I didn't say that.'

'You see a black girl, and your mind says, wham, there's an easy lay.'

'How the hell do you know what I'm thinking?'

'I read it in your eyes, whitey.'

Garnett said quietly, 'For the last time, do you know where I can find Inglis?'

'No, I goddamn well don't know where you can find your piece of tail. I told you to get out of here.' She paused for breath and then shouted, 'Now git.'

She had removed the belt and was holding it in her right hand. Appiah swung her arm back and lashed out at Garnett. The steel buckle just missed his eyes as he jerked his head out of the way. Appiah lurched forward off balance, Garnett grabbed her arm, twisted it up behind her back, prised the belt out of her hand and threw it across the room. He cupped his free hand over her mouth before she had a chance either to yell out or sink her teeth into his fingers. She tried back-heeling his shins but it didn't come off.

'All right,' he said, 'you've made your point. I'm leaving.'

It didn't make any difference. Sharp talons dug into his thigh, bruised the flesh and then groped upwards towards his groin. Garnett put his knee into the small of her back and shot Appiah across the room. She hit the divan bed with both legs and went over it head first. Garnett was out of the room and running down the flight of stairs before she had picked herself up off the floor.

'You bastard,' she screamed, 'you bastard.'

As he reached the front door, she came out on to the landing and heaved a glass ashtray after him. It shattered on the floor. Nobody took any notice. In that crowded slum tenement they had grown accustomed to a woman rowing with her man. Garnett walked out of the square and made his way to the tube station.

Paradise Street didn't live up to its name. It was just one

57

more of the countless number of streets full of semi-detached houses which the Victorians had bequeathed London. All of the houses looked solid, unimaginative and depressingly uniform. Chestnut trees, rooted in asphalt, lined the pavement on one side of the street like soldiers on parade, while opposite, a corrugated iron fence over three metres high enclosed one end of the football ground. The lamp-posts, some fifty metres apart, cast a narrow pool of light in their immediate area in an otherwise dark street. One abandoned Morris Oxford was parked in the road, its innards gutted by scavengers in search of spare parts.

The shop, which belonged to Bullivant and Son, stood on the corner of Paradise Street and Inkerman Road. A light was showing in the room above the shop.

Garnett walked down the narrow alleyway adjoining the shop, and found an iron staircase leading to the flat above. He climbed the steps and rang the door bell. Bath water gurgled down the waste outlet and then, in the comparative silence which followed this deluge, he could hear a radio close at hand competing with the T.V. He rang the bell again. The volume on the radio was turned down, and a woman said, 'See who's at the door, Ted.'

There was no reaction. The voice climbed an octave. 'The door, Ted, for God's sake.'

Feet in carpet slippers padded towards the door, the key turned in the lock, a bolt was drawn and the door opened a fraction. Framed in the crack was a long, wizened-looking face.

Garnett said, 'Remember me?'

Ted said, 'As if I could forget. Anybody follow you?'

'No.'

He opened the door wider and Garnett stepped into the light and began unbuttoning his coat. Ted re-locked and bolted the door. 'Planning on staying then?' he said.

'I want to see the man.'

'What man?'

'The one I talked to in your front room some months ago.'

'Oh, him.'

'Yes, him.'

'Have you got a name?'

58

'Garnett.'

'I'm Hall, Ted Hall. You don't want much, do you?'

'Can you contact the man?'

Hall scratched his large stomach. 'It'll take time.'

'How long?'

'A day, maybe two, depends on the runners. You want to stay here?'

'Yes.'

'I don't know what Marie will have to say.'

'Who's Marie?'

'The wife. She can be funny at times.'

Neither of them heard the kitchen door open. A voice said, 'Who can be funny?'

The woman was about thirty-five, a blonde whose hair was too yellow to be natural. Taller than her husband, she had a plump but still shapely figure. Under the red quilted-nylon dressing gown which hung open to her waist, she was wearing a plain black slip. The slip was a tight fit; it hugged the curve of her stomach and the swell of her breasts.

'Cat got your tongue, Ted?' she said.

'No.'

'Well then?'

'Mr. Garnett is staying the night,' Hall said tentatively.

Marie Hall looked at Garnett with renewed interest. A smile hovered on her lips. 'Good,' she said, 'we haven't had company for a long time. Have you eaten?'

'Very little.'

'Eggs and bacon okay?'

'Fine.'

Marie Hall walked over to the stove and lit the gas. 'Better check the front, Ted, to make sure no one is hanging around.'

'He said he wasn't followed.'

She broke two eggs into the frying pan and added a couple of rashers.

Hall said, 'You really think I ought to take a look, Marie?'

She clenched her teeth. 'Yes, Ted,' she said heavily, 'I do think you ought to.'

Hall shuffled out of the room. He seemed reluctant to leave them alone.

His wife said, 'He wasn't always like that. You wouldn't have recognised him a few years ago; full of confidence he was before he had the accident.'

'What accident?'

'Got knocked off his bike by a bus, broke a leg and fractured his skull.' She put the plate of eggs and bacon on the kitchen table and took a knife and fork out of the drawer. 'Sit down then,' she said. She bent over Garnett and placed the knife and fork on either side of the plate, brushing against him as she did so. She drew up a chair and sat down facing Garnett across the narrow table. 'Oh, yes, he was quite a man before he had the accident,' she said dreamily. A knee brushed against his, whether by accident or design he wasn't sure, but he had no intention of finding out.

Dane checked in at the Alton Hotel at six-thirty in the evening. She proposed to stay there until it was time to meet Garnett outside W. H. Smith and Son on Charing Cross Station the following Tuesday morning. She had taken a roundabout route from Appleby, staying the night in Leeds, catching a bus to Sheffield and then coming on to London by train. She was quite certain that she had not been followed.

In this, Dane was mistaken. Special Branch had had her under surveillance from the moment she boarded the train at Appleby, and they never let her out of their sight. O'Dwyer was in the next compartment all the way to Leeds and, when she left the train, a plain-clothes policewoman was waiting for her at the barrier. They had two Panda cars covering the hotel where she stayed the night, and the next day, another policewoman followed her into Sheffield and watched her board the London train. They covered every scheduled stop in case she decided to get off the train before it reached King's Cross where Stratton was waiting for her. Stratton followed her to the Alton, and after telephoning Hulf, booked a room on the same floor.

With Stratton inside the hotel, O'Dwyer watching the back, and a surveillance car parked outside the front, Hulf reckoned he had Dane boxed in tight.

8

On Sunday, Hall attended matins at St. Stephen's in Carisbrooke Grove. There were twenty-six people in the congregation and most of them were elderly. Occasionally, the numbers would fluctuate, usually when a couple's banns were being read, but more often than not there was just the same faithful flock.

Although Hall belonged to the regular faction, he paid little heed to the service, and it was always something of a relief when the sermon ended and the collection was taken. He used the church as a D.L.B., hiding the message in the sealed offering which he put on the collection plate. Frequently, his offertory envelope contained only money, but on this occasion there was a slip of filter paper stuck to the ten pence piece, on which was written, 'Garnett wants to see the man. Can you arrange soonest?'

The message would get to the head sidesman, and Hall was banking that he would be able to fix the meeting. If he couldn't, then Hall had a problem, because not knowing the next link in the chain, it looked as if he might be stuck with Garnett, and the idea didn't appeal to him at all. He didn't like the way Marie was fussing over Garnett, and he was pretty certain she would oppose any move to ease him out of the house if the sidesman failed to contact Vickers.

Hall left the church, called in at the Plough, and by the

61

time he had put away two litres of bitter he was no longer worried about Garnett. Belching cheerfully, he went on home, ate his usual large Sunday dinner and then, armed with the Sunday papers, took to his bed for the rest of the afternoon. A heavy meal on top of the beer ensured that he slept soundly until dark. He got up at seven, half hoping that Marie would tell him she had heard from the sidesman, and was disappointed when it became evident there wasn't any message.

Monday came raw, wet and cold. From the vantage point of the sitting room above the shop, Garnett could see most of Paradise Street, but in the two hours that had elapsed since he began his self-appointed vigil, nothing of note had happened. People came and went about their business pretty much as they did on any other day, and yet every time the shop bell tinkled, Garnett wondered if the caller had come for him. By midday he was half convinced that either Hall's contact had failed to get in touch with Vickers, or else Vickers didn't want to see him. And suddenly he realised how much he was depending on Vickers. He had just under forty pounds and the clothes he stood up in and, apart from Hall, there was no one he could turn to for help. He didn't believe forty pounds was going to take Dane and himself very far.

It was the first time he had really thought about Dane in several days, and it came as a bit of a shock to find that concern for his own survival had pushed all thought of Dane out of his mind, and for a moment he was reminded of Liz who, whenever they quarrelled, was apt to bring up the subject of his selfishness. It was an accusation which always left him feeling uncomfortably aware that there was more than a grain of truth to it. He had once tried to convince Liz that, at worst, he was just thoughtless, and she had said, 'You tell me where thoughtlessness ends and selfishness begins,' and there was no answer to that.

A sudden squall of hail bombarded the window, particles of ice bounced off the road and then settled to form a white layer on the tarmac. A postman in a khaki-coloured ground sheet stopped just short of the shop, dismounted, propped his bicycle against the kerb, and then became lost to sight as he walked down the alleyway. He re-appeared a minute or so later, got back on his bike and wobbled off down the street.

Garnett lit a cigarette and walked away from the window. He flopped into a chair, picked up the *Daily Express* and scanned the front page. He didn't feel up to reading it. Before the war, a headline like—'Extensive Police Raids in Greater London Area'—might have comforted the law-abiding citizens, but in this upside down world, it could only please the collaborators. He turned to the centre pages —James Bond had gone, to be replaced by a devoted social worker called Jane Powell who endeavoured to brighten the lives of all around her, especially the workers at the State Tractor Plant. Garnett hoped that one day the cartoonist would get drunk and let one of his strapping workers literally stuff Jane Powell and give her a problem of her very own to work on. The day that happened he knew he would be living in a free country.

Restlessly he tossed the paper to one side, eased himself out of the chair, and for want of something better to do, began to fiddle with Hall's transistor set. Saccharine music from Radio 2 filled the room. A girl sang 'I want to be loved by you'. He flicked on to Radio 4 and the Minister of Agriculture was saying '... Well, of course, it's true we had a bumper harvest last year, but the re-deployment of the Soviet Forces will entail some interruption of trade with Europe and therefore we must expect some temporary shortages...' And Garnett thought, 'They're going to cut the rations again.' He went back to Radio 2 again, and a syrupy voice said, '... and now for Mrs. Irene Harvey of Calshott Gardens, Streatham, who is the proud mother of two sons serving in the militia, here is an old favourite of hers—"Strangers in the Night".'

Hall said, 'The postman's just been.'

Garnett switched off the radio and turned round slowly. Hall was wearing a broad smile and was clutching an oblong-shaped manilla envelope in his hand.

'It's for you,' he said.

Garnett stubbed out his cigarette, took the envelope from Hall and noticed that it had already been opened. He shook out a circular and read it. Printed in red at the top was 'Nash and Stansfield, Estate Agents, 141 High Street,

Wembley', and underneath—'For Sale. Desirable Semi-detached at 88, Thurlby Road, Wembley, consisting of Lounge, Dining Room, Kitchen, Scullery; Bathroom, Lavatory and 3 bedrooms on first floor; Lavatory and 2 small bedrooms on second floor. Large Garden. Freehold £12,500. May be viewed weekdays between 2 p.m. and 4 p.m. by arrangement with agents.'

Garnett turned the envelope over and saw that it had been addressed to Hall. 'Thinking of moving?' he said.

Hall blinked. 'What are you talking about? It's for you. The sidesman set it up.'

Garnett said, 'You don't like me much. This could be a good way of getting rid of an unwanted guest.'

'It's on the level, ask Marie.'

'Maybe I will.'

Hall jerked the door open. 'Marie,' he shouted, 'come on up here a moment.'

'What is it? I'm busy.'

'It's important.'

She came up the staircase, walking heavily and muttering under her breath. 'All right,' she said, brushing a strand of brass coloured hair out of her eyes, 'I'm here, now what?'

Garnett said, 'You wouldn't be thinking of moving would you, Marie?'

'What?'

'To Wembley.'

She eyed the circular in his hand. 'Oh, that,' she said. 'It's for you. You have to be there between two and four.'

Hall said eagerly, 'It's nearly half past twelve now, I should get started if I were you. Trains on the Underground are few and far between at this time of day.'

'Where are your manners? Let him eat first.'

'There isn't time,' Hall said stubbornly.

'No,' said Garnett, 'you're quite right, there isn't time.'

He went along to the small box room at the end of the hall where they had put up a camp bed for him, and collected his coat. Marie followed him.

'You don't have to rush off like this,' she said.

'It's better this way.'

'Ted's no reason to be jealous.'

'I know.'

64

'Worse luck,' she said and smiled impishly.

Garnett grinned. 'Well, anyway, thanks for everything, Marie.'

'It was nothing. Look us up again sometime, won't you,'

'You can bet on that.'

Garnett held out his hand, but she stepped past it and kissed him warmly on the lips. 'Look after yourself,' she said quietly.

'And you.'

He walked quickly down the hall into the kitchen, opened the back door and ran down the iron staircase leading to the alleyway below. He turned into Paradise Street and started towards the Underground station. He looked back once and waved to Marie, who was standing in the window, and then he turned the corner and she was out of sight. The hail had changed to a light drizzle.

He played the usual game of tag on the Underground, doubling back on his tracks and using up an hour before he finally connected with the Bakerloo Line at Edgware Road. He got out at Wembley Central and started looking for Nash and Stansfield.

He found the estate agents next door to a bookseller's, which called itself 'The Sex Shop'. 'The Sex Shop' was one of the peculiarities of Occupied England. Part of a nation-wide chain of pornographic retailers, it secretly enjoyed a government subsidy, because someone from the Ministry of Propaganda had reasoned that, after a diet of pornography, the reading public would turn with some relief to novels which pushed the Party line. He might have had a point because 'The Sex Shop' wasn't doing much business. Garnett opened the door to Nash and Stansfield. They weren't very busy either.

A slim girl, whose dark hair was scraped into a bun on top of her head, was seated at a desk just inside the door. She was reading a book which was propped against the typewriter. Opposite her, behind a larger and more imposing desk, was a young man about twenty-four or twenty-five years old, who stood up as Garnett entered. The most striking thing about him was his hair. Garnett had never seen anything quite like it—cut short, it was the colour of silver sand. Pale blue expressionless eyes stared at him as though measuring him up. The alabaster skin was stretched as tight as a drum across his high cheekbones. He was a shade taller than Garnett, and although he must have been several kilos heavier, there was no spare flesh on his frame.

Garnett said, 'Good afternoon, Mr. . . . ?'

'Nash.'

'I'm interested in buying a house, Mr. Nash.'

'Of course. What price have you in mind?'

'Around twelve and a half thousand.'

'We have several properties in that bracket which might suit you.'

'I had my eye on 88, Thurlby Road.'

Nash said, 'I'm sorry, it's no longer available.'

'Why?'

'The owner decided against selling.'

'I received a circular this morning advising me it was for sale.'

'There must have been an error.'

Garnett said, 'I find that hard to believe.'

'Perhaps you'd like to have a word with Mr. Stansfield?'

'I'd like to very much.'

The thin smile was still there on Nash's face but he hadn't taken hold of Garnett's arm out of friendship. The grip on the tendons behind the elbow was painfully effective and ensured that, if Garnett was carrying a gun, he was in no position to use it. Still holding him firmly, Nash led Garnett into the inner office.

The room had a fitted carpet which toned in with the white walls. The furnishing was on the austere side. There was no desk, just a plain black-tiled coffee table, on one side of which was a Parker Knoll Statesman armchair upholstered in black vinyl and on the other a ladder-back upright chair. A reproduction of Shepherd's *Elephants at Amboselli* hung on the wall behind the armchair.

Vickers was relaxing in the armchair, rocking gently, and he hadn't changed a bit. The sardonic, half sad, blood-hound face looked no older; the same elegantly attired figure looked just as trim. Inevitably, he was smoking a cigarette in a long black holder. He looked up and said, 'Good of you to drop by, David.'

They hadn't met for five months. The prodigal son might

66

have returned to the fold but Vickers was never a man to kill the fatted calf.

Garnett said, 'Tell your friend I'd like my arm back, General.'

Nash released his arm and the blood started flowing again. Garnett sat down in the upright chair facing Vickers, rubbed his elbow and then flexed the fingers of his right hand. Nash remained standing behind Garnett.

'You've arrived at an opportune time, David.'

'I'm surprised you're still available. Surprised but relieved.'

Vickers said, 'I move around a bit.'

'So I've heard. Somewhere different every night.'

'A myth, David, but it helps to create the mystique.'

'We've been flushed.'

'So have a lot of other people.' Vickers ejected the cigarette from the holder and stubbed it out. 'It should never have happened, David, not with the Russians pulling out. We should have been looking forward to victory, not defeat.'

Garnett said, 'How did they know where to find Dane and me, General?'

'I told Seagrave to keep a check on your movements because I thought there was a chance you would come back to the fold one day.'

'And they got it out of her?'

Vickers raised an eyebrow. 'I don't imagine they had much difficulty,' he said. 'Do you know Moxham?'

'Who's he?'

'The Co-ordinator of Political Strategy. A month ago, the five of us—Cripps, Donnelly, Seagrave, Moxham and myself—met to discuss future strategy in view of the partial Russian withdrawal from this country. It was my turn to chair the meeting and there were three suggestions on the agenda. The first envisaged no change in policy; the second mooted the possibility of seizing control of selected areas as the Russian Occupation Force was run down; and the third advocated limited co-operation with the puppet government in the hope that we could induce the Russians to withdraw their last three Divisions. The second and third proposals were defeated, which left us stuck with no change in policy.

67

Seagrave voted with me in each case. Only Donnelly voted for co-operation.'

'And yet he was arrested after Seagrave was taken into custody.'

'If we are to believe what we read in the papers.'

'You think it might be a cover up?'

'I thought it possible until I heard you had been flushed. Only Seagrave could have supplied them with your address. I'd like to know who is supporting her.'

'Maybe she is acting on her own?'

Nash said harshly, 'We don't think so.'

Garnett turned and stared at Nash. 'Why?' he said.

'Because without help she would be too vulnerable.'

'It would seem,' Garnett said slowly, 'that by a simple process of deduction, either you or Moxham are involved, General.'

'I don't find that very amusing,' Vickers said icily.

'I wasn't joking.'

'I'm disappointed in you, David. You are viewing the situation with a narrow, closed mind. Why rule out those lower down in the chain of command? Perhaps others were aware of what happened at the last meeting. Certainly, more than one person in Political Strategy would know what was on the agenda.'

'You should have been a diplomat, General.'

Vickers placed the tips of his fingers together and looked at a point on the wall above Garnett's head. 'If I were Seagrave,' he said smoothly, 'I would make sure I had some form of insurance before I allowed Special Branch to get their hands on me, wouldn't you?'

Garnett said, 'With great respect, General, I didn't come here to talk about your problems. I have enough of my own. Tomorrow I meet Dane and we need somewhere to hide.'

Vickers carefully fitted another cigarette into the black holder and took out his gold Dunhill lighter. 'Where is your problem? You are with us now, David.'

'Can I count on you for help?'

Vickers smiled and said, 'If I can count on your help too, David.' The lighter flared briefly and a thin spiral of tobacco smoke curled lazily towards the ceiling.

In a flat voice, Garnett said, 'What do you want me to do this time?'

'I have a simple mind, David. If I went in with Special Branch, I would want a lever on Warner. In fact, I'd make very good use of every facility in my department to get something on him, and if I found he was incorruptible, I wouldn't have anything to do with him.'

Garnett nodded, but before he had time to speak, Vickers said, 'I'm so glad you agree. The number two in Security is Robin Kelso.'

'Yes?'

'Go and see him.'

'Why me?'

'It's just possible Special Branch may have him under surveillance, and Nash has been with me for some time, and do you know, he has become almost indispensable.'

'How nice for Nash.'

'He'll cover you, of course.'

'That is good news,' Garnett said drily.

'From a safe distance.'

'Naturally—I wouldn't want anything to happen to Nash.'

Vickers looked across at Nash and said, 'I think we had better make sure that David is suitably equipped, Peter.'

Nash inclined his head, pushed himself away from the wall against which he had been leaning in a deceptively nonchalant way, and left the room, closing the door quietly behind him. Garnett thought he would have made a good butler.

Garnett said, 'A question.'

'Yes?'

'Why are we so interested in what hold Seagrave may have over Warner?'

'I could put it to better use.'

'Oh?'

'Did you know they are planning to transfer all the political detainees to Russia?'

'No, I didn't.'

Vickers smiled, 'You know,' he said, 'I think it would be rather fun to send the present government to Russia instead of the detainees, don't you?'

'Hilarious,' said Garnett.

The smile was wiped clean. Vickers ejected the burning stub into the ashtray and crushed it with the cigarette holder.

'Kelso's surgery is at 23, Ladbroke Terrace, Hayes.'

'A doctor?'

'Dentist.'

'What about Dane, General?'

'We'll talk about her later. See Nash on your way out, he'll fix you up.'

Nash was waiting for him in the outer office with a coy little .32 revolver and a hip holster. It looked like a toy pistol but, as Nash pointed out, provided Garnett aimed for a vital spot, it was pretty effective. Garnett didn't care for the expression 'pretty effective' and said so, but Nash was unmoved. He gave Garnett an ignition key, told him where to find the Mini, and then briefly indicated how he proposed to cover Garnett while he was in the surgery and where they were to meet afterwards. The briefing didn't inspire Garnett with confidence.

The factories were emptying as he came through the centre of Hayes. Before the war, the High Street would have been jammed with cars at this time of day, but petrol rationing had solved that problem. Now the streets were infested with cyclists, myriads of them flowing out of the factory gates like salmon heading up river. They rode three, sometimes four abreast, weaving in and out of the traffic with an expertise that left Garnett breathless. The other drivers were seemingly used to it—he wasn't. Progress was first gear and a few metres at a time. It took him over three-quarters of an hour to get through the High Street, but once he was over the railway bridge, he hoped his troubles were over. He reached the traffic lights beyond the railway bridge just as H.M.V. closed down for the day. Still surrounded by cyclists, he turned left at the lights and was thankful when he eventually found Ladbroke Terrace. Compared to what he had just been through, Ladbroke Terrace was a haven of rest. Garnett parked the car outside number 23 and got out. It was still drizzling.

There are semi-detacheds and semi-detacheds—23, Ladbroke Terrace was a doll's house. Turning up his coat collar, Garnett pushed open the front gate and walked up the narrow path which was flanked on either side by weed-encroached rose beds. He rang the bell, and from somewhere inside the receptionist tripped the lock. The door swung open and he stepped into the hall.

A pert young face, framed by long, brown, silky hair, smiled at him from behind a desk angled under the stairs. A white smock added to the clinical air of freshness about the girl, and then she spoke, and the abrasive sound of her voice came as a shock.

She said, 'Can I help you?'

'I'd like to make an appointment.'

She frowned briefly. 'Are you on Mr. Kelso's panel?'

Garnett said, 'I've just moved here.'

The girl pointed at the door facing her. 'Would you like to wait in there,' she said, 'perhaps Mr. Kelso's partner can fit you in.'

'I'd like to have Mr. Kelso do an extraction. My mates at H.M.V. tell me he's painless.' Garnett smiled. 'I'm such a bloody coward, see. I'm willing to wait.'

The girl looked down at the desk and studied Kelso's list of appointments. 'You might have to wait a long time.'

'That's all right.'

'Well, all right,' she said, 'it's your tooth.' She pointed to the waiting room again. 'You'll have to wait in there though.'

Garnett went into the room. A ring of faces looked up, met his gaze and then, equally quickly, looked down at their magazines again. Garnett found an empty chair, picked up a copy of *The Practical Motorist* and read an article about how he could economise on consumption and make his petrol ration go further if he drove at a constant cruising speed and avoided sudden bursts of acceleration. There were graphs and statistical tables to prove the point. Garnett didn't understand a word of the technical data, but he was prepared to take the writer's word for it. Bored by the technological eloquence of the article, he put the magazine to one side.

A travel poster on the opposite wall caught his eye and Garnett studied it carefully. It reminded him very much of the Kenya coastline. There were indications of a coral reef and the sand was silver and the fauna was just right. He decided it must be one of the coves near Malindi and he got up and walked across the room to take a closer look, confident that he had got the location right. His face fell when he saw the poster was described as 'Coastline—Southern California'. He went back to his seat and picked up the motoring magazine again.

The waiting room gradually emptied and he was able to edge his way closer to the single-bar electric fire, until eventually he was warm enough to remove his coat. Twenty minutes later the receptionist said Kelso was ready to see him.

Kelso was a slight man with rimless glasses and a monk's patch in his fair hair. He was evidently the sort who didn't feel the cold; the sleeves of his white coat were chopped off above the elbows exposing slim arms thickly covered with fair hair.

Garnett climbed into the dentist's chair; the receptionist closed the door of the surgery and drew a chair up to the desk in the corner.

Kelso said, 'Miss Sleeman will want a few particulars.'

Miss Sleeman uncapped her Biro, glanced at the National Health Form and said, 'We need your name, present address and Social Security Number.'

Garnett said, 'Ronald Gibbs, 24, Sidmouth Drive, Hayes. My Social Security Number is TX 597840.'

The girl frowned, made him repeat the number, corrected what she had originally written down, and then left the room. Kelso lowered the chair and angled it so that Garnett was looking up at the ceiling. He tilted Garnett's head, opened his mouth, bent over him, pressed the tongue down with a spoon-shaped instrument and started looking for the bad tooth. He didn't find it.

Kelso straightened up. 'Why did you come to see me, Mr. Gibbs?' he said quietly.

'Because Charlotte Seagrave said you were good.'

'Oh?'

'Yes. She told me how impressed she was with the way you treated Mr. Warner.'

Kelso said, 'You know, I think that tooth will have to

72

come out, and I think it will be less painful if you had a general anaesthetic.' He pushed the trolley containing the cylinders closer to the chair.

Garnett slid the .32 out of the holster and pointed it at Kelso's stomach. 'No gas,' he said softly, 'and no extraction either. You know, and I know, there's nothing wrong with my teeth.'

There was a faint smile on Kelso's lips, and if he was alarmed, he took good care not to show it. 'All right, Mr. Gibbs,' he said calmly, 'suppose you tell me why you came here?'

In a minute, thought Garnett, I'm going to look damn silly. 'Seagrave is having trouble,' he said. 'We think it's time a little pressure was applied.'

Kelso lit a cigarette and leaned back against a filing cabinet. 'What sort of pressure?'

'We want to lean on Warner.'

Kelso turned round, unlocked the top drawer of the filing cabinet, brought out a slim envelope and tossed it into Garnett's lap. 'Is this what you want?' he said.

Garnett slid the .32 into the holster, opened the envelope, removed the dental card and tipped the snapshots out into his hand. The colour prints were sharp and clear. Two men smiling into the camera—one—young, slim with long, glossy black hair curling over his ears—the other—bigger, older, with short hair going grey, clipped moustache, square jaw—both naked—arms around each other's waists. The remaining three pictures showed them in various postures during intercourse.

Kelso said, 'It takes a special kind of pervert to photograph himself in the act, but then Warner is a very kinky bastard—A.C. and D.C., you know the type?'

'I've met them.' Garnett slipped the photographs into the breast pocket of his jacket, got up out of the chair and walked towards the door.

'They're not the only ones.'

'What?'

'Copies are held by other custodians.'

'So?'

'So, if you're from Special Branch, these prints won't

end the matter; there are others on the market and arresting me won't do you any good.'

'Do I look like a policeman?'

'I've seen some who are just like you.'

'Thanks a lot.'

Garnett opened the door and went out into the hall. He collected his coat from the waiting room, said good night to Miss Sleeman and let himself out into the street. The weather hadn't changed—it was still drizzling.

Garnett unlocked the Mini, slid inside, started up and pulled away from the kerb. He returned to H.M.V., turned left at the traffic lights, went over the M4, turned right on the A4 to Bath and headed towards Heathrow. He turned into the multi-storey car park by the main airport terminal building, took a parking ticket out of the vending machine and began circuiting the park until he found a vacant slot on the third floor. He parked, locked the Mini and then walked down to the second level.

Nash was waiting for him in a green Austin 1100, just as he said he would be. There was someone else with him, a dark-haired youngish man in a brown leather jacket who got out of the car as Garnett approached. The man held out his hand and said, in a hard flat voice, 'Keys and ticket.'

'Are you taking the Mini?'

'That's the general idea.'

Garnett handed over the ignition key and the parking ticket and got into the Austin.

Nash said, 'Did you get it?'

Garnett reached inside his jacket pocket and passed the snapshots to Nash. Glancing at the retreating back of the man in the leather jacket, he said, 'Who was that?'

'A man, just a man, his name isn't important.' Nash whistled softly. 'These are good,' he said. 'Any trouble?'

'No trouble. I'm surprised that sort of photograph cuts any ice these days.'

'The Russians aren't as broadminded as we are.'

Nash started up the car and reversed out of the parking space. 'You did all right,' he said.

'Think so?'

'Why the doubting tone?'

'It was too easy.'

'You're getting too old for this game.' Nash negotiated the final turn, stopped at the booth, paid the parking fee, and then, turning on to the A4 pointed the car for London. 'You're getting too cautious,' he said, 'that's your trouble.'

'I've been in this game, as you call it, for over six years, and I've survived because I don't take anything at face value.'

'Good on you. What do you want me to do, give you a medal?'

'I want a safe place for Dane.'

Nash smiled thinly. 'Vickers said we would get round to the dolly sooner or later.'

'All right, now we've got round to her.'

'Where's your rendezvous?'

'That's my concern.'

Nash pulled up for the traffic lights. 'It's also our concern.'

'Tomorrow, Charing Cross Station, outside W. H. Smith between eight-forty-five and nine o'clock in the morning.'

Nash eased off the brake as the lights changed. 'We'll be covering you just in case anything goes wrong.'

'Like you were covering me while I was in the surgery?'

'Closer, much closer—we want to make sure she is not being used as bait, with or without her consent.'

Garnett said, 'What did you say just now about being cautious?'

'This is different.' Nash pulled into the kerb and stopped the car. 'You get out here,' he said. 'There's a key in the glove pocket to Flat 53, Barbican Towers, Kennington. You'll find we've stocked the place up.'

Garnett took the key and pushed open the car door.

'We'll be in touch,' said Nash.

'I bet you will.'

Garnett stood there watching the tail lights of the Austin fading into the distance and then made for the nearest bus stop. It was some time before he realised that he was still carrying the .32, and he knew instinctively that it was no oversight on Nash's part.

Dane lay in bed staring up at the ceiling, her arms folded

75

behind her head. For thirty-six hours she had been stretched like a bow, and it had all started with a casual stroll round the block and seeing a reflection in a shop window. The reflection told her that she was being followed. Alert and watchful from then on, she had become aware of the tight surveillance net which had been thrown around the hotel. Anxious and alone, she had first thought of the fail safe telephone number, and then remembered that the Resistance would run a check to see if she was being followed, and she knew without doubt that, that being the case, no help would be given. There remained just one faint hope—the hall porter—an independent-minded old soldier who had fought at Arnhem with the 1st Airborne Division, and was openly contemptuous of the Russians, the puppet government and all collaborators, in that order. To ask for his help entailed trusting him implicitly, and that wasn't an easy thing to do, but there was really no choice. To stay put and do nothing merely invited arrest.

And so, in concert, they had hatched up this plan for the morning, and she couldn't help wondering how much reliance she could place on the old man. Tired of speculation, she reached up and put out the light. Sleep didn't come easy.

9

DANE RESISTED THE TEMPTATION to check her watch yet
again. The last time she had looked it had shown eight-
twenty, and barely a minute had elapsed since then. It was
unlikely that the saluki-bronze Capri with the black hard-
top would have moved from its position some twenty
metres along the road from the front entrance to the hotel.
Last night it had been an Avenger; yesterday morning it
had been a Rover 2000.

Picking out the Q car wasn't too difficult. In a line of
parked vehicles, the ones with occupants were suspect,
and by a process of elimination, it was possible to narrow
the choice down to one. Special Branch could switch cars
and parking places, but unless they had the manpower to
ring the changes every half hour or so, the risk of detection
was high once Dane was aware she was under surveillance.

Dane counted slowly up to one hundred, took a deep
breath and counted another hundred, and still felt the urge
to look at the creeping minute hand on her wristwatch.
She tried exercising her mind by recalling personalities
whose surname began with a Y, and finding it difficult to
think of any, switched to S and rapidly became bored with
the pointless game. She reverted to being a clock watcher.

At eight thirty-five, wearing the clothes she had acquired
in Appleby, she left the room and went down into the

lobby. The hall porter opened the door for her and followed her out into the street. They stood there on the pavement in the watery sunlight, looking anxiously up and down Craven Road, while the Special Branch agent in the Ford Capri kept on reading his paper as if unaware of their presence.

A taxi appeared at the top end of the road and cruised towards them. The hall porter raised an arm and flagged down the cab. The man in the Capri put his paper aside, started up the engine and began to pull out of the line of parked cars. A large delivery van beat the Capri to it and halted immediately behind the taxi. The cab moved off, the van stayed put, and there was no way for the Capri to get past. The van driver got out of his cab, gesticulated apologetically at the Capri driver, and then opened the bonnet and bent over the engine. The man in the Capri called the back-up car in Cleveland Square.

The cab turned into the Bayswater Road, dropped Dane at Lancaster Gate Station and immediately picked up another fare. By the time the back-up car had fought its way into the Bayswater traffic, the cab was on the move again. The back-up car followed it all the way to Oxford Circus, where the second fare got out. As a matter of routine, they took the cab driver in for questioning. He described Dane and said she had asked to be taken to Piccadilly and had then changed her mind at Lancaster Gate where he had been lucky enough to pick up another fare. Apart from that, Special Branch got nothing out of the cab driver.

Dane had no time to play tag on the Underground but she was counting on the rush hour traffic to give her some protection. Changing at Oxford Circus, she arrived at Charing Cross a few minutes after nine and, fighting against the stream of commuters making their way towards the Underground, she edged up to the bookstall. A sea of faces milled past her—middle-aged men in conservative suits, dark overcoats and bowler hats, younger men less formally attired, hatless girls in minis, midis and maxis, the plain and the attractive, the slim and the plump, and all of them moving purposefully, oblivious of each other and Dane.

The crowd gave her a sense of security and she found it easy to browse through the paperbacks seemingly without a care in the world. A few minutes later, Garnett appeared at her side.

'Everything all right?' he said.

'I think I might have been followed.' She spoke out of the corner of her mouth, scarcely moving her lips—a trick she had picked up in prison. 'I need a safe house.'

'I've got a place.'

'Where?'

'We go together.'

'It isn't safe. I shouldn't have come here, but I was afraid to stay at the hotel any longer.'

Garnett said, 'There's nothing to get alarmed about, we're being covered.'

He took hold of her arm and steered her towards the Underground but she was in a mood to argue. Walking quickly made her speak jerkily. 'You're a fool,' she said, 'they want me to lead them to you.'

'If they were going to take us, they would have done so at the bookstall.' He shoved her on to the escalator and stood behind her on the step above. Leaning forward, he said, 'Stop being noble.'

'And you can stop being pig-headed.'

They came into the booking hall, paused to get tickets from a machine and then went through the barrier. The monotonous run around began—Charing Cross to Leicester Square to King's Cross to The Monument to Kennington. No one followed them.

Barbican Towers was fourteen floors of concrete and glass with four apartments on each floor, making a total of fifty-six in all. Number 53 was on the fourteenth floor. It should have been on Floor 13, but in deference to superstition, the G.L.C. had numbered it the American way. A corner flat, No. 53 had a lopsided view of the Oval Cricket Ground on one side and Vauxhall Bridge and the river from the other aspect. It comprised two bedrooms, bathroom and lavatory, kitchenette and a lounge-dining room. Fittings included full central heating, pile carpets and a wall fridge. There was also a telephone.

Dane went into the master bedroom, removed her trench mac and flung it on to the bed. She unpinned her blonde hair and let it fall about her shoulders.

'What I need now,' she said, 'is a hot bath and some coffee.'

Garnett said, 'I thought I told you to do something about your hair?'

'I did, I pinned it up.'

'You should have dyed it.'

'That's easier said than done.'

'You were taking a risk.'

She sat down on the bed and removed first one black leather boot and then the other before she answered. 'Don't carp at me,' she said wearily, 'just go and see if there is any coffee.'

A restless night coupled with the strain of the last two hours had left her feeling bone-tired. Every movement was an effort of willpower. She stood up, unzipped her dress and let it fall about her ankles. In stockinged feet, Dane padded across the floor shedding her slip on the way to the bathroom. She ran the bath water, came back into the bedroom and hopefully searched through the drawers in the built-in wardrobe unit.

Garnett said, 'Where do you want your coffee?'

'I'll take it into the bathroom.' She closed the bottom drawer.

'Empty,' she said, 'and I've got nothing to wear except what I stand up in.'

'There's a clean shirt hanging in the wardrobe, if that's any use. The indispensable Nash slipped up on the feminine change of attire.'

'Will it fit me?'

'Swamp you.'

She opened the wardrobe and looked inside. 'Which one?'

'Take your pick.' He paused and then said awkwardly, 'Look Valerie ... I didn't mean to sound so off-hand.'

She turned round clutching a patterned blue shirt to her. 'I know that, David.'

'I love you.'

'I know that too.' She stroked his cheek lightly with her

80

forefinger, took the cup and saucer out of his hand and disappeared into the bathroom. 'You're just not very good at showing it sometimes,' she said as she closed the door behind her.

Garnett wandered over to the window and stood there looking down at the driver. Away to his left he could see the Battersea Power Station, whilst downstream he had an oblique view of the Houses of Parliament. London filled the horizon as far as the eye could see. How many people out there? Eight, ten, twelve million, if you included the whole of the Greater London Area? A man ought to feel safe in the middle of twelve million people, but he didn't.

Bare feet padded into the room and he turned away from the window, and there was Dane dressed in a shirt several sizes too large. Her blonde hair hung in damp ringlets about her face, and she still looked pale and tired. He had been very close to her now for over a year and he had come to depend on her, yet he knew there were times when he gave Dane the impression that he took her very much for granted. Some men can express their involvement in words but Garnett was not amongst them. The right phrases always eluded him, and when it came to it, he instinctively took an oblique approach.

'I'm glad you didn't dye your hair,' he said.

'Well, it wasn't a very practical idea, anyway.'

'I missed you.'

'Did you?'

'You know I did.'

He was close to her now and he gently straightened a ringlet of damp hair, only to release it and let it spring back again. He put his arms around her and felt the warmth of her body through the shirt. Gently, he kissed her cheeks, her lips, her neck, punctuating each kiss with the loosening of a shirt button.

'I've only just put it on,' she protested, but did not stop him when he slipped the shirt off her shoulders and drew her towards the bed. And afterwards, he could not remember who was the first to fall asleep, and when he heard the ringing sound, he instinctively reached out to shut off the alarum, and then it slowly dawned on his sleep-befuddled mind that it was the telephone in the next room.

81

He got out of bed and, still naked, padded into the lounge-dining room and lifted the receiver off the cradle. Nash said, 'Sorry to call you on your day off, Mr. Helm, but there's some trouble with the central heating in Charles Street.'

'Oh, yes?'

'Seems the civil servants aren't being very civil; they don't like the cold, so Mr. Stansfield wants you to look into it. We'll send the van round to pick you up from outside your place.'

'When?'

'Ten minutes.'

Garnett said, 'Make it fifteen.' He hung up, went into the bedroom and started dressing.

Dane stirred, pulled the blankets up under her chin, opened one eye and said drowsily, 'Where are you off to, David?'

'I'm not sure. It depends on what Vickers has in mind.'

'Why can't he leave you alone?'

'He wants his pound of flesh, love.' He leaned over the bed and kissed her.

'When will you be back?'

'Who knows? Sometime.'

A Bedford van belonging to the Department of the Environment was parked outside the front entrance to Barbican Towers. Garnett walked across the pavement, opened the sliding door and stepped into the van. Nash was in the driving seat. As they pulled away, he said, 'You look as though you've just rolled out of bed.'

'What's it to do with you?'

'You won't have seen the noon edition then?'

'No.'

'There's an *Evening Standard* in the back which might interest you.'

Garnett turned round and picked up the newspaper. The front page was carrying a picture of Dane and himself. Dane's wasn't flattering—taken nearly a year ago, after she had been sentenced to two months' detention for failing to register with the local police, it showed her in prison garb after they had shaved off her hair. His picture wouldn't have won any prizes either—a blow-up of a telephoto lens

82

shot, Garnett's eyes were half shut because the sun was playing on his face, and the enlargement made his skin look blotchy.

Nash said, 'You're getting very warm.'

Garnett tossed the paper over his shoulder. 'Who's going to recognise either of us from that? Dane looks like a freak in a side show, and I'm not much better.'

'I'm glad you're so confident. In the mood you are in, you won't mind putting the pressure on Warner.'

Garnett lit a cigarette. 'Vickers wants this?'

'Certainly.'

'He would. How do we set it up?'

'Warner has a sixteen year old daughter named Janet. Does that surprise you?'

'No. Kelso said he was A.C. D.C.'

'The girl goes to the Karl Marx Institute of Social Studies in Westbere Road, Hampstead. A man from Special Branch meets her outside the school at four-thirty and drives her home. We are going to lift her.'

'What for?'

'You've heard of double idemnity? We need the girl in case the pictures aren't enough.'

Garnett sighed. 'You kidnap that girl and you will have a hornet's nest about your ears.'

Nash shook his head. 'Nobody is going to miss her,' he said, 'not even her own mother. Two phone calls, that's all it will take.'

Garnett flipped the cigarette stub out of the window. 'I suppose you know your own business.'

'We do. A phone call from her mother to the deputy head asking if Janet can leave fifteen minutes early because they have to attend a reception at the Albanian Embassy in place of the Minister of Internal Security sets it up in one direction, and a phone call from the deputy head to Mrs. Warner telling her that Janet is working with the drama group until six-thirty will keep the Special Branch chauffeur out of the way while we pick her up.'

'And this is going to work?'

'Listen, the girl we're using could have made a fortune in the Clubs—she can take anybody off.'

'And is there a reception at the Albanian Embassy tonight?'

'Yes.'

'You're lucky.'

'Not as much as you would like to think. We would have come up with something else. The Albanians aren't the only socialites in town.'

'All right. So what happens when Janet discovers she is not being met by the usual chauffeur?'

'She won't be expecting him. The phone call to the deputy head will have taken care of that.'

Nash followed the traffic over Chelsea Bridge and then turned into the King's Road.

Garnett said, 'We've got enough on Warner as it is, so why bother with the girl?'

Nash snorted in derision. 'And Vickers said you were smart. Try using your brains and put yourself in Warner's shoes. Seagrave has already threatened to expose him; if he gets the idea that other people are using the same material, he might sit tight.'

'You didn't set this up overnight.'

Nash glanced at Garnett and sneered. 'You were a soldier once; even the army must have made contingency plans. If you are worried about the girl, forget it, nothing is going to happen to her.'

Garnett said, 'I'm glad to hear it, because while I am able to do something about it, no child is going to be hurt by you or anyone else.'

'I'm shaking in my boots.'

'You'll do more than that.'

Two spots of colour showed in the alabaster face and his knuckles turned white as Nash gripped the steering wheel, and then suddenly he relaxed and laughed. 'What are we getting worked up about? Nothing is going to happen to her.'

They swung off the main road into a side street and then turned right along a narrow dirt road which skirted the railway line. Bumping over the uneven ground, they made a U-turn in a factory yard and stopped between a couple of low, brick-built sheds. Empty tin cans and broken glass littered the yard; half bricks were lodged on the corrugated iron roofs of the sheds.

Garnett said, 'What's this, an adventure playground?'

Nash said, 'This is where you get out.'

Garnett pushed open the sliding door and stepped down into the yard. 'Aren't you coming too?'

Nash smiled thinly. 'Don't worry, you'll be met.' He banged the gear lever into first, gunned the engine and lifted his foot off the clutch; he was in top before he reached the factory gates.

Garnett walked over to the nearest shed, tried the doors and found them locked. He crossed the yard and tried the other shed with the same negative result. A stone sailed through the air and landed with a clatter on the corrugated iron roof above his head.

A shrill voice said, 'Bet that made you jump.'

The boy was about thirteen, round-shouldered and tousle-haired, under-weight and under-sized. He stood there, hands stuffed into the hip pockets of his jeans, wearing a faded green anorak over a grey open-necked shirt.

He smiled tentatively. 'Been watching you ever since you got out of the van,' he said. He swung his foot and sent a loose stone flying towards an imaginary goal-post, and then just as suddenly, turned and walked away from Garnett.

After a few paces, he stopped, looked back over his shoulder and said, 'Come on. What are you waiting for? We ain't got all day.'

He led Garnett through the factory yard and across a piece of wasteland which, at the far end, was bounded by a wire mesh fence. The boy climbed the fence and dropped down into an alley. Garnett followed him. The alley jinked to the right and passed between two rows of back to back houses. The boy stopped by a gate in the wooden fence which ran the length of the alley.

'Through here,' he said, 'shed on the left.'

Garnett opened the gate, walked into the garden and tapped on the door of the shed. It swung open.

The man with the dark hair smiled at Garnett and said, 'Surprise, surprise.'

Garnett said, 'You get around—last night Heathrow, this

afternoon a back street in Hammersmith. Maybe you've acquired a name on the way?'

'Keilly, Richard Keilly. Step inside.' He waved an arm in the direction of a crowded workbench. 'I'm doing a little soldering,' he said. 'Close the door behind you.' He picked up the electric soldering iron and bent over the vice. 'This is a tricky bit; got to solder the motor to the platform without melting the plastic. I built this railbus from an Airfix kit, see, and if I accidentally touch it with the iron the darn thing may crack.'

'Are you a model railway enthusiast?'

'Yes. You should see the layout in our loft. Got about a hundred metres of track up there. And rolling stock—just about everything Triang, Hornby and Basset Lowke ever put on the market, and Marklin as well.'

'Who?'

'Marklin, a German firm—very good—can't get their stuff now.' Keilly put the soldering iron to one side and admired his handiwork. He produced a packet of Park Drive cigarettes, stuck one in his mouth and lit it with a match. 'Nash told you what we have in mind?' he said.

'Only in broad outline.'

Keilly said, 'Your part is a doddle. You wait here with me until we know the fish has swallowed the bait. Then you telephone Warner from a public call box—don't worry, Warner won't be speaking from his ex-directory number, he'll be in a public call box too. You'll give him the run around so that we can make sure he is playing it straight, and then when we are satisfied everything is okay, you'll give him a rendezvous. Where and when is up to you, but after meeting Warner, you are to go to 21, The Station Arcade, Queensbury. We want to hear how you got on.' Keilly dropped his cigarette end on to the floor and scuffed it out with his foot. 'One thing more, when you speak to Warner, use your own name. It's important he knows who he's dealing with.' Keilly smiled briefly. 'At the moment you're the bogey man as far as Special Branch is concerned.'

'And what do I say to Warner?'

'I'll tell you just as soon as I hear we've got the girl.' Keilly unscrewed the vice and picked up the Airfix railbus. 'We'll go into the house and have something to eat.'

'Last meal for the condemned man?'

'Something like that. Are you carrying the .32 Nash gave you?'

'Why do you ask?'

'You might need it,' Keilly said grimly.

The night was cold and dark, and the high-level platform at Golders Green was exposed to the chill wind from the east. The mac Keilly had lent him offered little warmth and the waiting room was damp and cheerless. Even if it had been heated, Garnett would still have chosen to stay outside on the platforms—if things did go wrong, he didn't want to find himself trapped inside a room with only one avenue of escape. Not that there was much likelihood of anything going sour. They had, after all, put Warner to the test, sending him first to one call box and then to another to pick up fresh instructions whilst they observed his actions. Warner, they told Garnett, was playing it straight; and so he had fixed the final rendezvous, and now it was only a question of waiting for him to show up.

The train was a pinpoint of light in the distance, becoming larger as it closed rapidly. It clattered into the station and gradually screeched to a halt. Doors hissed open. A handful of passengers got out and made their way to the exit. As the train drew out of the station, one man remained behind staring at a poster advertising Brylcreem. The man wore a British Warm, a trilby hat and leather gloves. He looked towards the waiting room, and the overhead lights playing on his face picked out the square jaw and the neat moustache. Anthony Warner had arrived to keep his appointment.

An Up train pulled in, halted briefly and then moved out. Garnett made no move to join Warner. Five minutes passed, then ten, then fifteen. A young couple, arms entwined about each other, sauntered on to the platform, moved into the shadows at the far end, leaned back against the station signboard and embraced. Warner shifted his weight from one foot to the other, glanced up and down the platform, hesitated, and then walked a few metres to his right and studied the map of the Underground. It pleased

Garnett that he seemed to be worried and ill at ease.

The distant signal changed to green and the train appeared in sight. Warner turned and stared expectantly at Garnett. The train drew into the station and stopped. Garnett waited until the doors were open and then strode across the platform and entered a non-smoker. Warner followed and sat down in a seat opposite. The sweat was clearly visible on Warner's face.

There was one other occupant in their section of the carriage, an elderly man in a shabby raincoat who smelt of beer and was half asleep. As the doors started to close, the man came awake, got to his feet and lurched towards the exit. He failed to make it in time. Swearing continuously, he hung on to a strap until they reached Brent and then staggered out. Nobody else entered the compartment.

Garnett moved across the aisle and sat next to Warner. He said, 'You know who I am?'

Warner ran a tongue around his lips. 'Oh yes,' he said, 'you are no stranger to me.'

'Good. All you have to do is to listen carefully.'

'Where's Janet?'

'She's safe and well, and she's going to stay that way if you do as you are told. First thing tomorrow morning you will ring up the school and ask to speak to the deputy head. You will tell her that an unfortunate incident occurred during the reception at the Albanian Embassy which considerably distressed your wife and daughter. You will say that, while in the Ladies' Room, Janet was accosted by an older woman who made certain improper suggestions and later assaulted her. You will go on to say that you feel it will be best for the child if she has a change of scenery for a few days, and you have therefore sent her out of London for a short holiday with her mother. You expect her to return to school in a week or ten days time. Clear?'

Warner said, 'You've got a sick mind.'

In a harsh voice, Garnett said, 'We could hardly have said that a boy assaulted her, could we? I mean, your daughter is used to looking up at the ceiling, so it would hardly come as a shock to her if a man put his hand up her skirt.'

88

The anger showed in Warner's face. 'That's a damn lie,' he snarled.

'You think so? Not only can we give you names, but it might also interest you to know that Janet was unanimously elected by her fellow students as the girl most likely to come across.' Garnett paused, and then in a softer tone of voice said, 'Anyway, all this is irrelevant, isn't it? Tomorrow your wife will catch the nine-ten to Banbury, and we shall meet her at the station and see she is reunited with her daughter. It will help to authenticate your story.'

He broke off as the train arrived at Hendon Central. A couple with two children got into the compartment and remained standing near the doors talking softly amongst themselves. Garnett waited patiently until they got out at the next station and they had the carriage to themselves again. Then he said, 'We have some pictures of you.'

'So?'

'We also now have your daughter. We want three things from you—a means of contact, your co-operation and the hunt for Dane and myself called off.'

'What about Seagrave?'

'She's your problem, but I ought to warn you that we can't prevent the arty poses getting into wrong hands if you should decide to get nasty with her. You're riding two bicycles from now on; taking orders from us and playing along with Seagrave. Okay?'

Warner inclined his head.

'All right,' said Garnett, 'any ideas on the means of contact?'

'No.'

'No what?'

'No, meaning I have no ideas.'

Garnett smiled. 'You know,' he said, 'we rather thought you might take that line, so we cooked up a girl friend for you while your wife is away on holiday. She's Marcia Coutts and she lives in Knightsbridge—13, Belvedere Gardens—a nice girl, you'll like her. You call on her tomorrow night and she will give you your instructions and arrange a D.L.B.'

Warner said, 'I'm going to need some help. Hulf has been in on the Seagrave business from the beginning, and

89

he might get curious if I ordered him to stop looking for you and Dane.'

'Maybe we can do something about that.'

'And another thing. Suppose my wife doesn't like the idea of going to Banbury?'

'You tell her it would be bad for Janet's health if she didn't. You see, some of the people I have to work with don't share my scruples. They wouldn't think twice about giving her the chop.'

Garnett stood up as the train approached the next station. 'You stay on to the end of the line,' he said, 'we don't want any misunderstanding.'

Leaving the train at Burnt Oak, Garnett caught a bus outside the station which took him into Queensbury. Lights were burning in all the flats in the station arcade with the exception of the one above the tobacconist's. Glancing up at the windows, Garnett failed to notice anything which suggested that the flat was even occupied. He walked the length of the arcade, turned into the alley behind the shops and stopped outside the back gate to number 21. A faint light showed through the curtains in the kitchen. He tried the latch, pushed the gate ajar and gritted his teeth as it scraped against the uneven surface of the yard. Two doors down, a dog started yapping, but it must have been the sort of animal that barks at anything and everything, for no one took any notice. Garnett climbed the short flight of wooden steps and knocked on the back door.

Nash opened it almost immediately and stepped aside as Garnett entered the room. He closed the door, looked Garnett up and down, and said, 'I see you made it all right. How did Warner take it?'

Garnett lit a cigarette. 'He'll co-operate.'

'Good.'

'At a price.'

'Like hell.'

'He's worried about someone called Hulf—seems to think he could be a nuisance. Does the name mean anything to you?'

Nash pinched the bridge of his nose between forefinger and thumb. He gave the impression of being tired and confused. 'Oh, yes,' he said irritably, 'we know Hulf, he's the sort who never lets go.' The moment of uncertainty passed and he became brisk again. 'You and Dane will have to move on first thing tomorrow. I'll give you an address in Bagshot.'

'I'm running short of money.'

Nash reached into his hip pocket, pulled out a wad of notes, counted off twenty and gave them to Garnett. 'That enough?'

'It will do for a day or so.'

'Try economising. Money doesn't grow on trees.'

'I'll cut out the caviar and stick to bread and cheese, unless you've any other advice to offer.'

'Make it look as if you left in a hurry. Leave the beds unmade.'

'What?'

'Tomorrow, when you move out of the flat.' Nash smiled. 'You see, I'm planning a surprise for Hulf,' he said.

10

THEY WERE MOVING FAST because the tip was hot, and the Central Information Room had lost no time in channelling it to Special Branch, and Hulf was only too eager to follow up any lead which might bring him closer to Dane and Garnett.

If there was one fly in the ointment, it was that the informer refused to give his name and address, but this was not unusual since anyone who grassed got short shrift from the Resistance when they caught up with him—and they had an uncanny way of doing just that. Every police informer knew the risks involved, knew the police couldn't protect him once his cover was blown, knew the Resistance worked on a ruthless process of elimination of those who could or might have been in a position to betray them, and yet the informers still came forward if the money was right.

Hulf had dealt with a good many informers in the last six years and he respected their wishes. If a man wanted £5,000 mailed to an accommodation address as a reward for a really good tip, Hulf had no hesitation in complying. He was a successful C.I. man because he paid up promptly and didn't ask questions. Over the years he had developed an instinct for recognising whether the tip was any good or not, and this particular one seemed more than promising. Barbican Towers was not unknown to Hulf, because some months ago it had featured in the list of apartment buildings with a high turn-over of residents. It was the sort of place the Resistance might well use as a safe house.

The black Austin Westminster snaked through the traffic on Vauxhall Bridge, followed the one-way system through Kennington Lane and Durham Street and stopped just short of and round the corner from Barbican Towers. Hulf got out of the car and set off at a brisk walk. Stratton followed him like a well-trained dog.

Hulf took one look at Barbican Towers and wrinkled his nose in disgust. He saw fourteen storeys of concrete and glass adding up to a building which was stark and functional. It was, he thought, a large impersonal dormitory which the architect had tried to soften with a forecourt, Italian style, surrounding a lily pond and a bronze statue of Pan whose pipes were the outlet for the ornamental fountain. The fountain wasn't playing, the pond was murky and full of dead vegetation, and beneath the jungle of water-lilies, Hulf was willing to bet that he would find empty beer and coke bottles.

Hulf elbowed his way through the swing doors and found O'Dwyer waiting for him in the lobby with the caretaker in tow.

Hulf said, 'What do you make of it, Sergeant?'

O'Dwyer cleared his throat. He indicated the man in blue dungarees who was standing next to him, and said, 'From the caretaker's description of the couple, sir, I'd say they could be the ones we are after.'

Hulf rounded on the caretaker. 'What's your name?' he said.

The man was small and inoffensive. National Health steel-framed spectacles and a quiff like a question mark gave him an owlish look. A prominent Adam's apple showed above the frayed collar of his shirt.

He blinked his eyes rapidly and said, 'Norman, sir, Brian Norman.'

Hulf produced a mint lump from his pocket, unwrapped it and popped it into his mouth. 'Have you got the key to their flat?'

'Yes.'

'And are they in?'

93

'As far as I know.'

Hulf stopped chewing on the mint. 'What time did you start work?' ·

'Nine o'clock this morning.'

'How many lifts are there in this building, Mr. Norman?'

'Just the two.'

'And the fire escape?'

'Internal—leads down to the lobby.' The Adam's apple bobbed up and down. 'I'd have seen them if they left after nine.'

Hulf shoved the mint lump into his right cheek. 'All right,' he said, 'let's go and pay them a call.' The caretaker began to move away. 'You too, Mr. Norman,' said Hulf, 'we shall need your help to get into the flat if they don't answer the bell.'

The four of them trooped into a lift. O'Dwyer closed the door and then punched the button marked 14. 'Flat 53 is on the top floor, sir,' he said.

Hulf grunted, shifted the mint lump to the other side of his jaw and munched it. They rode up to the fourteenth floor in silence and then walked down the corridor with O'Dwyer leading the way. They stopped outside number 53 and O'Dwyer and Stratton took up station on either side of the front door. Hulf rang the bell and promptly stepped aside. Nothing happened.

Stratton said, 'I can hear a radio.'

'None of us is deaf, Sergeant,' said Hulf. He grabbed Norman by the shoulder and pushed him towards the door. 'All right, Brian,' he said cheerfully, 'you've got the key, you lead the way.'

Hands trembling, Norman unlocked the door and hung back. Hulf had other ideas. He pushed Norman into the hall and waited to see what sort of reception he got. All was peaceful. Less cautious now, and drawn on by the sound of the radio coming from the bedroom, they moved into the lounge-dining room.

Not one of them noticed the oblong box on the wall behind the dining table. If they had done so they would have assumed that it had something to do with the central heating. If they had touched it they would have found that the paint was still tacky, and they might have wondered

94

why the flex beneath the box was not stapled to the wall. And if they had bothered to trace the flex which ran under the carpet they would have found the pressure plate. But, of course, they did none of these things except that O'Dwyer found the pressure plate by accident. He trod on it.

The Claymore mine did the rest. A hail of needle sharp barbettes scythed across the room, tore through flesh and bone and ripped the opposite walls to shreds. The concussion blew the ceiling in and covered the floor in a thick layer of white dust.

O'Dwyer lay on his back, a pierrot in modern dress, covered from head to foot in a white shroud of plaster blemished in a dozen places by dark red stains which grew larger with each passing second. Stratton, legs splayed apart, was leaning against the wall for support while his hands cupped the entrails which were spilling out from what remained of his stomach. His head, which was tilted over to one side, seemed to be looking at Norman who lay face down on the carpet with one arm pointing straight ahead at the bedroom like an accusing finger. The arm was detached from the rest of the body. Hulf saw nothing. A barbette had severed both optic nerves, and another had so sliced his forehead that a flap of skin now hung down over his sightless eyes.

The noise of the explosion and the black smoke drifting through the shattered windows of the end apartment on the fourteenth floor alerted the Special Branch agents in the street below. At first stupefied, they then reacted and converged on the front entrance to Barbican Towers. One of their number, cooler and with more insight than the others, called for an ambulance.

The scene inside Flat 53 was something for the Chamber of Horrors. Cordite fumes still poisoned the air and the dust cloud blotted out the daylight. Three men had been butchered; the fourth, moaning softly, was crawling aimlessly round the room on his hands and knees.

Dane heard Garnett replace the phone in the hall, and judging by the slow measured tread of his footsteps, she suspected he had something on his mind. One look at his face as he entered the room confirmed it.

95

Dane said, 'Penny for your thoughts?'

He stopped tugging on the lobe of his left ear and sat down in a chair facing the gas fire. Dane shifted her position and leaned back against his legs.

In a tired voice he said, 'They've just told me that we don't need to worry about Hulf any more.'

'You don't sound very relieved.'

'Why should I? Vickers always expects his favours to be repaid.'

Dane twisted round and rested her chin on his knees. 'And now is no exception,' she said.

'Correct. I am supposed to collect a car from Speedways Garage in the village, drive out to the Green Man at Pirbright and pass myself off as a rep from the brewery. They've hinted I'll be away for two or three days.'

'When do you go?'

'Who says I'm going?'

'You won't refuse. You couldn't even if you wanted to. You once told me that loyalty worked two ways—up and down.'

Garnett said, 'In my case it seems to work in one direction only—upwards.'

'So?'

'So it's hard to break old habits.'

Dane stood up. 'Do I stay here while you are away?'

'Until they get in touch with you.' He kissed her on the mouth. 'Don't go chatting up any strange men,' he said.

Dane snorted. 'Some hope of that; nobody calls here.' With the door half open, Garnett looked back at Dane, grinned and said, 'Good, keep it that way.' He ducked through the door as Dane hurled a cushion at his head.

The Green Man was in a quiet backwater. Tucked in beneath the railway embankment, the nearest house was more than two hundred metres away. In the past, it had been very much a soldier's pub and the civilians had stayed away, but now the soldiers were long gone because the Guards' Depot had disappeared, and in its place there was a Youth Leader Training Centre whose Director of Studies had seen fit to place the pub out of bounds. The Green Man now catered for the locals, and not many of them used it. Garnett thought that perhaps the forbidding appearance of the pebble-dashed building with its dull slate roof and dark green drainpipes had something to do with the lack of custom. He parked the car, went round to the side entrance and pressed the buzzer.

A middle-aged man in brown pinstriped trousers, stained waistcoat, rolled up shirt sleeves and carpet slippers came to the door. Suspicion lurked in his narrow-set hazel eyes.

In a surly voice he said, 'What do you want?'

Garnett said, 'I'm the rep from Warren and Bristow—I understand there is some complaint about the last consignment of our draught beer.'

The man stood to one side. 'In the cellar,' he said.

'What?'

'The barman's in the cellar, he'll tell you all about it. You'd best follow me.'

Garnett followed him along the dark hall until the man stopped by a staircase which led to the cellar. 'Down there,' he said.

Down there was a small whitewashed cellar illuminated by a naked sixty-watt bulb dangling at the end of a long flex. Down there were beer barrels, shadows, cobwebs and a musty warm smell. Down there Nash was waiting for him with a stranger.

The stranger was in his late fifties. He looked fit and hard, there was no sign of a middle-aged spread and he carried himself well. His chin was thrust forward almost aggressively as though daring the world to hang a punch on it. He had the Celtic build—small, dark and wiry.

He shook hands with Garnett and said, 'I'm Moxham, perhaps you have heard of me?' The Scots burr was noticeable.

'Co-ordinator of Political Strategy. Right?'

'Yes.'

Garnett lit a cigarette. 'How do I know you're Moxham?'

Nash said, 'I can vouch for him.'

'That might not be good enough.'

Moxham smiled. 'I admire your caution, David. It is David, isn't it?'

'It is.'

97

'I can't prove my identity; suppose we take each other on trust?'

'All right.'

'Aren't you curious to know why I wanted to meet you?'

Garnett leaned back against a beer barrel. 'You'll tell me in your own good time,' he said.

'Quite so.' Moxham snapped his fingers. 'Does the name Blackwell mean anything to you?'

'No. Should it?'

'Harry Blackwell was next in line to be President of the T.U.C.'

Garnett stubbed out his cigarette. 'I never was enthralled with quiz games.'

'I'll come to the point.'

'You do that,' Garnett said pleasantly.

'The fact is, David,' he said, 'very few of our leading politicians and intellectuals have survived six years in a Soviet concentration camp, but there are at least five others still alive besides Blackwell who could be said to have an international reputation. I'm thinking of people like Adrian Schonfield, one time Ambassador to the U.N., Stephen Walker, the Shadow Chancellor, Cory Wendell-Lewis, the Attorney-General in the last freely elected government, Wallace Newman, the Minister for Europe, and Ian Gordon, Leader of the House of Commons. These men could form a government in exile.'

Garnett said, 'The trouble with governments in exile is that they stay that way.'

Moxham ignored the comment. 'At present, these men are split up among a number of detention camps up and down the country, but Warner is going to ensure that they are all concentrated at Proteus—that's near Ollerton, north of Nottingham on the A614.'

'When is this likely to happen?'

'By Friday of this week. Round about the middle of next week, every political prisoner at Proteus will be put on a special train and taken to a port of embarkation where they will be loaded on to a ship bound for Leningrad.'

'Why not fly them out?'

Moxham said, 'There are something like twenty thousand political detainees in fifteen separate camps. The Russians are operating their A.N. 22 fleet out of Brize Norton and Heathrow only, and they need all their transport aircraft to evacuate the army of occupation. That's why the political prisoners are going by sea.'

'And you want me to lift these six?'

'Yes.'

Garnett said, 'Listen, I'm not very good at getting people out of prison. I tried it once at Parkhurst with a man called Pollard, and he was dead before I got him through the wall.'

'I'm quite sure you will succeed this time. In any case, this is only part of a plan to discredit the puppet government in Soviet eyes.'

'Oh yes?'

A thin smile appeared briefly on Moxham's face. 'In your case,' he said, 'we shall show that the escape of the political prisoners was engineered with the active help of the government. If I know anything about the Russian C.-in-C., Andreyev will react violently, and the government will fall, and our nominees will step into office.'

'How?'

'The details need hardly concern you,' Moxham said airily.

Garnett lit another cigarette. 'Reading between the lines, I get the impression that failure on my part will be acceptable providing we can still implicate the government.'

'You're wrong. We want those six men in the United States to lobby Congress. When the Russians pull out, and believe me, they have no intention of leaving anything more than three cadre-strength divisions behind, we shall want all the help we can get.'

'From the States?'

'Precisely.'

'And we can get these men across the Atlantic?'

'I think we stand a damn good chance. I plan to use one of the Royal Navy Hunter class submarines to pick them up. Three ships of this class slipped across to Canada before the Armistice was signed.' Moxham paused for effect and then said, 'Naturally, there will be a berth for you and Dane on board the submarine if you pull it off.'

Garnett dropped his cigarette on to the floor and stepped

on it. 'That's a good carrot,' he said.

Moxham smiled. 'You'll do it?'

'Provided all the arrangements are left to me.'

Moxham cleared his throat. 'We'll have to exercise a certain amount of co-ordination,' he said.

'Such as?'

Nash said, 'I'll tell you once you've looked the job over.'

'You?'

'Me and Vickers.'

'That's better.'

'The trouble with you ex-professionals is that you're so damn touchy. You lost a war and yet you still think you're bloody marvellous.'

Moxham said sternly, 'I won't have this bickering; both of you can save your anger for a better target.' He turned to face Garnett and said, 'I'm going to send you up to Nottingham tonight to plan the job in outline. You will pose as a sergeant in the Field Security Police. Nash will provide you with the necessary documents, uniform and cover story. With your background, you should be able to pass it off without any difficulty, and the uniform will give you considerable freedom of movement. I want you back by Saturday at the latest.' Moxham walked towards the staircase. With one foot on the bottom step, he turned and said, 'By the way, you can forget any ideas you might have about trying to lift these men while they are inside the detention camp. Do it while they are in transit.'

'I don't call that having a free hand,' Garnett said as Moxham started up the stairs.

'Perhaps not, but that is what I mean by co-ordination.'

Nash smiled. 'That put you in your place,' he said.

'Didn't it.'

'All right, first things first.' Nash extended a hand, 'Let's have the .32 back; this is going to be a peaceful reconnaissance.'

Eleven people got off the train which arrived in Nottingham at 23:45 hours. Garnett was amongst them yet apart. The uniform did that, because nobody wanted to be seen talking to a sergeant in the Field Security Police. It didn't worry Garnett. He walked up the two flights of steps, gave his ticket to the collector, and then turned towards the R.T.O.'s hut which was opposite the booking office.

The hut was manned by a doughy-looking corporal in the Military Police and a W.A.C. sergeant. The sergeant was definitely attractive. The green Cossack tunic suited her slim figure and she had obviously gone to some lengths to make sure the uniform fitted perfectly. Usually the leather waist belt pulled the tunic in tight and made the average girl look like a sack of potatoes. Her auburn hair was short and trained forward over the ears to leave two slim fingers on either side of the cheekbones. She had the sort of face which would look striking on a recruiting poster. The name tag on her tunic was Edwards J.

Garnett placed his movement order and I.D. card on the counter. He said, 'Sergeant Byass, F.S.P., detached for special duties in Nottingham.'

The military policeman said, 'What duties?'

'A case involving deserters.'

'That's not the job of Field Security.'

'I'm not chasing the absentees, I'm after the ring that's helping them.'

The girl franked the movement order and pushed it across the counter. 'Where are you staying?' she said quietly.

'I was told you might arrange that.'

The green eyes widened in surprise. 'Oh?'

'There is a transit hotel in Nottingham, isn't there?'

'Yes,' she said faintly, 'the Sheriff of Nottingham Hotel in Maid Marian Way.'

'Subtle.'

'What?'

'The connection.'

Her hand strayed to the phone. 'How long will you be staying?'

'A day, maybe two—depends on the progress I make.'

The girl began dialling. 'Your O.C. should have let us know you were coming,' she said.

Garnett said, 'We've got a new man, he probably didn't know the form—a real pistol, you know what I mean?'

The military policeman said with feeling, 'Don't I just.'

The conversation died. The M.P. sat down in a chair,

picked up a dog-eared copy of *Parade* and admired the chesty birds. The girl spoke softly into the telephone but her eyes didn't leave Garnett. He didn't like it. She seemed to be weighing him up as if there was something about him which didn't ring true. The girl hung up. 'All fixed,' she said, 'if you stay more than two nights you will have to be taken on the ration strength.'

'Of course.'

'I'll give you a lift.'

'That's very kind of you but I can get a cab.'

'Not at this time of night you won't,' she said firmly. 'Besides, it's no trouble, I live there and I'm just about to go off duty.' She opened the side door of the hut and stepped out. 'Come on,' she said, 'my relief should be here by now.' Garnett picked up his grip and followed her into the station yard. Like Dane, she carried herself well, although she was fractionally shorter. She had nice legs too, but the black jackboots were a sinister overtone.

A Mini-van swung into the driveway and pulled up in front of them. A plain girl wearing glasses and a shapeless overcoat got out of the Mini, smiled sheepishly and said, 'Sorry I'm late, Jo.' She saw the look on Edwards's face and corrected herself, 'I mean, Sergeant,' she said apologetically.

'You're sloppy,' Edwards said coldly, 'if this happens again you'll do extra duty.'

The girl stood to one side, Edwards got into the van, leaned across the seat and opened the other door for Garnett.

As they moved off, Edwards said, 'I suppose you think I'm a bitch?'

'No, I don't.'

'I'm in charge of three other girls and Martin is the sloppiest of the lot.' She went up through the gear box as if to demonstrate her masculine competence.

'You can't have much time to yourself,' Garnett said idly.

'We work an eight-hour shift, which usually gives us one day off in four. Have you eaten?'

'I had a snack at the station.'

'St. Pancras?' she said quickly.

'No, my train left from Euston.'

102

'Sorry,' she said blithely, 'I'm being stupid. I must be over-tired.'

'Neat,' he thought, 'she's checking up on me to see if I did come through London.'

'It's a good thing you did have a bite to eat because you won't get anything at this time of night.' She swung off the road, pointed the car down the ramp and slid to a halt in a reserved parking place. 'We're in the basement of the hotel,' she said cheerfully.

Garnett waited for her while she removed the rotor arm and then locked the doors.

'Can't be too careful,' she said.

By God, you can't, thought Garnett, not with you around —you're too bloody clever by half.

There was one sleepy porter on duty in the lobby, otherwise the place was dead. Garnett signed the register and collected the key to his room. He was conscious of the fact that she was watching him closely all the time, and it made him feel uncomfortable.

'I thought I'd wait,' she said, 'we're on the same floor.'

All the way up in the lift he could smell her perfume. It wasn't overpowering or anything like that, but for some intangible reason he had a feeling that he was being stalked.

The lift seemed to take a very long time to reach the third floor.

Edwards said, 'Put your bag in your room and come and have a nightcap with me. My room's just down the corridor from yours.'

It wasn't an invitation so much as a royal command. Garnett did as he was told, although Edwards's interest was unwelcome and he had an uneasy feeling that the attraction wasn't entirely physical. Edwards opened the door to her room, put on the lights and then carelessly flung her forage cap on to the bed. She waved an arm in the direction of one of the two basket chairs in front of the electric fire.

'Make yourself comfortable,' she said. She stooped, opened the fitted cupboard and brought out two glasses and a bottle.

'Whisky okay?'

'Fine.'

'I haven't got any soda.'

'Water will do.'

Edwards part-filled both glasses under the tap and gave one to Garnett before she sat down in the chair facing him.

'Cheers,' she said.

'Salut.'

'You know, I think you're a bit of a fake.'

The glass froze halfway to his lips.

'I don't think you are a sergeant at all.'

'No?'

'No.'

'Because I look too old?'

'Partly.'

'Some of us get passed over for one reason or another—answering back once too often, that sort of thing.'

'Is that true in your case?'

'Yes.'

'I would say you were about thirty-five or so.'

'There are times,' Garnett said, 'when I feel a whole lot older.'

'You were outside the age bracket when selective service began, so what made you join up?'

'I suppose I like an organised life. I did a six-year stretch before the war.'

'In what?'

'S.C.L.I.'

'And then you joined up again?'

'Why not? The Red Army used to be stiff with men who had served the Czar.'

'And I thought you were an officer.'

Garnett swallowed his whisky. 'Why?'

'Because it would be typical of your lot. You use infiltration techniques to check up on our loyalty. You should take us on trust.'

'I'll remember that.'

She smiled. 'The lecture's over,' she said.

'Thank God for that.' His heart started beating at the normal rate again.

'My friends call me Jo. What's your first name?'

'David.'

'Have you been to Nottingham before?'

'No.'

'Will you be working flat out all the time?'

'I have to eat.'

'I know a nice place.'

'Yes?'

'I finish duty at 1600 hours tomorrow.'

'I'll take you out to dinner.'

'It's a date,' she said.

'Yes, it is,' he said thoughtfully.

'Good night then, David.'

Smooth, he thought, very smooth. I've been conned into doing something I don't want to do.

'Good night Jo,' he said.

Garnett went back to his room, undressed and got into bed. He lay there in the dark, his mind too active for sleep. He came to the conclusion that Jo Edwards was a very sharp and dangerous woman, and he wished like hell that he had thought of a plausible excuse to avoid meeting her again.

11

BREAKFAST WAS A DRIED-EGG omelette, a slice of frizzled bacon and a piece of fried bread which disintegrated when Garnett attempted to cut it. The coffee was the best part of the meal. There was no doubting that the Sheriff of Nottingham Hotel had seen better days before it had been commandeered by the government.

Garnett lit a cigarette and opened the newspaper at the centre page. Jane Powell, social worker, was in trouble. Busily lecturing one of the former directors on the joys of Communism and pointing out how fortunate he was to be allowed the opportunity to prove himself afresh on the shop floor, she had failed to notice that all the workers had gone home. The capitalist lackey wasn't listening to Jane P., and the leer on his face indicated that the opportunity he saw differed radically from Jane P.'s. Rape was in the air, but unfortunately it was going to stay that way, for Garnett remembered that some months previously the starry-eyed heroine of the strip cartoon had taken up karate.

Garnett folded the newspaper, stubbed out his cigarette in the ashtray and strolled out of the dining room. He walked leisurely up the stairs to his room, and having put on a trench mac and forage cap, went down by the lift. He had deliberately wasted time because he did not want to hang around in the hotel lobby. The car came for him a few minutes before nine.

The driver was a warrant officer in the Field Security Police. It was not easy to judge his age. His face, lined and sallow, presented a false picture. The olive, almost jaundiced complexion was the result of a mixed marriage between his white father and a Kenyan-born Hindu. Defensive by nature, he had learned to take care of himself from the day he had started primary school. An all-round athlete, his strong points were swimming, hockey and boxing—particularly boxing. He had had over two hundred bouts as an amateur in the Light and Light Welter Class and had lost on five occasions only. He relied on speed, stamina and skill, and nearly all his fights had gone the distance because he lacked a heavy punch. His name was Wally Pugh; he was twenty-eight and happily married to a woman three years older than himself who had given him three children, all of them girls. He was also an undercover man who had volunteered to penetrate the militia. It was a risky job and he had much to lose. Nobody knew why he had chosen to do it, nobody bothered to ask.

Garnett said, 'How much have you been told?'

'Enough to account for your presence here.' Pugh brought the car to a halt for a pedestrian on a zebra crossing. 'My O.C. is Lieutenant Vallance. When you meet him, don't make the mistake of thinking he's as stupid as he looks. He may not be clever but he's thorough.'

He eased the car through the knot of pedestrians in Theatre Square, whipped into Sherwood Street and turned right on Burton Street to feed into Milton Street, which in turn led into the Mansfield Road.

Pugh said, 'Make a statement which sounds false to Vallance and he will run a check on you which I won't be able to stop.'

'Do I have to meet him?'

'You do. I slipped a fake letter into his tray this morning warning him to expect you. I rang him up before I left, told him about the letter and said I had just had a message to pick you up from the transit hotel.'

Garnett said, 'The more I think about it the less I like it.'

'I had to cover myself.'

'What am I going to say to this man of yours?'

'That's up to you. If it's any help, they are moving all the detainees out of Proteus early next week. We have had a warning order to stand by from midnight on Tuesday. You might like to talk about that. My faked letter merely said you were conducting a security check and we were to afford you every facility.'

They were moving through the centre of Sherwood now, and there wasn't much traffic on the road. Dark clouds scudded before a keen wind and a few raindrops spattered against the windscreen.

Casually, Garnett said, 'Know anything about a girl called Jo Edwards?'

'No.'

'A sergeant in the W.A.C.—good looking, very sharp— works in the R.T.O.'s office.'

'I may have seen her about. Have you got your eye on her?'

'It's the other way round.'

'Lucky you.'

'She said something which I thought odd, something about trusting people. It made me think that perhaps she is working for Field Security.'

'If she is,' said Pugh, 'it's news to me.'

Sherwood was behind them now and they were running along the edge of Arnold. They went through a gentle S-bend, started climbing and then turned sharp left into Bestwood Lodge Drive. The house was just visible above the bare trees.

Bestwood Lodge had had a checkered history. Edward III had used it as a hunting lodge. Nell Gwyn had it given to her by Charles II for services rendered, and then subsequently it had stayed in the St. Albans family until the army acquired it cheaply in the early fifties. Once a district headquarters, the police had taken it over during the second year of Soviet occupation and turned it into a Regional Control Centre. The house was a red-brick Gothic building standing on high ground and enclosed by a belt of trees on three sides.

A barrier and sentry box had been placed at the point where the road curved sharply round to the front of the house. The policeman on duty carried a Sterling sub-machine-gun and a .38 Lee Enfield pistol in a black leather holster. There was also a handler and guard dog to keep him company. Pugh turned off to the left before they reached the barrier, sounded the horn as they went through the narrow archway and parked in the yard next to a line of five Land-Rovers.

'Field Security is the poor relation here.' Pugh smiled. 'We get to live in the stables.'

He got out of the car, waited for Garnett to join him and then led the way across the yard to a door on the right of the archway. A spiral staircase led to the floor above where Vallance had an office at the far end of the landing. Garnett left his mac in Pugh's office and then waited outside the door while Pugh went in to see Vallance. It was a short wait. Pugh came out and said softly, 'He'll see you now.'

Vallance was no oil painting. The bloated round face, double chin and pot belly reminded Garnett of a bullfrog. He also thought that Vallance was probably the oldest lieutenant in the army. The oldest lieutenant possessed a dog, a black and white mongrel, the offspring of a bull-terrier and some other unidentifiable breed. The dog, lying under the desk, looked up at Garnett, showed his fangs and growled. Vallance kicked the animal in the rump and the dog grunted once and then lowered its head. Garnett saluted and handed his I.D. card to Vallance.

Having scrutinised it, Vallance chucked it back at Garnett and said, 'Why are you here, Sergeant Byass?'

Garnett said, 'Security, sir.'

A vein throbbed above Vallance's right eye. 'Jesus Christ, Sergeant,' he snarled, 'that's fucking obvious even to a layman. Whose security are you looking into? Ours? The Detention Camp? Or is this just another bloody documents check?'

The dog added his bit. He rose up, advanced on Garnett and started barking.

Vallance shouted, 'Shut up.'

The dog did so.

'It's to do with the transfer of political prisoners at Proteus, sir.'

'Where's your problem? The Russians will provide the train guard, and the militia and police will be responsible for their safe custody from the camp to the railway station. You needn't worry your head about the Resistance—a few slogans on the wall, leaflets pushed through the door— that's about their mark.'

Garnett said, 'I'm worried about the militia.'

'You made a slip, Sergeant.'

'Sir?'

'You said "I'm worried". Now, if you had been sent up here by your O.C., I would have expected you to say something like "we are worried" or "my O.C. is worried" not "I'm worried"—that makes it too bloody personal. And another thing, you're obviously not used to calling people "sir". Just who are you, Sergeant Byass?' A plump hand crawled towards the phone. 'I think I'll call your O.C. 2984 F.S. Detachment, Aldershot, isn't it?'

Garnett cleared his throat. 'Sir,' he said, 'it was a slip of the tongue on my part. The fact is that I have been attached to Special Branch. I work with the Controller, Mr. Warner.'

'Do you expect me to believe that?'

Garnett shrugged his shoulders.

'Can you give me one good reason why I should, Sergeant?'

'Do you know about the transfer of V.I.P.s to Proteus?'

'What V.I.P.s?'

Garnett said, 'Suppose I were to tell you that within the next twenty-four hours you will receive a tele-printer message informing you that a number of V.I.P.s are being transferred from other detention camps to Proteus for despatch to Russia. Would you believe that?'

'I might if you were to give me some names.'

'I'll give you two—Schonfield and Wendell-Lewis.'

'Now that is something I can check on.' The plump hand grabbed the phone.

Garnett said, 'Sir, even if you do have a secure telephone link I don't think you ought to mention any names. Just talking to you has been a breach of security and we could both get into trouble.' Garnett allowed the implication to hang in the air for a minute, and then pressed the advantage he had won. 'I wouldn't want to implicate you, sir. I would suggest you have nothing to lose by waiting—

inside twenty-four hours what I have said will be confirmed on the teleprinter, and I am not going anywhere in the meantime.'

'All right, Sergeant,' Vallance said slowly, 'you were asking about the militia?'

'I'm worried about the state of their morale.'

Vallance picked up a ruler and turned to face the map on the wall behind him. 'Clumber Park,' he said. The ruler hit the map firmly. 'Headquarters of 19 Mechanised Regiment with 55 and 56 Motor Rifle Battalions.' The ruler side-stepped. 'Newark—57 Motor Rifle Battalion, the junior battalion in 19 Mechanised Regiment. Make no mistake, the 19th is a top-class formation, one of the oldest and the best there is in the militia, one hundred per cent reliable, they've virtually had no absentees and certainly no cases of desertion in the last two years. You might say that the political instructors have done an excellent job of indoctrinating the soldiers. Does that put your mind at rest?'

'It is on that point. I'd like to go over the route—take a run out to Proteus, that sort of thing.'

'I'll come with you.'

Garnett said, and he didn't mean it, 'That's very good of you, sir.'

'Just as soon as I have been through the rest of the mail. You can wait for me in the sergeant-major's office next door.'

Garnett saluted, turned about and made for the door. The dog started to follow him, thought better of it and settled for a deep-throated growl instead.

The shirt was damp on Garnett's back and the roof of his mouth was dry. He leaned against the filing cabinet in Pugh's office and was surprised to find that his legs were shaking. He smiled weakly at Pugh and said, 'He gave me a hard ride.'

Pugh didn't look up. 'Feel like a cup of coffee?' he said.

'Yes, please.'

'Put the kettle on then.'

Pugh held up a slip of paper for Garnett to see. On it he had written—Be Careful what you say, this room is bugged— He turned round in his chair and fed the piece of paper into the automatic shredding machine.

Garnett said, 'Where do you keep the coffee, Sergeant-Major?'

'Top shelf in the cupboard by the window.'

The cupboard held a jar of coffee, a tin of dried milk, three plastic beakers and one teaspoon. Garnett measured out the coffee and added one heaped spoonful of dried milk to each cup while he waited for the electric kettle to boil. Knowing that the office was bugged put a damper on conversation, and Pugh was no help. He had a bulky file in front of him which he was reading with an air of intense concentration. It took him almost three minutes just to get through one page.

Garnett unplugged the kettle, poured the boiling water into each mug and stirred the mixture. For some reason the coffee smelt of acorns and the powdered milk coagulated into little hard lumps which floated on the surface. It tasted as vile as it looked.

He placed a mug on Pugh's desk and said, 'I wouldn't drink it if I were you.'

Pugh didn't have to. The squawk box on his desk came to life. In a grating voice Vallance said, 'I want you and Sergeant Byass to meet me in the yard with a Land-Rover. We're going to take a look at Proteus. Who have we got left to look after the office?'

Pugh said, 'Sergeant Yates, sir.'

There was an answering grunt and then the intercom went dead.

Garnett ended up in the back of the Land-Rover with the dog. Neither of them liked the arrangement much, and the dog showed it by growling every time he moved. Long before they reached the first roundabout beyond Arnold, Garnett was nursing a growing hatred for the animal as well as its owner. It was almost impossible to get a clear view of the road through the hunched up figures of Pugh and Vallance, and the rain, which was falling steadily, didn't help matters because the windscreen wipers weren't functioning properly. A fine spray thrown up by the rear wheels soaked the right side of his mac. But the dog was all right—he had enough sense to make sure that Garnett was shielding him from the worst of the spray.

The countryside was just a blur. In fine weather Garnett was prepared to concede that it was probably very attractive, but on this miserable winter's day beauty didn't enter into it. It was also a dead loss from the practical viewpoint. Along the entire stretch of road from Arnold to Proteus, Garnett failed to see one good ambush site. Either the killing area was too small or else the withdrawal route for the ambush party was too exposed.

Pugh slowed the Land-Rover and pulled into the lay-by just short of the entrance to Proteus Camp.

As the vehicle came to a halt, Vallance looked back over his shoulder at Garnett and said, 'Seen enough, Sergeant?'

Garnett forced a smile on to his face. 'I'd like to run up to Clumber if it's convenient—sir?' He added the 'sir' as an afterthought.

It clearly wasn't convenient, and the expression on Vallance's face showed his feelings on the subject, but he signalled to Pugh to move on without comment, and they pulled out of the lay-by when there was a break in the traffic.

The tyres hissed over a carpet of water, the rain kept up a steady tattoo on the canvas canopy and a following wind, gusting now and then, drove the rain into the back of the Land-Rover. Through half-closed eyes, Garnett caught a fleeting glimpse of a stone archway, and beyond it a watch tower on stilts overlooking a compound of grass-covered mounds. Less than one kilometre farther on, he saw a signboard displaying a large silver-coloured mailed fist and the title, Headquarters 19 Mechanised Regiment.

The road curved downhill, skirted an ornamental lake and then he spotted the unit tactical signs of the 55th and 56th Motor Rifle Battalions in the woods on either side. Vallance said, 'There's a roundabout ahead. We can go left to Worksop, straight on to Bawtry, or right to Newark, or,' he added heavily, 'we could turn round and go back, Sergeant Byass.'

Garnett said, 'I'd like to go back, sir.'

Vallance muttered something under his breath which sounded like, 'Thank fuck for that.'

They covered the return journey at an average speed of 120 k.p.h. and they were almost aquaplaning. Garnett

113

hinted that he was not in any particular hurry to get back for lunch, but his innuendo fell on deaf ears.

Pugh dropped Vallance off under the archway so that he could reach his office without getting wet, but Garnett wasn't as lucky—he still had one leg over the tailboard when Pugh moved on into the yard, and he had to wait until the Land-Rover was reversed into its slot before he could get out.

Pugh said, 'I suppose it's too early to go to the canteen?'

'Sod the canteen,' Garnett said irritably.

'What's eating you?'

'What's eating me? I would have thought that was obvious. I can't go anywhere without Vallance. I might just as well be under arrest.'

'Oh come on, it's not as bad as that.'

'I'm glad you think so.'

A window opened above them and Vallance leaned out.

'Sergeant Byass,' he called, 'come up to my office, I want a word with you.' He closed the window before Garnett had a chance to reply.

Vallance was still standing by the window when Garnett entered his office. Without turning round, he thrust back his right hand which was clutching a flimsy piece of paper. 'Here,' he said tonelessly, 'you'd better read this teleprinter message. It's about those V.I.P.s of yours—six of them are being shipped up here tomorrow.' Vallance rested his forehead against the window pane. 'It seems I was wrong about you, Sergeant,' he said.

Garnett said, 'I see they are going with the others on Wednesday morning, time of train to be confirmed later.'

Vallance turned to face him. 'I'd better tell you now, I haven't been exactly straight with you.'

'Oh?'

'No. 19 Mechanised Regiment had to post out a lot of their best men to form new units when the militia was expanded. I wouldn't like to say how good that regiment is now.'

Garnett placed the message in the Out tray. 'Can you elaborate please, sir?' he said.

'The absentee rate has soared and there has been a significant increase in the number of courts martial. I also

114

gave you a misleading impression of the local Resistance. They have been quiet of late, but I have a feeling that they are just biding their time. Security checks have shown that the militia is losing arms and ammunition at an alarming rate, and although I can't prove it, some of the thefts reported look to me like the Resistance had inside help.' Vallance smiled bitterly. 'Still,' he said, 'if the worst comes to the worst, you might get some help from the 84th Soviet Airborne Battalion. You probably noticed they were guarding the nuclear warhead stockpile at Clumber. They've only got a few atomic demolition munitions left on the site, so they ought to be able to spare a company or two.'

The outlook couldn't have been more bleak. It struck Garnett that either Moxham or Vickers or both were living in a fool's paradise. No one in his right mind would think of organising an escape operation in the vicinity of a nuclear arms dump. For one thing, security would be much tighter, and for another, there were a damn sight too many soldiers around.

Vallance said, 'Did you hear what I said, Sergeant?'

'Yes, sir. I was just thinking that we could always fall back on the police in an emergency.'

'Oh, we are certainly going to have to rely on them a lot, Sergeant. At least their Regional Control Centre links the county police forces of Nottinghamshire, Derbyshire, Lincolnshire, Leicestershire and Northamptonshire.'

Garnett said, 'No chance of that Ops Room being put out of action, is there?'

'You mean if there was a power cut?'

'Something like that.'

Vallance said, 'Come here.' He pointed across the yard at a building which was just below the main house. 'You see that funny little doll's house over there, that's where they keep the generator for just such an emergency. Nothing can put the police radio net off the air unless it's jammed, and they would have to know the frequencies to do that.'

'They could search the waveband.'

'They would have one hell of a job, we cover a very wide frequency waveband.'

'We?' said Garnett.

'This detachment is on the police command net. I get a

115

copy of their scantlist—I keep it in that safe over there.'
Vallance smiled. 'Don't worry, Sergeant, I am the only
person who knows the combination.' He glanced at his
wristwatch. 'Nearly time for lunch,' he said. 'Have you
seen all you want to?'

'I'm quite happy.'

'What makes you happy, Sergeant?'

'A lot of things. For instance, there isn't a suitable ambush
site between Arnold and the detention camp.'

'I assume that factor was taken into consideration before
it was decided to transfer the V.I.P.s to Proteus?'

Garnett said, 'We weren't consulted, sir. I understand it
was a political decision.'

'I see. What else comforts you?'

'Well, there are the two battalions right on the spot and
there is a third one available at Newark. Maybe their
morale isn't all that hot, but if my department wasn't aware
of it, I'm damn sure the Resistance isn't any better informed.
On top of that, we have three other factors going for us—
the Russians, the police and the element of surprise.'

'Surprise?'

'Nobody, apart from the addressees on the signal, knows
about the transfer of prisoners or when it will take place.'

'There's nothing like being optimistic,' Vallance said.

'That doesn't mean to say that we won't take additional
security measures.'

'Such as?'

Garnett shrugged his shoulders. 'That rather depends
on what London thinks is necessary. At a guess, I'd say we
will draft in extra agents.'

'You?'

'Possibly, amongst others.'

'When are you going back to London?'

'Tomorrow.' Garnett coughed. 'Sir,' he said, 'do you
think Sergeant-Major Pugh could run me back to the hotel
now?'

'Yes, see him on your way out.'

Garnett thanked him and saluted. He was halfway to the
door when Vallance called him back.

'You know, Sergeant,' he said, 'there's something familiar
116

about your face. You remind me of someone and I can't think who.'

'So my mother used to say.'

Vallance flushed. 'Are you trying to be funny?'

'No sir,' said Garnett. He saluted a second time. On his way out he collected Pugh from his office.

Sitting there in the car, nursing the sodden trench mac on his lap, Garnett came to the conclusion that, either Pugh was in a hurry to get back home in time for lunch, or else he was anxious to get rid of him. The speed limit might not have existed as far as Pugh was concerned, and he remained silent and withdrawn throughout almost the entire journey until they reached Maid Marian Way when he then obliquely revealed what was uppermost in his mind.

He said, 'Will you be up this way again?'

'Why?'

'I just wondered.'

'It depends on a number of things.'

'I see.'

'No you don't, but if I do come back you can be sure of one thing—you will probably have to kill Vallance.'

Pugh's knuckles turned white as he gripped the steering wheel. 'That's not my line of country,' he said tightly, 'I'm an undercover man.'

'I have news for you,' said Garnett, 'you'll be a dead undercover man if you don't.'

Pugh drew up outside the hotel and turned to face Garnett 'I shall just have to hope that you don't return,' he said quietly.

Garnett stepped out of the car. 'I'm not anxious to come back,' he said, 'but don't bank on it.'

He went inside the hotel and took the lift up to his floor. Once inside his room, Garnett stripped off and, while the bath water was running, rang down for a drink. He decided to skip lunch.

Edwards had planned the evening in some depth. They had dined at the Saracen's Head in Southwell, and then she had taken him on to the Leg of Mutton before finally winding up at the U.S.C. The fact that she was misusing army department transport didn't seem to worry her at all, and judging by the number of military vehicles parked outside the United Services Club, Garnett knew that she was not the only one faking the vehicle work ticket. Even the military police were in on the racket.

The U.S.C. was a wooden building not unlike an outsized cricket pavilion. Overlooking the Trent at West Bridgford, it enjoyed a secluded position with playing fields on three sides and the river on the fourth. The club had been open for three years and its membership was limited exclusively to the armed forces and the police. It boasted a small restaurant, a bar and a discotheque. Edwards made straight for the discotheque.

The room was dark and intimate and the music was deafening. It might have been tolerable if it hadn't been for the ultra-violet strip and the plastic decorations. He wondered what was the attraction of ultra-violet apart from the see-through effect it had on nylon. Whatever it was, Jo Edwards wasn't showing anything. She was wearing a simple knee-length green velvet dress and low-heeled black patent shoes. It was effective; heads had been turning in her direction all evening, but if she was aware of the admiring glances, she certainly didn't show it.

She was dancing very close to him, her face nuzzling against his chin. Every now and then she would raise her head, smile up at him and squeeze his hand and sigh. He had no way of knowing how much of it was an act. They were scarcely moving from the spot, yet her body was constantly in motion pushing against him. Whenever they turned, she would arch her back and thrust her pelvis forward and somehow entwine her legs in his. She hardly spoke a word, but then it wasn't really necessary—her body was saying more than enough.

It was like being inside a hothouse. The sweat ran down Garnett's face and the shirt clung to his back like a wet dish-cloth. The haze of tobacco smoke made his eyes smart and the endless tape music went on and on and on, and he longed for a breath of fresh air.

She read his thoughts accurately. 'Let's go outside,' she said, 'it's getting stuffy in here.'

Outside was damp and raw cold compared with the

118

discotheque, but at least the air was fresher and it had stopped raining. They walked slowly along the line of parked cars towards the river.

'Have you got a cigarette?' she said.

Garnett lit two and gave one to her.

'It'll be foggy tomorrow,' she said absently.

'How do you know?'

'Local knowledge. What time are you leaving in the morning?'

'I'm catching the eight-fifteen.'

'I'll miss you.'

'I'll miss you too,' he lied.

She stopped opposite a Ford Zephyr and pointed at the side window where someone's back was in full view. 'Look at that,' she whispered and then giggled softly, 'someone is having it away.'

There was only one safe answer to that one, and Garnett made it. 'Good luck to them,' he said.

Edwards shivered. 'I'm getting cold.'

'Shall we go back inside?'

She flipped her cigarette away, and the burning stub described an arc through the air and then went out like a dud rocket.

'Let's go back to the hotel, David.'

She unlocked the Mini, got in behind the wheel, leaned across the seat and tripped the latch on the passenger door. As Garnett settled into the seat beside her, she said, 'Damn and blast.'

'What's the matter?'

'I've laddered my tights.'

The dress was bunched up in her lap and she was showing just about everything. She pointed to a tiny run near the red lace trim on her pantie girdle. 'See,' she said, 'my last pair too.'

'You can always get another pair tomorrow.'

'I'm almost out of coupons,' she said.

He wound down the window and threw his cigarette out into the car park. She was giving him the come-on and they both knew it.

'Shall I write to you, David?'

'What?'

119

'I've got your unit address.'

'I'm going to London to attend a conference; I might not get it before I am back up here.'

'You'll be back by Saturday?'

'No. Monday, maybe Tuesday.'

'Are you married?'

'No.'

'Then why the reluctance?'

'I'm not reluctant, I want to see you again, Jo.'

'It doesn't sound like it, you don't want me to write to you.'

'It isn't like that,' he lied. 'Listen, I'll be back on Monday or Tuesday, it depends on how long it will take me to complete the security check.'

'What check?'

'I have to visit the School of Military Intelligence at Ashford first thing Monday morning.'

'I'll write to you care of that address. The letter will be waiting for you when you get there.'

'Jesus,' he thought, 'this is a bloody nightmare. A letter to Ashford addressed to a non-existent Sergeant Byass is all I need.' 'I'll ring you,' he said.

'When?'

'Tomorrow night when you come off duty.'

'It's my day off.'

'All right, I'll phone at six.'

She leaned towards him her mouth half open. 'You do that, darling,' she whispered.

Her arms went around his neck and her warm, soft mouth pressed against his. Her tongue darted and probed and she bit his lip and then the lobe of his left ear, and he wondered how the hell he was going to ditch the woman. Almost convinced that Edwards was playing a devious game, he figured that there was one sure way of finding out. He dropped his left hand and moved it up under her skirt, and that did the trick.

She drew back and grabbed his wrist. 'Hey,' she said weakly, 'that's the limit for tonight.'

He withdrew his hand and she straightened her skirt.

'You're pretty fast,' she breathed.

'You're not exactly slow yourself.'

She fumbled with the ignition key, found the slot and turned it on. 'Shall we go back to the hotel? I really am rather tired.'

'Let's do that.'

'It's been a wonderful evening,' she said.

Soldiers have an apt name for girls like Jo Edwards, but he didn't feel deprived.

12

THE TRAIN GOT INTO St. Pancras at 10:48. Garnett went straight to the Gentlemen's, locked himself in a cubicle and changed into civilian clothes. He then found an empty booth and telephoned Nash at the estate agent's and, working to a pre-arranged code, enquired if they had any unfurnished flats on their books. A negative response coupled with advice to call back next week, gave him the all clear to go to the R.V. Leaving the call box, he made his way to the Underground. He observed the usual precautions; he got out at Leicester Square, walked down to Piccadilly and caught a Bakerloo train out to Stanmore.

Keilly was waiting for him outside the station with a Corsair.

Garnett dumped his grip on to the back seat and got inside. 'Where are we going?' he said.

'North Harrow.'

'That's nice,' Garnett said, 'I've always wanted to go to North Harrow.'

'Lucky you, your dream's come true.'

Fifteen minutes and one cigarette later they had reached the centre of North Harrow and were stuck at the lights. A short distance up the road from them, Garnett spotted a large squared-off building, which at first sight he took to be a bingo hall until he noticed the gilt lettering below the parapet which said 'Bowling Alley'. The lights went to green and Keilly, turning right, saw a gap in the oncoming traffic and shot through. He turned left almost immediately and pulled into a private car park.

Keilly pointed out the rear entrance to the bowling alley. 'Through there,' he said, 'and on into the manager's office —you can't miss it.'

Garnett said, 'Aren't you coming?'

'No, I'm just the chauffeur.'

'What about my kit?'

Keilly said, 'You go on in, they're waiting for you. I'll see to your bag.'

Ten-pin bowling had crossed the Atlantic to become all the rage, and then, in common with a long list of imported pursuits, its popularity had withered and died as quickly as it had been born. Bowling alleys had mushroomed to meet the initial craze and then had folded overnight when the fad wore off. A few survived supported by a dwindling band of enthusiasts. This was one of them. He walked down the entire length of the silent, empty hall and opened the door to the manager's office. Nash and Vickers were waiting for him but, Garnett noticed, not Moxham.

Vickers said, 'How did you get on?'

Garnett sat down in a vacant chair. 'In a word—lousy. It's no go because Moxham wants them lifted whilst they are in transit, and there isn't a suitable ambush site between Arnold and Proteus. It's no go because there are two militia battalions at Clumber and a third one in Newark, not to mention a Russian airborne outfit guarding a nuclear warhead depot, which, I might add, Nash omitted to draw attention to in his briefing. It's no go because the police operations room at Bestwood controls five county constabularies and they can block every exit out of Nottingham. It's no go because the prisoners are being moved out of Proteus early on Wednesday morning which means that we don't have the time to plan this job thoroughly, and I am averse to taking part in something which I know is going to be a balls-up. I can also think of a few other reasons if you're still not convinced.'

Vickers said, 'Moxham might be persuaded to change his mind so that we go for them while they are still inside Proteus.'

'He might be persuaded, General, but I wouldn't. I wasn't able to get near the place, I don't know the layout, nor do I know where to find these six V.I.P.s of Moxham's even supposing I managed to get past the outer perimeter. And another thing—don't ask me to take them while they are moving through the city. They could alter that one-way system if they chose to, and we'd be sitting high and dry with an ambush on the wrong street. In the early hours of the morning they won't have a traffic problem on their hands so they can do what they like about one-way streets.'

'Which leaves us with Nottingham Station.'

'Yes.'

Vickers fitted a cigarette into his long black holder; Nash was ready with his lighter at just the right moment.

Vickers said, 'Surely you can think of at least one snag, David?'

'There are several.'

'I rather thought there might be.'

'We're after six men, right? And they are shifting fifteen hundred out of Proteus—that gives them a lot of scope. They could split the six up amongst the fifteen hundred and we could be looking for a needle in a haystack, or they could make special arrangements to bring them in under heavy guard at the last moment. They are not short of soldiers, in fact Nottingham is going to be stiff with them.'

'But the station is the best bet?'

Garnett said, 'I'd put it another way—the station is the best of a lousy set of alternatives.'

Vickers said, 'Supposing we decided to go ahead, how would you set it up?' A thin smile appeared on his face. 'I mean we could always get someone else to execute your plan if necessary.'

'Who?'

'Me,' said Nash.

'I wouldn't trust you to organise a piss-up in a brewery.'

In a sharp voice, Vickers said, 'That was uncalled for, Garnett.'

'My apologies.' He didn't mean it and Vickers knew it and Nash knew it, but both of them were prepared to accept it.

Vickers said, 'All right, let's hear your ideas, David.'

'Nottingham Midland is a fairly small station considering the size of the city, and it stands on a T-junction, so that if you are approaching it from the Mansfield direction, you have to make a sharp left turn into the station yard. There are two entrances to the main hall and these are about thirty metres apart. If you stood with your back to the first entrance, the booking office would be on your left and the R.T.O.'s hut would be on your right, while behind you would be W. H. Smith and Son. The ticket barriers are about twenty metres in from the entrance archways, and beyond the barriers there is a broadwalk approximately ten metres wide before you come to the steps leading down to the platforms. Control that concourse above the platforms and you control the station.'

Vickers looked up at the ceiling. 'If you took over the booking office and the R.T.O.'s hut you would have the entire concourse in a cross-fire.'

'I figured that too, General, but it might not be that easy. According to the teleprinter message, the Brigadier commanding 19 Mechanised Regiment has been made responsible for co-ordinating the operation. Now he has been told to hold a conference on Tuesday morning, and it's possible he might decide that the R.T.O.'s staff aren't required. In fact, he might want the entire station staff dismissed.'

Nash said, 'All I hear is ifs and buts.'

'Ignoring the ifs and buts is the quickest way I know of getting yourself killed.'

Vickers ejected the stub of his cigarette into the ashtray. 'Despite what you say, David, I still think it is a feasible operation.'

'You're forgetting the police Regional Control Centre.'

'We can take that out,' said Nash.

'How?'

'They need electricity for light and to power their static wireless sets, don't they? So we take out the power station.'

'There's more than one power station feeding the city, and the police also have their own generator—and don't talk about blowing that up because the bloody thing is too well guarded. If we are going to fix them, we have to jam

125

them, and that means we have to know their frequencies, and those frequencies are contained in a scantlist which is kept in a safe, and only Vallance knows the combination.'

Vickers said, 'Ah, yes, Vallance.'

'Yes, Vallance, General. I don't know what Pugh has told you about him but he's a bad one. He is sly and cunning, and I think he might be on to me.'

'Safes can be opened, David.'

'Of course they can, but Vallance isn't the only fly in the ointment. There's a girl called Jo Edwards, a sergeant in the W.A.C. who works in the R.T.O.'s office. I think she may be an undercover F.S. agent. She's too friendly for my liking, and she tried to catch me out. I don't think she was sold on my cover.'

'What you are saying is that you want out,' Nash sneered at Garnett, 'I told you before, you're too old for this game, dad—you're a has-been.'

In a level, calm voice Garnett said, 'We don't stand a chance because there are too many unknown factors, their security is too good, we don't have the time to plan the job properly, and the prize doesn't warrant the risks involved. We're out to bring a government down, right? Now you tell me how snatching six men will do that.'

'It won't,' said Vickers, 'but there are other operations taking place simultaneously, and together they will have the desired effect.'

'What other operations?'

'I can't tell you, you know that.'

'If I am going to do this job, I'm entitled to know what you have in mind.'

Vickers said, 'I need a drink, how about you, David?'

'Whisky.'

Vickers looked up at Nash. The glance was enough—Nash crossed the room and opened the cocktail cabinet.

'All right, David, I'll let you in on one aspect. A few hours after you have lifted the prisoners from Nottingham Station, the 57th Motor Rifle Battalion at Newark will receive orders to take over the nuclear warhead depot. The Russians won't like it. In fact, I can guarantee that there will be a very nasty incident—both parties will open fire on each other.'

'How can you be so sure?'

'The expansion of the militia offered us a unique opportunity. We used it to infiltrate some of our better men into the army.'

Nash handed a glass to Garnett. 'We think of everything,' he said.

Garnett sipped his whisky thoughtfully. 'If this plan works, General, are things going to be any better? I mean, can you trust these nominees of yours who are going to step into the government?'

Nash laughed. 'He wants a written guarantee that there will be free elections.'

Vickers said quietly, 'The situation could hardly get worse, could it, David?'

'I suppose not. We really intend to send these six men to the States?'

'We do, and as Moxham promised, there will be room for you and Dane.'

'If we do this thing, I am not going to make a dash for the coast. We lift the prisoners and then we lie low for six, maybe eight weeks before we rendezvous with the submarine.'

'I agree.'

'Good. I also want to work with people I know I can trust.'

'You can trust me, David.'

'Oh I do, General, but you are not going to be with me. Is Dinkmeyer still available?'

'Well, I don't know about that, he's not altogether suitable—I mean there is that handicapped daughter of his to consider.'

'And he is also an American, General, which means that we shall have to find two extra berths on the submarine, but I worked with him in Salisbury and I trust him. He will handle the escape route.'

'If you insist.'

'I insist. I also want to see a list of safe houses and I'll make my own choice. Nobody, apart from Dinkmeyer and myself, will know which ones have been selected. Dinkmeyer is also going to be the man who tells the navy where and when to pick us up, and he will need a one to one link with the submarine. The navy might not like that but they can lump it.'

Vickers said acidly, 'What else have we got to lump?'

'I'll need a safe-breaker and someone to take the place of the W.A.C. on duty in the R.T.O.'s office and . . .'

'Use Dane.'

'Dane has done enough.'

'No one has done enough, Garnett, that's why we are still an occupied country. You will use Dane.'

'All right, but only if she agrees.'

'She will have to agree.'

Garnett ignored the pointed comment. 'I will need at least three other men with me inside the station, and a diversionary force outside—and drivers, good ones who know Nottingham and the surrounding area. Do you think you can raise that lot in three days?'

'We'll have to, David. You can have Keilly and Nash as a start.'

'I thought Nash was indispensable?'

'Nash, my dear boy, is going to keep you on the straight and narrow in case you have second thoughts. He will call for you this afternoon and introduce you to the staff so that you can run your eye over them.'

Garnett drained his whisky. 'Where's Dane?' he said.

Nash said, 'I'll show you, I'm going that way.'

Garnett stood up. 'Will I see you again, General?'

'Naturally, there are still a number of details to be ironed out.'

They went out through the back way and walked on down the road in silence. There was ten years and a wall of animosity between the two men which Vickers could hardly have failed to notice. Garnett thought it probably suited his book to have Nash there to needle him. Nash stopped outside a semi-detached and pushed open the front gate.

'This is it,' he said, 'ring the bell and Dane will answer. The house belongs to the manager of the bowling alley, but he is taking a few days off on our orders. I'll call for you at two.'

'I'll be ready.'

Nash smiled—it wasn't a friendly smile. 'I've got to hand it to you,' he said, 'Valerie Dane in London, Jo Edwards in

128

Nottingham—you've got crumpet waiting for you at both ends of the line.' He saw Garnett ball up his fists and the smile faded. 'Don't try it,' he said harshly, 'there are too many people about.' He turned on his heel and walked away.

Eastcote Road was part of the old section of Harrow. Its terraced houses had seen two world wars, a depression and an occupation, and yet outwardly nothing had changed significantly. The baker's shop on the corner had been there since the Boer War but the grocer's shop had gone. The street had seen hobbled skirts, cloche hats, square shoulders, wedge shoes and the mini. It had neither gone up in the social order nor had it gone down. In the affluent days before the occupation the street had been a convenient place to park the car if the car parks were full. It was a street which people moved out of when they earned enough to do so. It was a street which took in lodgers.

Nash pushed open a wrought-iron gate and walked up the short front path. The porch was a Gothic arch framing a chocolate-brown door which made the house look not unlike a mission hall. He banged the knocker and waited. No one came to the door.

Garnett said, 'They couldn't have heard you.'

Nash banged again. Footsteps shuffled in the hall and the door opened slowly. The old woman was in her seventies and crippled with arthritis. The joints of her hands were swollen and distorted and one leg was marginally shorter than the other. She wore a built-up heel to compensate but it didn't improve her mobility.

Nash said, 'May we see Mr. Taylor?'

'I won't have visitors in my rooms,' she said. Her dentures were a bad fit and they clacked like castanets.

Nash pressed a pound note into her hand. 'We won't be long and we promise not to make a noise.'

'I should think not.' She pursed her lips. 'How long?'

Nash gave her another pound. 'About ten minutes.'

'He's in the back room upstairs. Mind how you go on the stairs, there's a loose rod.'

Wallpaper which had once been cream-coloured was now turning yellow with age. A gilt-framed picture of a rose-covered cottage fought a game but hopeless battle to brighten the gloomy landing. They tried the door to Taylor's room but it was locked on the inside.

Nash rattled the door knob and called, 'Come on, Ernie, open up, you've got company.'

A voice said, 'Go away, I'm busy.'

'This is business, Ernie.'

'What kind of business?'

'Money business.'

A spring creaked, bare feet padded across the floor and the bolt was drawn back. As they entered the room, Taylor leapt into bed and pulled the clothes up to his chest, almost hiding the girl who was sharing his bed.

Stale tobacco smoke hung in the air, adding to the general impression of slovenliness—a cupboard door hanging open, Taylor's clothes draped carelessly on a chair, and a pair of dark blue panties and laddered tights lying beside a crumpled newspaper on the floor.

Taylor was thin, sallow and hollow-chested. Lank hair covered both ears. According to his I.D. card he was twenty-six, but he looked a good ten years older. The girl was plain, round-faced and plump. Straggly brown hair hung down over her bare shoulders and partially concealed the swell of her breasts. Long false lashes added to the illusion that her eyes were bulging out of their sockets.

Nash said, 'We're here on business, tell your bird to go and powder her nose.'

The girl opened her mouth in shrill protest. She had big, strong, evenly spaced yellow teeth.

'Who do you think you're talking to?' she shouted.

Taylor scratched his nose. 'You can say anything you like in front of the wife.'

Nash stared at him coldly. 'We're talking about money, Ernie. Women have a habit of relieving you of it before you've had a chance to earn it. Send her out of the room before she spends it for you.'

Taylor shrugged his shoulders, turned to the girl and said, 'Hop it.' The girl opened her mouth to protest again. 'Go on, hop it, like I told you.' He raised his hand as though to hit her across the face and she scrambled out of bed, grabbed a dressing gown and fled out of the room.

'You've got to show them who's the boss,' Taylor said modestly.

Nash said, 'How old is she, Ernie?'

'Seventeen.'

'Liar.'

'Well, she looks seventeen.'

'They'll have you for carnal knowledge yet, Ernie.'

'Yes, well, that's a chance I've got to take.' He rubbed the stubble on his chin. 'Haven't seen you in a long time, Mr. Rogers. How did you know where to find me?'

'The word gets around in the trade, Ernie.'

The eyes became sly. 'Who's your friend, Mr. Rogers?'

Nash smiled. 'He's heard all about you, Ernie, and he's impressed.'

'Is he?'

'Oh yes, you're one of the few safe-breakers who's never done bird; never pulled a really big job but never been short of the bread for long. Tell him why you've never done bird.'

Taylor reached under the bed and came up with a packet of Embassy. He stuck a cigarette between his lips and lit it. 'I don't have a trademark, see. Some blokes are petermen, some are drillers and some are cutters, and they get so specialised that the fuzz can recognise their handi-work. Now me, I go for the small stuff, and I use jelly, or a drill or a torch. I'm flexible.' He blew a smoke ring towards the ceiling. 'Have you got a safe in mind?'

Garnett said, 'It's an out of town job.'

'I'd need to look the place over.'

'You won't have to, it's a daylight job and you will be wearing uniform.'

'What sort of uniform?' Taylor said suspiciously.

'Army.'

'That's not for me.'

'You might not have to do it, but you'll still get paid.'

'Now look, Mr. Rogers, you tell your friend I draw the line at playing heroes. If he wants to lift an army payroll, let him find somebody else.'

'This isn't a payroll, Ernie, and like the man said you could get paid for doing nothing.'

'How much?'

'Five hundred.'

'Seven fifty.'

'Five hundred plus whatever's in the safe.'

'I thought this wasn't a payroll job, Mr. Rogers?'

'They always keep money in safes, Ernie.'

Taylor stubbed his cigarette out on the floor. 'All right,' he said, 'what do I have to do?'

Garnett said, 'You get your hair cut and then we pick you up on Sunday night.'

'Hair cut?' Taylor echoed, 'my mates will die laughing.'

Nash grabbed Taylor by the throat and slammed his head against the wall. 'You say one word of this to your mates, Ernie,' he said quietly, 'and I'll kill you.'

Taylor felt his throat tenderly. 'There was no need for that, Mr. Rogers,' he complained, 'you know I've never been a gabber.'

Nash said, 'You just keep it that way, Ernie.'

He signalled Garnett to follow and then walked out of the room. They passed the girl friend on the landing as she came out of the lavatory and nipped back into Taylor's room.

Garnett waited until they were outside the house before he said his piece.

'I wanted a reliable man,' he said coldly, 'and you give me Taylor. What makes you think we can use a man like that?'

'Ernie is reliable. I've used him before.'

'What for? A personal job?'

Nash said, 'You professionals make me sick. Listen, a Resistance organisation needs money, right? We can't run a flag day so we take it from wherever it's available. In the beginning we hit banks until they started arming cashiers and we had to switch to supermarkets and small businesses, and if you're smart you want the police to think it's part of the normal crime pattern and that way Special Branch doesn't get interested. So we use people like Ernie Taylor who have been on the fringe of the trade all their lives. You don't have to worry about Ernie Taylor—he'll do a good job for you.'

They caught a bus to Mill Hill from outside Sopers Department Store, got off at Bunns Lane and then walked to Harrison's coal yard. The man they wanted was bagging anthracite and loading it on to a truck single-handed.

He was known as Michael Allen. Before the war he had been a police constable stationed at Hendon. Of above-average intelligence, he had been earmarked for accelerated promotion, but he had resigned from the force on the grounds that his wife, who was of a nervous disposition, didn't like being left alone at night. He got out just in time. Three months after he resigned, the puppet government took out emergency powers prohibiting voluntary retirement. Pre-war he had been a member of a small-bore shooting club. He was, in fact, a natural marksman who had found no difficulty in adjusting to full bore. He became an active member of the Resistance shortly after his wife took an overdose of sleeping pills, and the Resistance had made good use of him. He was known as 'the assassin' and secretly he was rather proud of the title. His hatred of the Russians was deep, personal and lasting, and dated from the time when two drunken Russian soldiers had broken into his bungalow while he was out, and having raped his wife had then beaten her up. It didn't matter to him that subsequently these same two Russians had been court martialled and shot—what mattered was that his wife had committed suicide, and nothing could erase that. Few people inside the Resistance realised that Allen was fast becoming a dangerous psychotic.

Allen spotted Garnett and Nash standing outside the coal yard as he dumped the last bag on to the truck. He approached the fence almost lazily, wiping his hands on his hips. He was a powerfully built man, and considering what he had been through, Garnett thought he looked remarkably cheerful.

Nash pointed a finger at Garnett and said, 'This is the man you'll be working under.'

Garnett said, 'I've heard a lot about you.'

A broad smile appeared on Allen's face. 'Have you?' he said proudly.

'I've been told you prefer working alone.'

'What of it?'

'This time you will have to follow my orders.'

'That's no sweat.'

133

'You've got to think, act and look like a soldier.'

'We did plenty of square-bashing when I was a recruit in the police.'

'This is going to be a messy job.'

'When do we go?'

'Sunday.'

'I'll be ready.'

He turned and walked back to the truck. The vacant smile which had been hovering on his lips all the time they had been talking worried Garnett.

Nash said, 'Come on, let's call it a day.'

Garnett called Edwards at six-thirty and she sounded as if she was pleased to hear from him. She kept him talking until he had run out of loose change, and in that seemingly endless ten minutes, he had committed himself to calling her again the following evening. He didn't want to, but equally he didn't want her writing to the School of Military Intelligence. Keeping Edwards happy was an insurance policy, but he didn't like the premium he was obliged to pay, and he knew that if he told Dane about it, she wouldn't like it either.

13

THE PHONE RINGING IN the hall dragged Garnett from a deep sleep. He scrambled out of bed, thrust his feet into a pair of old slippers, grabbed his dressing gown, and shivering with cold ran downstairs and picked up the receiver.

A cheerful voice said, 'This is Sunscape Tours, Mr. Thrush speaking. I believe you have been enquiring if we have any cottages to rent at Easter. I think you said you wanted a quiet place in the country not too far from the sea?'

'That's right.'

'Good. It so happens that we have one or two attractive cottages which are still available at a reasonable rent. Perhaps you would like to call round to our offices in Regent Street sometime today?'

'Yes, we will.'

'Ask for me—Mr. Thrush—okay?'

'Yes, thank you for calling.'

'It's my pleasure,' said Thrush and hung up.

Garnett replaced the phone and turned round to find Dane standing on the bottom step of the staircase.

'I thought I might as well get up and make breakfast,' she said. 'What do you fancy with your eggs, tea or coffee?'

'Whatever we have most of.'

'It will have to be tea then.'

He followed her into the kitchen, raked the stove, banked

it up with coke and put it on the draw. The kitchen was the warmest place in the house.

Dane said, 'I presume it was a business call?'

'Yes.'

'Do you have to do this job in Nottingham?'

'It's one way of guaranteeing we get on the boat.'

Dane banged the frying pan down on the gas stove. 'Do you really believe that fairy story?' she snapped.

'I don't know what to believe any more.'

'Am I to be involved?'

'Vickers thinks you ought to help.'

'He would.'

'You don't have to.'

She cracked a couple of eggs and dropped them into the pan to join the three rashers of bacon. 'You don't like the idea of going back to Nottingham, do you David?'

'Not particularly.'

'Why?'

'Because it's too risky.'

'Then why go?'

Garnett said, 'It's difficult to explain. I think we are at a turning point, and I have a feeling that we've got a lot of ordinary people behind us. I've had more help from people outside the Resistance in these last few days, than I have had in years. I think we can topple this puppet government with one good push, and I think the Russians will be only too happy to pull out if we play our cards right. And so, even if there isn't a bloody submarine waiting for us, I still believe we should go through with it.'

Dane said, 'That was quite a speech for a man who doesn't know what to believe.' She arranged the bacon and eggs on the plate and placed it on the kitchen table. 'You'll want a knife and fork,' she said.

Garnett got them out of the kitchen drawer. 'Aren't you eating?' he said.

'I'm not hungry.'

'Have I said something to upset you?'

'No.'

'You've got something on your mind.'

'I was wondering about Kelso, your dentist friend.'

Garnett put down his knife and fork. 'What about him?'

136

'When the Seagrave business looked as if it was going sour, Vickers told you to go to Kelso and find out what hold Seagrave had over Warner.' Cradling the warm cup of tea in both hands, Dane drank from it slowly. 'I find that very odd, don't you?' she said.

'Kelso was Seagrave's deputy, it was logical to call on him first. Perhaps we just struck lucky.'

'You don't sound very convinced, David.'

'I had my doubts at the time.'

Dane put the cup down on the draining board. 'It may be feminine intuition, but I think someone on the Central Committee knew what Seagrave intended to do. In fact, I'll go further—Seagrave had their approval, and that's why it was so easy to find those photographs.'

'That's a hell of an assumption.' He pushed the plate away and drank his tea quickly.

'Aren't you going to finish your eggs and bacon?' she said.

'I've suddenly lost my appetite.'

'What are you going to do?'

'Do?' he said, 'I'll tell you. We shall get dressed and then we're going to call on the tourist agency.'

'After all I've said, you are still prepared to go ahead?' she said angrily.

'I'm not saying you are wrong. Maybe Seagrave did have someone's approval, but things can change. Perhaps the plan backfired and the sponsor got cold feet and changed his ideas and doesn't like to admit it.'

Dane compressed her lips. It was on the tip of her tongue to point out that very few people knew she had been inside and yet the *Evening Standard* had carried a picture of her, shaven-headed and in prison garb. Someone was being very co-operative. Aloud she said, 'At least promise me you will go and see Kelso again before you finally commit yourself.'

'I'll think about it,' he said.

The travel agency was sandwiched between a Gas Board showroom and a dress shop. The display in the long plate-glass window had changed little over the years. Gone were the coloured layouts extolling Cannes, the Rhineland, Italy and Greece; in were Scarborough, Hastings, Edinburgh and Tenby under the heading, 'Holiday at home—Discover beautiful Britain'. There was no option but to have a holiday at home—travel abroad was prohibited.

Garnett opened the door for Dane and then followed her inside. The stark white counter which filled the width of the room was staffed by a row of neatly dressed guides wearing name-tag brooches in the lapels of their wine-coloured blazers. Racks stuffed with brochures lined the walls; tiny speakers disguised as air vents relayed taped music at an agreeably quiet volume. Conversation was conducted in a low key. Garnett spotted Thrush at the far end of the counter.

'Mr. Thrush,' he said, 'I took your advice and came to see you. You called me earlier this morning, remember?'

Thrush favoured him with an artificial smile. 'Ah, yes,' he said brightly, 'you were looking for a quiet place in the country not too far from the sea. Have you anywhere in mind?'

'I hoped you might be able to suggest a likely spot.'

Thrush reached under the counter and produced a looseleaf notebook. 'You might like to browse through that,' he said.

The list was short and deflating to read. Garnett had not known what to expect but the scarcity of safe houses alarmed him, until it occurred to him that it would be typical of Vickers to give him a very foreshortened list to choose from, and in a way he didn't blame him. No one in his right mind would allow one man to walk around carrying an exhaustive list of addresses in his head. Garnett closed the book and pushed it back across the counter.

Thrush said, 'Did you find anything suitable?'

'May be.'

'Of course, it's not good practice to refer you to our competitors, but I do know of someone who might be able to help you.'

'I'd like to meet him.'

'He lives some way from here, in Charlton—34, Dene Park Road, Charlton, near the football stadium.'

'Who is he?'

'I think you know him, he used to run an agency in Salisbury.'

Garnett said, 'Thank you, you've been most helpful.'

Thrush bowed his head. 'It's my pleasure,' he said.

As soon as they were outside on the pavement Dane said, 'That was cosy. I hope you got what you came for.'

'I did. I've got a list of safe houses and I know where to find Dinkmeyer. Nobody could ask for more than that.'

The houses in Dene Park Road backed on to the railway line. The sitting room in number 37 had a view of the ground belonging to Charlton Athletic, a view limited to the main stand and the floodlights on top of the gantries.

Paul Keith, alias Dinkmeyer, had put on weight in the six months since they had last worked together in Salisbury but otherwise he hadn't altered much. There was only a little more pepper and salt in the curly red hair and the sagging waistline was now definitely obvious, but his face was still unlined and young for a man in his middle forties. As an American citizen, he had been in the wrong place at the wrong time when the war had started, and in return for a new identity, he had gone to work for Vickers. It was an arrangement he often regretted. He didn't appear to be overjoyed to see Garnett, perhaps partly because he was suffering from a heavy cold which showed in his reddened sore nose. His voice too had almost gone and he spoke in a hoarse whisper.

'I didn't expect to see you again,' he said.

'I suppose not. How's Sue?'

'All right,' Dinkmeyer said guardedly, 'she's gone out for the afternoon.' He reached for the glass of whisky at his elbow. 'Knowing you as I do, you didn't come here to pay a social call. Vickers said you had a proposition which would interest me.' He drained the whisky and then refilled the glass. He didn't bother to offer Dane and Garnett a drink.

Garnett said, 'How would you like to go home?'

'What's the catch?'

'We propose to send six men over the water to form a government in exile.'

'Have they got wings or something?'

'They will be picked up by a Hunter class submarine. There will also be room for you, Sue, Dane and me.'

'And where are these six men coming from?'

'A prison camp.'

'And you're lifting them?'

'Correct.'

'Where do I fit in?'

'You arrange the pick-up. I've got three safe houses, one at Seend, another at Glastonbury and the third at Chard. I'll deliver the V.I.P.s to these houses and you will take them on from there.' Garnett lit a cigarette. 'I plan to stay put in the safe houses for about six to eight weeks while the situation cools off. In that time I want you to buy a place near the coast which we can use as a final R.V. You can choose whatever location takes your fancy, but I suggest you ought to buy a small hotel or a caravan site or something in that line. There could be as many as fifteen of us.'

Dinkmeyer said, 'Where do I get all the money for this?'

'Vickers will provide it. And do your own conveyancing, we don't want anybody in the firm knowing where to find us.'

Dinkmeyer swallowed the rest of his whisky. 'Okay,' he said harshly, 'so you're very security conscious and no one on our side is going to know where we are. But we have to speak to the submarine, and how are we going to do that without someone eavesdropping? Someone has to allot the frequencies, tell the navy when to listen out and decide what code is going to be used.'

Garnett said, 'I could use a drink.'

Dinkmeyer looked sour. 'Sorry chum,' he said, 'I've only got a drop left in the bottle and I need that for medicinal purposes—and anyway, suppose you answer my question.'

'Vickers will provide you with necessary communications.'

'And that makes it all right?'

'He is one of the few people I know I can trust.'

Dinkmeyer said, 'Alleluia. Now tell me how I will know when to call the boat in?'

'We'll meet—five weeks from next Wednesday—at the London Palladium—you get the tickets and send one to me addressed to the Reverend Cadbury, The Old Vicarage, Church End Road, Seend.'

'People are going to take us for a couple of queers.'

'Dane will keep the date with you, she will act as the go-between.'

'And supposing you get yourself killed?'

'You'll read about it in the papers, and then you'll check out the safe houses, see how many of us have made it and take it from there.'

'I'll need to know the other addresses.'

'I'll write them down, you memorise them and then burn the paper.'

Dinkmeyer poured himself another whisky. 'While you're at it,' he said, 'you'd better make a note that Vickers wants to see you tomorrow afternoon, three o'clock—The Church Hall, Avenmore Drive, Ealing. You're both invited to tea.'

Low cloud hid the stars and made the night dark. There was a chill wind in the air which sent a shiver down his back and made Garnett wish that he had gone home with Dane instead of traipsing out to Hayes. He pushed open the front gate of 23, Ladbroke Terrace and walked up the narrow path. No lights were showing in the front and he wondered if Kelso had gone out for the evening. There was only one way to find out—he rang the bell and waited. A light came on in the hall and then Kelso opened the door. Garnett was inside before he had a chance to object.

Garnett said, 'I haven't come about my teeth.'

'Obviously.'

'I want some information.'

Kelso opened the surgery door and put on the light. 'We can talk in here,' he said. He leaned against the filing cabinet and folded his arms across his chest. 'I hope this isn't going to take long.'

'About Seagrave.'

'What about her?'

'The story I have is that she allowed Special Branch to pick her up for the purpose of making a deal with Warner. I'm also told she did this with the approval of certain people.' Kelso inclined his head. 'I want to know whose blessing she received.'

'I don't know,' said Kelso.

'Moxham?'

'I told you I don't know.'

141

'Vickers?'

'Are you deaf? How many more times do I have to repeat myself?'

'She didn't go it alone, Kelso, so who on the Central Committee supported her?'

'The Committee was on the point of collapse, it no longer enjoyed the support of all the Resistance leaders. Several people on the fringe of power were in favour of an approach being made to the puppet government.'

'Name one person.'

'I only know their code names.'

Garnett said, 'Okay, give me one.'

'The Angora Rabbit.'

'Pull the other leg.'

Kelso shrugged his shoulders. 'I'm not responsible for these ludicrous code names.'

Garnett said, 'She betrayed people in the Movement.'

'Only those fascists who opposed our policy.'

'Cripps is a fascist?'

'Yes.'

'And Donnelly?'

'Yes.'

'Have you got any proof of that?'

'No.'

'Well then, how do you know Warner didn't sweat the names out of her?'

'Because of the safeguard.'

'The photographs of Warner?'

'That amongst others.'

'What others?'

'If Warner didn't observe the rules, Seagrave planned to leak certain false information which would put us wise.'

'Such as?'

'Dead letter boxes. The moment Special Branch started checking those out we'd know our plan had miscarried.' Kelso smiled. 'I can see you regard Seagrave as a traitor.'

'Don't you?'

'No, she's a patriot.'

'God help us if there are any more like her around.'

'I disagree. We needed someone to make contact with

142

those people in the government who are just as eager as us to see the Russians go.'

'They are already on their way, or haven't you heard.'

'As I remember it, a token occupation force was to remain behind.'

'We should throw them out.'

The smile on Kelso's face became condescending. 'The trouble with you hawks,' he said, 'is that you think force is the only answer. Force never solved anything.'

'That's a nice cosy philosophy to go to bed with.'

'The Resistance should adopt Gandhi's principles and become non-violent.'

Garnett said, 'Gandhi was dealing with us, we've got the Russians, there is a difference.' He said good night and left before Kelso could think of another debating point.

He found a call box in the High Street, sorted out a pile of loose change and then rang up Edwards. It was a full minute before she answered and he thought he had struck lucky and had missed her.

Reluctantly he said, 'It's me, David.'

'I'm so glad. I was beginning to wonder if you would ring tonight.' Her voice sounded breathless; there was a little-girl-lost touch about it which sounded false.

'Why so?' he said, 'it's still quite early.'

'Later than yesterday though. What have you been doing today?'

'This and that.'

'Such as?'

'Business.'

'What business, darling?'

The darling bit almost threw him. 'I can't tell you, you should know better than to ask.'

'I see,' she said slowly.

'I hope you do.'

'I hope so too. When will I see you again?'

'Monday night.'

'Promise?'

'I promise.'

'What time?'

'About eightish.'

'Not before?'

143

'I'll try and make it earlier.'

'Do you miss me?'

'More than you know,' he lied. The pips started up and he added quickly, 'I've run out of loose change, Jo. See you Monday.'

'Will you be staying at the hotel?'

'Yes.'

'I'll book a room for you.'

'Do that...'

The phone went dead on Edwards as the line was automatically cut off. She replaced the receiver thoughtfully and then sat down on the edge of her bed. There was, she thought, something about David Byass which didn't ring true. He was cagey and always seemed to be on his guard. But, of course, those characteristics were common enough amongst Field Security Agents, but all the same, she felt he was trying to hide something. She had checked him out with Vallance and had been given a short but reassuring answer and told not to meddle in affairs which didn't concern her. Byass, she told herself, was a genuine F.S. agent even though he did bear a resemblance to one of the men on the Wanted List.

She opened the evening paper and again studied the Wanted List which the newspapers were compelled to print as a supplement at regular intervals. The lists were, as often as not, a piece of propaganda, for they included a large number of Resistance workers who had been killed and captured, and it was the practice to super-impose a black cross over the photographs of those who had already been accounted for, on the theory that this would convince the civil population that the security forces were getting on top of the Resistance.

She stared at the photograph of the man whose eyes were screwed up against the bright sunlight, and she could see that there was a slight similarity between David Seymour, alias David Garnett, alias George Abel, and the man she knew as David Byass. There was however a matter of the black cross which meant that he had either been killed or captured, and that might have put her mind at rest but for the fact that the adjacent photograph depicted a bald woman known as Evelyn Rogers, alias Valerie Dane who, it was stated, had been known to be associated with George Abel. She had a feeling that David Byass was hiding something from her and instinct told her it was a woman. It was best, she decided, to check whether David was a single man before she made a fool of herself, and it would be quite a simple matter to send a signal asking the Records Office to verify the service details of one, Sergeant Byass. Tomorrow was Sunday, but there was no immediate hurry—the signal could wait until Monday.

The door opened quietly and Martin sidled into the room, carrying a pair of black jackboots and a leather belt.

She blinked her eyes several times and then in a nervous voice said, 'I've bulled your kit, Sergeant.'

Edwards turned to face her. 'Bring them over here,' she said coldly.

Martin came forward anxiously. She cringed before Edwards like a puppy who knows it is about to be beaten. 'I did my best, Jo—I mean, Sergeant.'

Edwards inspected the boots and the belt. 'Your best isn't up to much, but they'll pass muster.'

'Can I go now?'

'Why? You're confined to quarters.'

'There's a film on at the Odeon which I wanted to see.'

'Forget it.'

'The other girls say it is against regulations.'

'What is?'

'My batting for you. They say you could get into trouble.'

Edwards said, 'Which do you prefer, to be dealt with by me or face a court martial?'

'I haven't done anything wrong.'

Edwards stood up and stared at Martin. 'You're idle, invariably late for duty because you oversleep, you can't be trusted to do anything without the closest supervision, you are untidy and you are stupid, and I also have good reason to think that you are politically unstable. If I preferred charges on those counts, you could go to prison for anything up to six months, and if I really tried hard, I daresay it would be six months with hard labour. Now—do you still wish to make a formal complaint for redress of grievance, or are you prepared to accept my punishment?'

Martin looked down at her large feet to hide the tears which were welling in her eyes. 'I'll accept your punishment, Sergeant,' she whispered.

Edwards said, 'All right, now get out and don't let me hear you complaining again.'

Edwards sat down on the bed and thrust her feet into the snugly fitting jackboots. She got up, slipped the quilted housecoat off her shoulders and opened the wardrobe door. She stood there in her stretch bikini panties and matching bra admiring her reflection in the full-length mirror, and she tried to imagine how David Byass might react if he was with her in the room, and then the cautious streak in her came to the fore and she felt guilty. It was wrong for a Party member and security agent to nurse such decadent ideas. She stepped into her uniform skirt and zipped it up, and then carefully pulled the cossack tunic over her head taking care not to disarrange her hair. She cinched the belt around her waist and then checked her appearance in the mirror once more. She looked composed, confident and definitely attractive. Jo Edwards was intelligent, ambitious, twenty-four and still single. If the Records Office gave David Byass a clean bill of health, she didn't intend to remain that way for long.

14

SUNDAY AFTERNOON WAS COLD and grey and the streets were practically empty. Thin plumes of smoke rose up from the chimney pots along Avenmore Drive and hung almost motionless in the still air. The road, straight as a ruler, led into a small square dominated by the church. The church hall, a low wooden hut, looked out of place beside the imposing façade of St. Mark's. The faint buzz of conversation which reached their ears as they approached the hut puzzled them both until Garnett indicated the poster on the door which said—'Ealing O.A.P.s' Church Social— All welcome.' He opened the door, stood to one side and allowed Dane to enter first.

Coloured streamers hung from the rafters, clusters of balloons were tied to the lamp brackets on each wall, card tables formed a hollow square around the room, and just below the stage at the far end of the hall, four trestle-tables placed end to end supported rows of white cups and saucers and plates piled high with buns, cakes, sausage rolls and sandwiches. The room was full of old people absorbed in cards, dominoes and Beetle. The women outnumbered the men by more than two to one.

A youngish man with tousled hair falling untidily over his right eye detached himself from a group of card players and rushed forward to meet them. The starched white collar above the black vest was too large for his thin neck.

With a nervous gesture he swept the offending strands of hair back in place.

'I'm so glad you were able to come and help,' he said. He swivelled on his heel, pointed to a door on the left of the stage and said, 'You'll find the others in there making tea.' He beamed. 'Do please excuse me, I shall have to dash, I'm making up a fourth at bridge.'

As if to substantiate the truth of his statement, a querulous voice from the back of the hall called, 'Come on Vicar, you're holding up the game.'

The helpers in the small oblong-shaped room consisted of two middle-aged women and the urbane Vickers. The women were gazing intently at the huge kettles perched on the two-ring Baby Belling almost willing them to come to the boil. A chromium-plated tea urn was balanced pre-cariously on the narrow counter next to the electric cooker amid scattered breadcrumbs, crusts and empty paste pots.

Vickers waved a slim hand indicating the two women. 'My assistants,' he said with a charming smile. 'Mrs. Roscoe is the lady in the red dress, and her friend is Miss Levy— meet Mr. and Mrs. Shuttleworth. Now that you two are here they will be able to take a well-earned break from their chores.'

The ladies got the drift. They smiled, said how pleased they were to meet Mr. and Mrs. Shuttleworth and then left to tend the food-laden tables.

Vickers said, 'How are things coming along?' He made the question sound as though it was a mere formality, his breezy confidence suggesting that he didn't expect any problem to arise.

'I don't like a last-minute change in plan, General. I told my people I would collect them tonight, and then I get word from Dinkmeyer that I'm expected to be here.'

'What are you worried about? Nash is collecting your team together, I thought he could save you the trouble, and after all, we still do have several important details to tie up. Incidentally, how was Dinkmeyer?'

'Apart from a bad cold, he was fine.' Garnett paused to light a cigarette. 'He will need a lot of money and secure communications. I'd like you personally to take care of that side of the business.'

'Oh, come now, David, I've got more important things to attend to in the next few days.'

'I'd like you to do it,' Garnett said evenly, 'because this job smells. I can't quite put my finger on it but there is something wrong somewhere, and you are one of the few people I am prepared to trust, General.'

Vickers smiled easily. 'All right, David,' he said, 'if that is what you want. I can't risk sending you in with one eye looking back over your shoulder.'

'What about the Nottingham end? I don't know these V.I.P.s of yours by sight.'

'Nash will, by now, have delivered an envelope through your letter box containing a number of press cuttings. You will find them quite a help.'

It was on the tip of Garnett's tongue to ask when Nash would be taking over, but he thought better of it. In a quiet tone he said, 'Do I get any help from Nottingham?'

'You'll meet the local Resistance leader in the Broken Wheel near Brackley for lunch—tomorrow at one o'clock. He will be waiting for you in the saloon bar with the drivers. You will recognise him by the pile of advertising literature at his elbow.'

'Any other recognition signal?'

'Yes. You will say, "I hope I haven't kept you waiting", and he will say, "Not a bit, we've only been here a few minutes ourselves." Happy about that?'

'It sounds innocent enough. What about the team?'

'Nash will see that they are kitted out, and we shall keep them out of the Nottingham area until late on Tuesday. We've got a good hide to the north of York on a disused airfield at Sutton-on-the-Forest, a bit far out and off the beaten track but safe enough.'

'Why don't you send them to the North Pole while you're at it? Sutton-on-the-Forest to Nottingham is over 140 kilometres.'

'I can't help that,' Vickers snapped, 'we had to find an isolated place with enough accommodation to house your team and conceal the two Land-Rovers, and Sutton-on-the-Forest filled the bill.'

Garnett looked around for an ashtray, and not finding one, pinched the cigarette out with his finger and thumb.

Vickers looked pained. 'Must you do that?' he said.

Garnett smiled cheerfully. 'It's a legacy of my lower middle class background.'

'Quite.'

The smile faded on Garnett's face. 'Where do you plan to send Valerie?' he said coldly.

'Dane is the exception. She will be in Nottingham staying at the Victoria Hotel under the name of Vaudrey. Allen will collect her from the hotel at whatever time you think is best. Allen, of course, will be dressed as a military policeman and will say that he has an urgent message for a Sergeant Vaudrey of the W.A.C. that her mother in London has been taken seriously ill. The reception staff will be a little puzzled at first because Dane will not have disclosed that she is in the army, but Allen will give them her home address and then the penny will drop. Dane will travel up to Nottingham in civilian clothes and will not report in to the R.T.O.'s office. Nash thought up the scheme. I think it's rather clever, don't you?'

Garnett said, 'Who is running this show?'

'You are, David.'

'Good. Let's keep it that way.'

Vickers raised an eyebrow. 'I assume you have no objection to joining the others at Sutton-on-the-Forest?'

'I have to stay in town at the Sheriff of Nottingham.'

'Why?'

'Because of Edwards.'

'Where does she fit in, David?'

The 'she' was the time bomb. Garnett could sense that Dane was going to take it badly. 'Sergeant Edwards is a bloody menace, she has a nasty suspicious mind.'

Dane said, 'She's not the only one who's suspicious.'

Vickers smiled. 'What's this?' he said lightly. 'A lover's tiff?'

'Edwards has been keeping track of me,' Garnett said quietly, 'she knows I am coming back to Nottingham, and if I don't appear tomorrow night she will start checking to see where I am.'

'And she can have you,' said Dane.

Garnett struck the counter with his clenched fist. 'For Christ's sake, get it through your thick heads that this bloody woman is a Field Security agent. I told you,' he said, pointing a finger at Vickers, 'I told you she didn't buy my cover story, and you passed it off with a shrug of your upper-crust shoulders. I have no alternative but to go to Nottingham, and Nash and Taylor will have to pick me up from the transit hotel on Tuesday morning.'

'We can easily arrange that.'

'Good. And while you're at it, get word to Pugh not to do anything about Vallance.'

'I don't understand.'

'I told Pugh that if I came back, he would have to kill him.'

'How very inconvenient.'

'Isn't it.'

Vickers said, 'Oh well, it's just a small detail. You will find a Vauxhall Viva AMV 4954 parked round the corner from the church. It's yours. Leave it in the car park behind the bowling alley when you've finished with it. Nash will pick it up from there.'

'I'll say it again, General, who is running this show?'

'You are, David. I'm just trying to make things easy for you, everyone is—Warner—even Hulf.'

'Hulf?'

'Yes. He died this morning, seems a splinter from the Claymore mine had entered his brain.' Vickers held out his hand and said, 'Good luck, David.'

Garnett said, 'Thanks, I'll need it.'

He knew a storm was about to break, and it started right there in the hall as soon as he had closed the door after picking up the envelope from the mat.

Dane said, 'Why don't you leave now?'

'What?'

'For Nottingham. You could still keep your appointment in Brackley and you would be able to sneak an extra night with Edwards.'

Garnett shook his head. 'You've got it all wrong.'

'I've never been more right. All that nonsense you spouted yesterday about this being a turning point. My God, I must have been naïve to swallow that rubbish.

You've been in touch with her behind my back, haven't you?'

'Yes, I telephoned her.'

Her eyes became wider. 'I knew it,' she said. 'I sensed something was wrong when you came back on Friday. You were distant and withdrawn, but I told myself it was because you were worried—and all the time it was another woman.'

Garnett placed both hands on her shoulders. 'Listen to me,' he said intensely, 'there isn't another woman, Valerie, at least not in the way you think there is.'

Dane removed his hands from her shoulders. 'Is she attractive?' she said coolly.

'What has that got to do with it?'

'Everything. It might explain why you didn't tell me about her.'

'I don't know why I didn't tell you.'

'You hoped to keep it a secret.'

'Keep what a secret?'

'The fact that you have been regularly telephoning her.'

Garnett said, 'I'm not staying the night in Nottingham from choice.'

'I'll pin a medal on you,' she said bitterly.

'For Christ's sake, can't you get it through your head that Jo Edwards doesn't mean a thing to me?'

'It's Jo now, is it?' Dane said cuttingly. 'Perhaps in future I won't always be there when you need me.' She turned away and ran upstairs. From the landing above, her voice was fainter but still angry. 'And another thing,' she said, 'you can get your own bloody supper.'

'I'm not hungry.'

'Well, that's all right then, isn't it.'

The bedroom door slammed and the key turned in the lock. He stood there in the silent hall and wondered if he should go upstairs but the locked door suggested that she didn't want him near her and morosely, Garnett went into the kitchen, took a knife from the drawer, slashed open the envelope and extracted a wad of press clippings.

He couldn't identify the newspapers, but one of the clippings was printed on glossy paper and he thought it might have been taken from the *Tatler*. Years old, it showed a distinguished-looking man talking to an attractive girl. The caption underneath said, 'Also present Sir Adrian Schonfield, home for a brief holiday from New York where he is Britain's representative at the U.N., seen here talking to his niece, Miss Katherine Forbes-Windsor.'

Katherine Forbes-Windsor was tall, blonde and beautiful. Katherine Forbes-Windsor was Valerie Dane. And now he knew why Vickers wanted her there in Nottingham.

15

BEFORE THE WAR, GARNETT had seen a painting in the Chaplains' Retreat House at Bagshot which had made a lasting impression. The artist had wanted to depict the aged Duke of Wellington presenting a loving cup to the infant Duke of Connaught with a landscape filling in most of the background. Queen Victoria, however, had strong views about drinking and, at her express wish a casket was substituted for the loving cup. Albert too, had to be in the picture, and thus his disembodied head and shoulders appeared like a lost spirit in the blue sky above Victoria's shoulder, and, as a final touch, she had insisted that the Crystal Palace be included and this duly appeared in spidery outline beneath an oak tree. The picture was a mess. The business in Nottingham would probably turn out like the picture, enough people had monkeyed with the plan to practically guarantee it.

The pub had green wooden shutters, whitewashed walls, a thatched roof, coach lanterns either side of the nail-studded door and chintzy curtains in the narrow windows. A white Corsair and a maroon-coloured Singer Vogue were parked on the forecourt. Garnett drew up beside them and got out.

In the days when, during bank holidays, cars were almost bumper to bumper on the roads, the Broken Wheel had been on to a good thing; nowadays its isolation was bad for business. There were just the four men in the saloon bar and they looked the part right down to their briefcases. A casual observer would have taken them for a group of salesmen having a lunchtime session. The sales literature on the bar served to confirm the initial impression.

Garnett said, 'Hope I haven't kept you waiting?'

A man in a double-breasted grey pinstripe turned to face Garnett. 'Not a bit,' he said easily, 'we've only been here a few minutes ourselves. What will you have to drink?'

Garnett eyed the row of glasses on the bar. 'I'll have a half of bitter,' he said.

The man turned to the barmaid and said, 'Half of bitter, please, and have something yourself, May.'

May said, 'Thank you, Mr. Rainbow, I'll have a coke.'

Rainbow smiled at Garnett. 'We're very enthusiastic about your plans, David. We really think London has come up with a good idea for once. It's about time we launched a really big sales campaign and expanded our market. I thought we might talk about it over lunch. May's given us a room to ourselves.' Rainbow handed the glass of beer to Garnett and started to edge away from the bar. The others followed him in a snake-like procession which wound its way through a narrow dark hall towards the kitchen before jinking left into a room which was just large enough to seat five in comfort around an oval-shaped dining table. The threadbare carpet, the faded wallpaper and its proximity to the kitchen suggested that it was normally in use as a rest room for the staff.

Rainbow said, 'Let's get down to business.'

There was an air of crisp authority about Rainbow, coupled with the ability to weigh people up, which he did openly and was reflected in the way he watched Garnett over the rim of his raised beer glass. A solicitor by training, he had a needle-sharp mind.

'I hear you have a small problem on your hands,' Rainbow said quietly.

'I need help.'

'That's why we are here, David.'

'You could be letting yourself in for more than you bargained.'

Rainbow lowered his glass. 'Suppose you tell us what you

155

want. You don't have to worry about hidden mikes or anything like that, we've been over this place with a fine toothcomb.'

Garnett said, 'I am going to take over the Midland Station with a view to lifting six very important political prisoners before they are put on the special train. I need a group of men who are willing to cover us while we get out.' Garnett picked up a fork and drew a rough sketch map on the tablecloth. 'This,' he said, pointing to an oblong shape, 'is the station with the dual carriage-way in front of it. The station is overlooked by a multi-storey car park which is set back at an angle about 200 metres from the dual carriage-way. If you get up to the fifth deck of the car park, you've got a clear view of the entire frontage of the station. You can also stop anyone coming across the road bridge from the direction of the town centre.'

Rainbow took the fork out of Garnett's hand. 'From the third deck,' he said, 'we could get across to the flat open parking space above the filling station and we would have an even better view.'

'And you would be more exposed.'

Rainbow smiled. 'If I were in their shoes, I should be worried about that car park. I would check it out before the prisoners started to arrive.'

'I think they will, they may even leave a few sentries behind.'

'How many?'

'At a guess—about a section, say eight or nine men.'

'If there are any more than that we could be in real trouble.'

'I doubt if they will be able to spare more than a section.'

'They've got a mechanised regiment spread between Clumber and Newark.'

Garnett said, 'One regiment equals nine rifle companies. Just to move the fifteen hundred prisoners they will need something in the region of thirty-five coaches with say four escorts to each coach. The bill for that alone is about one and a half companies, and then they will have to keep at least one company on stand-by at Proteus in case there is trouble when the prisoners are brought out of their huts. Add to that the requirement to picket twenty-five kilometres of road and provide personnel for traffic control and mobile patrols, and they won't have much left over.'

Rainbow said, 'I believe you could sell a pair of binoculars to a blind man.'

'The question is, are you buying what I'm selling?'

'Of course. Did you think there was any doubt?'

'Not really.'

'Well then, let's have the details.'

'I want you to cover the front of the station and the crossroads away to your right. The minute we start shooting, you open up on the pickets outside the station. You can take out the B.T.R. 60p armoured personnel carriers with R.P.G.7s.'

'Except that we haven't got any,' Rainbow said drily.

'What have you got in the way of anti-armour missiles?'

'A couple of Carl Gustavs and a round dozen M72 rocket launchers.'

Garnett said, 'You'll be 200 metres away from the target, so you can forget the Rocket launchers because they haven't got the range.'

Rainbow looked up at the ceiling as if seeking help from the Almighty. He remained absolutely motionless and not a muscle moved in his face. He could have been in a trance, like the guru Garnett had seen outside Agra when he had come down on leave from the Staff College at Quetta, except that there wasn't any banyan tree to shade Rainbow and the temperature outside the pub was only just above freezing point.

In a dreamy voice Rainbow said, 'We'll go for the armoured personnel carriers first with the Carl Gustavs and then hit the occupants with the G.P.M.G.s and grenade launchers as they bail out. The moon is in the last quarter and we haven't got any Starlight Scopes, which means that we shall have to use Schermuly flares to light up the place.' He smiled fleetingly, 'It's going to rival Guy Fawkes night.'

'The cars,' said Garnett.

'What about them?'

'I want the Zephyrs left in that car park tonight. I presume that isn't going to be difficult? I mean, some people do leave their cars there overnight, don't they?'

'I believe so.'

'Good. I'll use a mitre radio set on channel alpha to call for the cars when I need them. When you get the word, the cars will move up to the crossroads and wait for us there. Don't try sending them into the station yard because it might be blocked. If all goes well, there will be twelve of us coming out of the station and we won't be dawdling.' Garnett lit a cigarette. 'We split up, four to each car, and my group will travel in the end one. Bear in mind that half the party will be dressed in militia uniform, so don't let's have anyone shot in error by our own side. We are making for three separate hideouts, and I'm afraid the drivers can look forward to a protracted holiday.'

Rainbow said, 'Where are my drivers taking you?'

'You don't need to know, and they won't know either, at least not until we join them when each car will get a navigator from my team.'

Rainbow said, 'If you have bad luck, there might not be enough navigators to go round.'

'If it's as bad as that,' Garnett said, 'we won't need as many cars, and the odd drivers, left over can go on home.' Garnett smoothed out the tablecloth with the palm of his hand, carefully erasing the sketch map. 'Any other questions?'

'Yes,' said Rainbow, 'what time do you want us in position?'

'That rather depends on what time the special train is due to arrive.'

'Naturally, we wouldn't like to be there too early,' Rainbow said drily. His eyes narrowed as the penny dropped. 'You don't know exactly when they mean to start entraining the prisoners, do you?'

Garnett stubbed out his cigarette. 'Not yet I don't, but I will by this time tomorrow, and then I will get in touch with you again.'

'How?'

'I was hoping you would tell me.'

One of the drivers said, 'He could use the T.V. rental service.'

Rainbow scratched his beaky nose. 'I suppose he could. You'd better ring 2660341 when you have the right answer.

Say your name is Adams, give a fictional address and tell them your set has gone wrong. The girl will ask when it will be convenient for the engineer to call round and you'll give the time. Don't use the twenty-four hour clock, and for God's sake don't specify a.m. or p.m. We know we've got to do the job in the hours of darkness and we are quite capable of putting two and two together.' Rainbow looked down at his well-kept hands and said, 'I only hope we don't get our fingers burned.' His face broke into a beaming smile. 'At least we shan't be able to offer little Willie's excuse.'

Garnett said patiently, 'Go on, I'll buy it.'

'The teacher asked Willie why he had been absent from school on the previous day and the boy said, "Please Miss, my Dad got burnt," and she said, "Oh dear, I hope he wasn't badly hurt," and Willie said, "They don't fuck about down at the Crematorium, Miss." '

Rainbow sat back, the drivers laughed politely, Garnett managed a smile—he'd heard it before—so it seemed, had the drivers.

Garnett arrived in Nottingham just as it was getting dark, and he was lucky enough to find a vacant parking space in the basement garage of the Sheriff of Nottingham. Because he would never use the car again, he spent some minutes carefully wiping the steering wheel, gear shift and offside door handle in the pious hope that he would obliterate his fingerprints. He observed this precaution more out of habit than conviction, but since the *Evening News* had shown Dane and himself among the deceased on the Wanted List, it was just as well not to take any unnecessary risks.

He checked in with reception and found that Edwards had booked him an adjoining room and left a message that she had been ordered to attend a briefing session. He was grateful for that small mercy.

The reprieve lasted longer than he expected. He even managed to dine alone and still had time to linger in the bar. By the fourth large whisky, he decided he didn't give a damn about Josephine Edwards; by the fifth, he was inclined to include Valerie Dane or Katherine Forbes-Windsor, or whatever she preferred to call herself, in the same list. Dane, he thought fuzzily, had an unnaturally suspicious mind. Accusing him of being deceitful was like the kettle calling the pot black. In all the time they had been living together she had never told him anything like the truth about herself. A small-town girl with a bank clerk for a father and a school teacher mother no longer added up, and now when he looked back over the months they had been together, he realised that she hadn't told him a single fact which could be checked. Her parents were both allegedly killed in a car crash just before the war, and she had never mentioned the address of their house in Worthing. It was as if Valerie Dane had been born the day he started working for Cobb, Coleman and Varley, and she had been promoted from the typing pool to become his secretary. Only Vickers, it seemed, knew the truth about her, and that made him feel raw.

'Jesus,' he said under his breath, 'I've been had.'

The barman said, 'Did you want another drink?'

'What?'

'I thought you were after another whisky.'

'That's a good idea,' Garnett said thickly.

The barman, a mild little man with a face like a wizened apple, looked doubtful. 'It'll have to be something other than whisky.'

'Why?'

'You've had more than your ration.'

'I'm not drunk, if that's what you're implying,' Garnett said belligerently.

'I didn't mean that, the whisky's rationed, you see, and I'm not supposed to let anyone have more than four single tots.'

'And I've had five doubles.'

'More like trebles. I knew you were waiting for Sergeant Edwards, and anyone who's a friend of hers is a friend of mine, like. She's a nice girl is Sergeant Edwards.'

'Oh, that she is,' said Garnett. The barman seemed to be rocking on his heels as though he were dog tired, and suddenly Garnett also felt worn out. 'Oh, she's a nice girl all right,' he repeated slowly, 'you tell her I said so when she comes in.'

He slid off the bar stool. 'I'm going up to my room.'

The barman said, 'Mind how you go, sir.'

The lift, of course, finished Garnett, but his legs held out until he was safely inside his room. He hit the bed with his knees and fell forward on to his face, and then someone put the switchback in motion and he was climbing slowly and then hurtling downwards, and he could see the rail curving up again in front of him, and his stomach rose up to meet it. He rolled off the bed and started crawling across the floor, and it was just as if he was out in a dinghy on a choppy sea and the bloody washbasin was the other side of the Atlantic. He reached up, grabbed hold of the basin, and dragged himself to his feet. He didn't need to put his fingers down his throat. Legs feeling like jelly, he leaned over the bowl and was violently sick. He ran both taps, closed his eyes and unblocked the sink. The sweat was standing out on his forehead, and yet he felt cold and shivery. He carefully filled the tooth mug with cold water and, holding it in both hands, rinsed out his mouth. He began to feel a little better. He put the mug back on the glass shelf above the washbasin and then walked over to the window and rested his forehead against the cold pane. Either the whisky was rotgut or else the barman had spiked his drink. He wondered why that seemingly harmless old man should want to doctor his drink, unless in some curious way he believed he was helping Edwards, protecting her from something. From what? And then Garnett began to laugh as the thought struck him that the old man reckoned that he was going to bed her.

The door opened and the light came on, and there was Edwards standing in the doorway wearing the inevitable green skirt and cossack tunic.

She stared at him open-mouthed, and then recovering said, 'Are you feeling all right, David?'

'Your friend the barman, he doesn't like me. He thinks my intentions aren't honourable.'

'Are they?' she said quietly.

'What do you think?'

'I think you need a cup of strong black coffee. You wait in my room while I go down to the kitchen.' She smiled, and it was a very warm inviting smile. 'I won't be long, darling.'

Her room was neat and tidy almost to the point of being fussily so, and Garnett thought that she was going to make some man an ideal wife provided he could put up with a woman who practically worshipped cleanliness. On impulse he went through the drawers in her dressing table, turning over the freshly laundered underwear. He found the bank pass book underneath the sweaters in the bottom drawer, and was surprised to see how much she had in credit. Thrift, it seemed, was another of her virtues. He put the bank pass book back in its hiding place and closed the drawer.

Her shoulder bag was lying on the bed where she had thrown it and Garnett hesitated, debating whether or not to open it, and then he decided that it was a bit late in the day to start developing a set of scruples. Keeping an eye on the door, he unzipped the bag and sifted through the contents. The special I.D. card was in a pocket behind the mirror and it was about the size of a driving licence; embossed on the front cover was an acorn, the symbol adopted by the Intelligence Corps. He heard the door knob begin to turn and he just had time to zip up the bag and sit down in the fireside chair before Edwards came into the room.

'How do you feel now?' she said.

'Not too bad.'

'Drink the coffee and then you'll feel even better. Would you like an Aspirin? I've got some in my bag.'

'I'll be all right,' he said.

She moved past him, opened the doors of the wardrobe, and standing behind them began to undress.

'I'm sorry about this evening, David. We had rather a long message come through on the teleprinter and I had to call the girls together for a preliminary conference.' Her voice became muffled as she pulled the tunic over her head. 'And then I had to re-arrange the duty roster.'

'Oh yes?' he said vaguely.

'I decided that I would have to take the twelve to eight shift, and then just as I was about to leave, Vallance arrived with the O.C. train.' She broke off and drew in her breath sharply as though suddenly aware she was treading on dangerous ground.

'It's all right,' Garnett said easily, 'you haven't let the cat out of the bag. I know all about the special train. As a matter of fact, I shall be on hand to see that six rather special prisoners get on the train.'

She appeared from behind the wardrobe door wearing a violet-coloured jersey silk blouse over a white nylon slip. 'Vallance told me that we had to ensure that the station staff were sent home before the special train arrived at oo: 30 hours. He didn't mention you at all.'

'That's hardly surprising, he won't know I'm coming until tomorrow. London will let Vallance know in good time.'

She sat down on the bed and removed her jackboots. 'I hope for your sake London also remembers to tell the Russians, because they only expect to find two Brits inside the station, myself and C. S. M. Littlewood of the military police, and the whole reason for meeting the O.C. train was so that he would be able to recognise us next time we met.'

Garnett said, 'Then he will have to meet a second Field Security agent, won't he?'

'Are you what you say you are, David?' she said quietly. She looked down at her lap and nervously picked at the lace hem of the slip. 'You see, I've been in doubt for some time —in fact, today I even went so far as to send a signal to Records querying your service details. I'll admit that my real reason for doing so was to find out whether or not you are married.' A cold shiver went down his back but somehow Garnett managed to laugh. To his own ears it sounded false but Edwards was taken in.

'Oh my god,' he spluttered, 'first the barman thinks I am a bloody lecher and now you think I am a bigamist.' He caught hold of her hand. 'Listen,' he said, 'if you really want to be reassured, try calling Commissioner Warner, I work for him.'

Relief showed in her face. She stood up, took a pace forward and then sat down on his lap. Her arms went round his waist and she brushed her lips against his mouth.

'I love you, David,' she whispered. She burrowed into his chest, hugging him close to her and her silken legs rubbed against his, and he sat there like a stone.

163

She raised her head, and in a puzzled voice said, 'What's the matter?'

'I was just wondering if you were leading me on.' As soon as the words were out of his mouth he knew it was a mistake.

'It's cold in here,' she said. 'Don't you think it's cold?'

'Maybe it's a little chilly,' he said, and that was another mistake.

She got up from his lap, switched on the electric fire, hesitated for a moment and then strode purposefully across the room and put out the lights. She was somewhere near the door but he couldn't see her. He heard something crackle and then it dawned on him that she had removed her blouse and slip, and then, as the fire bars glowed red, he could see her vague white shape coming towards him. And then in the half light she tripped over the bedside rug and sprawled forward, and before he could save her, her head slammed against the wooden arm on the fireside chair. She cried out in pain, and as he cupped his hands to her face, his fingers became sticky. He scrambled out of the chair, strode to the door and put on the lights.

She was sitting on the floor one hand pressing together the lips of the gash above her right eye, and a thin bloody red line was coursing down her cheek to join the thin stream between her naked breasts. Garnett lifted her up and laid her gently on the bed. He found a face flannel, held it under the cold water tap, and used it as a compress. He soaked his handkerchief and wiped away the blood, and she said, 'Oh God, it hurts, it hurts.'

He searched the medicine cabinet and found a Band-aid which he taped over the cut, and then he went through her shoulder bag, found the packet of Aspirins and gave her three with a glass of water. He pulled back the bedclothes, and she slipped inside and he tucked her in.

'I am a damn fool,' she whispered. 'That's what comes of trying to prove myself.'

'What?'

'I thought you wanted to sleep with me, and so, even though I didn't want to do it, I thought I would make it easy for you.' She bit her lip and the tears appeared in her eyes, and he didn't know whether the pain had caused them or not. She reached out and took hold of his hand.

'I didn't mean it to turn out like this,' she whispered. 'Everything's gone wrong, but at least we are together.'

And he sat there at her bedside while she talked to him about herself, and she thought he was bloody wonderful, and his head was splitting and fear was growing in his belly because the chances were that this attractive bitch of a girl who was already half asleep had done for him. He wondered how long it would take Records to come up with the answer that they could find no trace of a Sergeant Byass in Field Security.

16

IT WAS ANOTHER COLD, raw day. The weather forecast had predicted snow showers over the Midlands with freezing fog persisting in the south-west, which was just one more bad omen to start the day with.

Garnett had breakfast before Edwards was up and about, and then hung around outside the hotel until Nash arrived to collect him a few minutes before nine. The Land-Rover was still moving when Garnett opened the door and scrambled inside. A voice behind him said, 'My word, we are in a hurry this morning.'

He turned round and saw Taylor grinning at him.

Nash said, 'Are we in a hurry?'

'No. Just drive around, I need time to think.'

'Trouble?'

'Yes—Edwards. Yesterday she sent a signal to Records querying my service details.'

Nash whistled tunelessly through his teeth. 'That's nasty,' he said. He signalled and then pulled out into the stream of traffic.

'Meaning?'

'The service details of Sergeant Byass won't stand up to a close check.'

Garnett said, 'Edwards will go to Vallance as soon as she knows I've conned her.'

'Or the police.'

'No. She'll go to Vallance because she's a Field Security agent herself, and I'm no longer guessing about that because I've seen her I.D. card.'

Nash said, 'Will she connect you with the job?'

'I told her I had an interest in making sure that six important prisoners got on the train.'

'You prick,' Nash said coldly. 'Other men can have a screw without giving their life history to the bird but not you, you have to open your mouth.'

Garnett kept his temper. In the circumstances it was quite a feat. 'Listen,' he said curtly, 'Edwards had just blurted out the time when the special train was due to arrive and she was about to clam up. I had to kid her along, I didn't know she had already sent a signal to Records—that came later.'

Nash said, 'If we know the time of the train, we don't need to see Vallance. We might even anticipate the signal.'

'What are you talking about?'

'I mean we get Pugh to ring Edwards to say that he has a Sergeant Byass under arrest.'

'She'd smell a rat straight off.'

'Not if he made it sound convincing. He could say that you had been picked up in the prohibited area of Proteus and that he was checking up to see if the R.T.O.'s Office knew anything about a Sergeant Byass. If she knows you are in custody, she will stop worrying and what Records say in their signal won't matter a damn. It's either that or we pass the job up.'

Taylor said, 'If it's all the same to you, I vote we give it a miss. You can drop me at the station and I'll catch a train back to the Smoke.'

'If that is supposed to be a joke,' said Nash, 'it's a lousy one.' He glanced sideways at Garnett. 'What do you think of the idea?'

'It has possibilities.'

'Now look,' said Nash firmly, 'you avoid seeing Vallance, we lie low until it's time to pick up Dane and then we do the job. No problem—no problem at all.'

Garnett said, 'You'd be right except for two major snags. We have to know the frequencies so that we can jam the police net.'

167

'Jamming their net is a refinement.'

'If we are going to make a clean break we need that period of confusion which jamming can give us. And another thing, Edwards and C. S. M. Littlewood of the military police met the Russian train-commandant last night—they were introduced to him for one reason and one reason only. There will be just two Brits on the station, and the Russian wanted to know who they were.'

Taylor said, 'Let's call it a day and go home.' The request fell on deaf ears.

They were moving along the Boulevard now with the Castle above them and heading towards the University, and they were drawing farther and farther away from Bestwood Lodge because nobody could decide what to do. Nash made up their minds for them. As they hit Clifton Boulevard he turned right and picked up the signs for Mansfield on the ring road.

'Okay,' he said, 'we'll do it your way, we'll go and see Vallance.'

It started to snow when they reached the outskirts of Arnold. Large wet flakes swirled in a cone-shaped funnel and splattered against the windscreen, making it difficult to see more than a few metres ahead so that they were forced to move at a crawl. They turned off the main road and still in second gear edged up the lane towards the Lodge.

Garnett said, 'If this is just a shower, God help us if it should turn into a blizzard.'

Nash sounded the horn as they drove in through the narrow archway. A couple of drivers working on their Land-Rovers in the yard, showed no interest in their arrival. Nash reversed into a vacant parking space and switched off the engine. He looked at Garnett and said, 'It's all yours, we'll wait here.'

'Have we got any weapons handy?'

'We've stashed a couple of 9mm. Makarovs and three A.K. 47 automatic rifles under Taylor's seat, but you won't be needing them just yet.'

'I won't?'

'No. Take a good look round the yard and then tell me if you think these people are expecting trouble.'

A glance round the yard showed that Nash was right. No

one was showing any interest in them.

Garnett said, 'All right, I'll signal you from the window when I want you to come up.' He got out of the Rover and crossed the yard.

At the top of the spiral staircase Garnett paused and looked up and down the corridor. The door of Vallance's office was closed and the landing was empty. He opened Pugh's door and went inside.

'Where is everybody?' he said quietly.

Pugh jumped. 'You bloody fool,' he snapped, 'what do you want to creep up on me like that for?'

'Where's Vallance?'

'He left to see the Commander of 19 Mech Regiment about ten minutes ago. Something about a final co-ordinating conference.'

'Will he be long?'

Pugh shrugged his shoulders. 'Who knows? It could last an hour or most of the morning.'

'Anyone call him before he left?'

'I wouldn't know—like me, he has an extension number on the main switchboard but can dial out. I can't monitor his calls.'

Garnett said, 'All right, we'll chance it. I want you to ring the R.T.O.'s Office and ask for Edwards. If she is not there, find out where you can reach her.'

'And if she is there, then what?'

'And then you ask her if she knows anything about a Sergeant Byass who has been detained on suspicion.'

'One of us is crazy and it isn't me.'

Garnett picked up the phone and thrust it at Pugh. 'Don't get flip with me,' he snarled, 'just do as you're bloody well told, and be careful, very careful what you say to her because Edwards is damn sharp.'

Pugh hesitated and then dialled the number. His finger-tips beat a nervous tattoo on the desk while he waited for someone to answer the call.

Pugh said, 'Is Sergeant Edwards there, please?' He looked down at the blotter while the voice at the other end spoke briefly, and then said, 'I'll hang on.'

Garnett lit a cigarette and peered out of the window. The snow hadn't settled and it looked as if the shower was beginning to ease up. At least the forecasters had been right about that.

He heard Pugh say, 'Sergeant Edwards? Oh, this is Warrant Officer Pugh 464 F.S. Section. I wonder if you could tell me anything about a Sergeant Byass? Did he check in with your office?'

There was a pause, and then Pugh said, 'We're holding him on suspicion, I'm afraid I can't tell you more than that over the phone.' There was another pause, a long one this time before Pugh said, 'Just a minute, Sergeant Edwards, someone's come into the office.' Pugh cupped his hand over the mouthpiece and turned to face Garnett. 'She asked if there was anyone with you—she says you were picked up outside the hotel this morning by a Land-Rover. She's also waiting on a signal from Records which might answer some queries as to your identity. What do I say now?'

Garnett snapped his fingers. 'Tell her to ring you as soon as the signal comes through, and say that we will then send someone down to get a statement from her.'

Pugh took a deep breath and then spoke to Edwards again. He sounded calm and unruffled and he gave the impression of being efficient and helpful. He practically had Edwards eating out of his hand before he hung up.

Garnett said, 'That was a very smooth performance, as good as any Foreign Office spokesman. Did she say if she got the number of our Land-Rover?'

'No. You were seen by the hall porter getting into the Land-Rover, but he didn't think to take the number down.'

'First break we've had this morning.' Garnett lit a cigarette.

'Where are the rest of your crowd? I've only come across two drivers in the yard working on their vehicles.'

'Vallance briefed them last night and then stood them down. They're free until 2200 hours unless he calls them together for further orders. I expect most of them are in the Sergeants' Mess.'

Garnett went over to the window and gave the all clear signal to Nash. The phone call had given them a temporary breathing space and he intended to make good use of it. His first priority was to ensure that Edwards wasn't able to contact Vallance direct.

Garnett said, 'I hope Vallance hasn't locked his office.'

'He has,' Pugh pointed to the key board on the wall, 'but he left the key—room number 6.'

Garnett stubbed out the half-smoked cigarette and unhooked the key. 'When a moth-eaten character by the name of Taylor arrives, tell him I want to see him in Vallance's office.'

The easiest way of fixing a telephone is to rip out the leads. It is also the most obvious, and in the circumstances, Garnett figured a little subtlety was called for. He selected a file from the pending tray, lifted the handset off the cradle, and wedged the file across the buttons to keep them depressed and so prevent a light coming up on the operator's switchboard. At that juncture, the last person he wanted to converse with was the operator. He unscrewed the earpiece and neatly severed the red and green coloured leads at the point where they disappeared beneath the handgrip, replaced the cap and then put the handset back on the cradle. No one was going to be able to speak to Vallance in a hurry.

Taylor said, 'You wanted me?'

Garnett turned to face him. 'I want you to have a look at that safe and tell me if you can open it without anyone knowing it.'

'Like I told your friend, I use jelly, or a torch or a drill, and when I've been at a safe there's no disguising the fact.'

'All right. How long will you need to get into that one?'

Taylor ran a professional eye over the safe, clinically itemising its characteristics. 'Bricked in,' he muttered, 'can't get at the back where it's weakest, unlocking handling, probably three locking bars each as thick as my thumb, front plate is about 40mm. thick—take a long time to cut or drill your way through that, and if I blow it, I'll need quite a bit of jelly—could be a tricky business trying to muffle the sound of the explosion.' He peered closely at the safe and then stood back rubbing his chin. 'It's an odd one this,' he said, 'they've welded a hinge bracket over the key-hole and mounted a combination lock on it. To open the safe, you need to unlock the combination and swing it back on its hinge and then fit the key into the lock to free the locking bars. Of course, if we had the key, I could cut the hinge bracket off and then weld it back on again after we had been into the safe, touch up the blistered paint and fresh welding, and that way nobody would know that we had been inside. Quicker too, only take me about an hour to an hour and a half from start to finish.'

'And without the key?'

Taylor said, 'I don't recommend blowing—too noisy. If I had to cut my way in, say just over three hours.'

'All right, I'll think about it.'

'Shall I fetch my gear?'

'No, you go and wait in the Land-Rover, I'll call you when I'm ready.'

Garnett looked the room over to satisfy himself that nothing had been disturbed. Vallance struck him as the sort of man who would immediately pick on anything which looked out of place, and he had quite enough problems to deal with already without the oldest lieutenant in the army adding to them. He closed and locked the door behind him and stepped into Pugh's office.

Nash was leaning against the radiator, his body at a sharp angle to the floor with his feet crossed casually at the instep. Both hands were shoved deep into his trouser pockets, his forage cap was tucked into the cloth belt round his waist and the top button of his tunic was undone. He looked bored and insolent. Garnett knew that if Vallance saw him like that he would hit the roof. Pugh, he thought, should have pulled Nash up, and then he noticed the tight-lipped expression on Pugh's face and guessed that Pugh had done just that and Nash had told him what he could go and do to himself. Garnett said, 'Smarten yourself up and try not to look like a drooping wallflower.'

Nash made no effort to move. 'This place is lousy with military maniacs,' he said.

Garnett looked at Pugh and shrugged his shoulders. The gesture seemed to imply he had no control over Nash, and Pugh was disappointed in him, and like Nash, he wasn't prepared for what followed. A scything right foot chopped the legs from under Nash and Garnett cuffed him across the face with his open hand as he went down.

Neither the blow nor the fall hurt Nash but his pride suffered. Hate showed in his narrow, pale eyes and thin compressed lips but he kept silent. He got up from the floor, buttoned his tunic and set the forage cap on his head. 'Does that suit you, Dad?' he said softly.

'It'll do.'

'Great. You pulled a fast one just then, and I can see that I underestimated you, but I won't make the same mistake again.'

Garnett said wearily, 'Suppose you make us a cup of coffee. You'll find everything you need in the cupboard.'

As a peace move, it lacked something, but it served to defuse the atmosphere. After hesitating briefly, Nash went along with the suggestion and Pugh, who had been noticeably on edge, relaxed a little.

Garnett said, 'Vallance has already issued his orders for tonight, right?'

'Yes,' said Pugh, 'subject to any last-minute changes which might arise as a result of the conference he's now attending.'

'I'm interested in his orders. What did Vallance tell you?'

'He gave us our tasks which are to provide a number of mobile patrols to cover Arnold and Sherwood, and briefed us on the composition and grouping of the road convoy and then...'

'Let's hear about the convoy,' said Garnett.

'It's a big one, forty-two coaches with three escorts to each coach, plus twenty one B.T.R. 60p armoured personnel carriers organised into packets each consisting of not more than ten vehicles, twenty metres between each vehicle, two minutes only between packets. A packet of ten comprises a B.T.R. 60p in the lead, followed by seven coaches with another B.T.R. 60p bring up the rear. The order of march is three packets, then battalion headquarters, another four packets and then the special.'

'The special?'

'One prison van sandwiched between three Armoured personnel carriers.'

'My V.I.P.s?'

'Unless it's a decoy,' said Pugh.

'Is that likely?'

'Your guess is as good as mine. Anyway, you won't have to wait all that long to find out. Convoy speed is thirty k.p.h., head of column is timed to reach the station at 01:15 and the time past a given point is thirty-eight minutes. Your special van ought to arrive outside the station at 01.53.'

Garnett said, 'Sunrise tomorrow is 07:55, first light say thirty minutes before that, which means we have five hours and thirty-two minutes of darkness to play with from the time the special packet arrives at the station.'

Nash unplugged the kettle, measured a teaspoonful of coffee essence into each mug and then added the boiling water. 'You are building one of those complicated detective plots,' he said, 'the sort where the murderer kills his victim with a runaway steam roller and has timed every move to the split second, and you know damn well that if anybody had so much as farted out of turn the whole deal would have collapsed like a pack of cards.'

The phone began to jangle. Pugh answered it. The caller did most of the talking but Pugh managed a sentence or two towards the end of the conversation. He said, 'That's very interesting, Sergeant Edwards.' He looked at his wrist-watch. 'I'll come down to the station and take a statement from you, and perhaps we could borrow the signal? It may help us with the interrogation. I'm afraid Sergeant Byass isn't being very co-operative.' There was a pause and then he said, 'It's no trouble, I'll be with you in about twenty minutes.'

He hung up, looked at Garnett and said, 'Records just blew your cover apart.'

'How did she take it?'

'She sounded bloody vindictive.' Pugh stood up. 'I'll take a statement from her and obtain that signal, and perhaps that will help to keep her quiet. It's now ten to eleven— even if I'm away for an hour and a half I should be back before Vallance. Okay?'

'Don't worry about us,' said Garnett. He sat down in Pugh's chair, picked up a pencil and drew a series of clock faces on the blotter.

'He didn't wait for his coffee,' said Nash.

Garnett stopped doodling. 'He never does,' he said absently.

Edwards was the key, there was no getting round that. The train commander might accept the last-minute substitution of C. S. M. Littlewood by one of Garnett's team, but if Edwards was also replaced he was going to be more than a little suspicious. Edwards would have to keep the Russian happy, and she wasn't going to do that voluntarily. Edwards had put herself down for the twelve to eight shift; the special train came in at 00:30, and the railway staff were to be sent home before then. As Garnett saw it, there were two problems—where and when to remove Edwards. He eliminated the station because too much help was at hand, which left him with the hotel, and that more or less set the time.

'What time are Keilly and the others supposed to arrive?' said Garnett.

'They're waiting to hear from me.'

Garnett took a sip from the coffee and pulled a face. 'I think you had better instruct them to meet you outside the Victoria Hotel at 00:15.' Nash reached for the phone but Garnett brushed his hand aside. 'Don't call them from here,' he said, 'go out and find a telephone box and take Taylor with you. He's probably feeling lonely.'

Nash said, 'Who cares if he is.'

'I do. I don't want him chatting up the other drivers in the yard.'

'You'll be here when we get back?'

'Of course. Any reason why I shouldn't be?'

'You've got rid of Pugh and now you're getting rid of me, perhaps you are thinking of doing a bunk?'

'Close the door behind you on the way out,' Garnett said coldly. He swallowed the rest of the dubious coffee and immediately felt the need of a cigarette to kill the taste. He brought out a crumpled packet and was relieved to find that there was still one left.

As he sat there behind the desk watching the cigarette smoke drift up to the ceiling, he thought about Dane. It would be some joke if she had carried out her threat. He pictured Allen walking into the Victoria Hotel to collect her, only to find that Dane had never turned up. A few days ago the idea that Dane could do such a thing would not have occurred to Garnett, but now he was no longer certain of her, and he had Edwards and Vickers to thank for that. Mere speculation, he decided, was fruitless. He picked up the phone, dialled 2660341 and waited.

A girl said, 'Instant T.V. Rental Service, good morning, can I help you?'

Garnett said, 'My name is Adams, 13 Rillington Gardens, Daybrook. I'm having trouble with the set I rented from you. The picture keeps revolving and I've tried the horizontal hold but it had no effect.'

'I think we had better send a man round to look at it. When would it be convenient for our engineer to call?'

Garnett said, 'I shall be back home at a quarter to one.'

'All right, Mr. Adams,' she said brightly, 'I've made a note of the time. I don't think there will be any problem.'

Garnett started to thank her but she had already hung up on him. He stubbed out the cigarette, clasped his hands behind his head and put his feet up on the desk. He had no doubt that in the same situation Vickers would have experienced no difficulty in unwinding, but he wasn't like Vickers, and he was no good at playing the waiting game. Garnett told himself it was silly to worry, because the list of things that could go wrong on this job was endless. He needed luck to pull it off and luck was something you couldn't budget for. He yawned, cupped his hand over his mouth and then yawned again. The yawn, he knew, was symptomatic—he always did it when he was nervous. He made a determined effort to doze but he couldn't blot out his thoughts. Pugh returned just as he reached the stage of feeling drowsy.

Pugh said, 'Are you in a trance?'

Garnett swept his feet off the desk. 'You were quick,' he said.

'Edwards doesn't beat about the bush. She had a statement already prepared by the time I got there.'

'And?'

'I think I convinced her that she didn't need to take any further action.' He dropped the signal from Records on to the desk. 'Take a look at this,' he said, 'London should have given you a better cover story.'

176

The signal would have left no one in doubt. It said: REFERENCE 14484443 SERGEANT BYASS D STOP NO TRACE OF THIS NCO IN FIELD SECURITY STOP FOR YOUR INFORMATION SERVICE NUMBERS BEGINNING 1448 WERE DISCONTINUED AFTER 1945 STOP.

'It doesn't make sense.'

'What doesn't?'

'London isn't normally that careless. You'd think they would get the service number right if nothing else. I've never known the forgery section to make such an elementary mistake before.'

'You were lucky Edwards didn't spot it straight away.'

'Yes,' he said slowly, 'yes, I suppose I was lucky, but Nash provided me with the cover story and it is beginning to look as though he intended me to be caught.'

'That's crazy, he wouldn't be up here with you now if that was the case.'

'You're probably right, except that I don't believe Nash expected Vickers to send him up here.'

A horn blaring repeatedly drew Garnett to the window. In the courtyard below, a Land-Rover pulled up sharply and a short, fat man got out of the passenger seat. He was joined by a black and white crossbred bulldog.

Garnett said, 'Here comes the oldest lieutenant in the army. A second Land-Rover came through the archway and just missed hitting the dog. Vallance didn't like it. He summoned the driver and made him stand to attention while he gave him a piece of his mind. The driver didn't like it either, but then Nash wasn't used to being harangued. Garnett heard their raised voices coming up the spiral staircase. Vallance was shouting and the dog was barking and Nash didn't sound exactly calm either. The door to the office burst open and there was Vallance red in the face and shaking with anger.

He pointed his swagger cane at Nash and said, 'Sergeant-Major Pugh, I want this N.C.O. charged...' He stopped short as he caught sight of Garnett. 'Does this corporal belong to you, Sergeant Byass?'

'Yes sir,' said Garnett.

'There are signs up all over the place clearly stating that the speed limit is twenty k.p.h. There's a bloody great sign

177

outside the entrance to the courtyard which says Drive slowly—Sound horn. This idiot corporal of yours thinks this is Brands Hatch and speed limits don't apply to him. You are to charge him, understand?'

'Yes sir.'

'What are you doing up here anyway?'

'Special reinforcement, sir.'

Pugh cleared his throat and said, 'What time do you want to see the N.C.O.s, sir?' His hand crept towards the tell-tale signal lying on the desk.

Vallance glared at him. 'I don't want to see them, Sergeant-Major. My orders stand, there has been no change in plan.' He rounded on Garnett again. 'Why didn't London tell me they were sending you up here, Sergeant?'

Pugh's groping fingers had almost reached the slip of paper when Vallance spotted them out of the corner of his eye. He snatched up the signal before Pugh had a chance to whip it out of sight.

Vallance said, 'What the hell is this?'

Garnett said, 'I wouldn't advise you to try anything. You are alone and there are three of us.'

Nash had the switch blade open in his hand before Garnett realised what was happening. The blade was no fatter than a knitting needle but it was razor sharp and Nash knew how to use it. He slipped it through the rib cage and into Vallance's heart with the practised skill of a butcher, and in that split second the army lost the services of its oldest lieutenant. The dog launched itself at Nash aiming to take him in the leg, but the animal was past its prime and it moved stiffly. Nash casually stepped to one side and slammed his right foot into its ribs and then savagely kicked it in the skull as the dog fell over. It grunted once and then lay quite still; the blood was running out of its ears.

Pugh said hoarsely, 'Christ, you've really blown it now.'

17

IT WAS LIKE A tableau in a waxworks. A fat man in a bottle-green uniform lay face down on the carpet and near him in a pool of blood a dog with glazed eyes, and looking on, three men one of whom was holding a blood-stained knife in his hand.

Garnett was the first to move. He walked to the window and looked down into the yard.

'What's that driver doing?' he said quietly.

Pugh cleared his throat. 'He's probably waiting to take Vallance home to lunch.'

Nash laughed softly. 'He's going to have a long wait.'

'Feeling proud of yourself?' said Garnett.

'He was on to us and you were both too shit-scared to do anything about it.'

'You might just get the chance to demonstrate your efficiency again.'

Pugh scuffed his feet. 'What do you mean by that?' he asked huskily.

'It's obvious, isn't it?' said Garnett. 'We can't leave that driver hanging about in the yard. Sooner or later he is going to wonder why Vallance hasn't appeared, and then he's going to come up here. Better he should come when we are ready for him. I suggest you open the window and tell him Vallance wants to see him in his office.'

'I'm an undercover man,' Pugh said faintly, 'I can't afford to become involved...'

'You are involved,' Garnett said harshly, 'right up to your ears.' He turned to Nash and said, 'Hide yourself in Vallance's office, and bear in mind that the door opens inwards. I want a quick clean job with no noise.'

Pugh said, 'How the hell are we going to cover this up?'

'We'll do one thing at a time, and the first step is to get that man up here without him suspecting anything.'

Pugh hesitated, as if in doubt, and then reluctantly he raised the window and leaned out.

'Ballentine,' he shouted.

A voice from below said, 'Sergeant-Major?'

'You won't be needed, Ballentine. Lieutenant Vallance isn't going home for lunch; he has some work to do in the office. You are free until we parade at 2200 hours. Okay?'

A hand waved in acknowledgment and Pugh closed the window.

'After that gesture,' said Garnett, 'I hope you are feeling all noble inside. I don't know what you think you have achieved, but if you are out to make life bloody difficult for us, you're on the right lines.'

'It wasn't necessary to kill Ballentine,' Pugh said excitedly.

'I'm not interested in your expert opinion. Get on that damn phone and tell your people in the Sergeants' Mess that there is no change from previous orders, and then contact Mrs. Vallance and say that her husband won't be coming home to lunch or supper. And understand this, if you make another foul-up, I'll borrow that flick knife from Nash and personally cut your throat from ear to ear.'

'You can trust me. I won't get in your way again.'

'All right,' Garnett said wearily, 'just get on that phone and do your stuff.'

Searching Vallance was not the pleasantest job in the world. Garnett thought there was something obscene about thrusting his hands into the dead man's pockets. The fleshy thighs were still warm to the touch through the cloth, and in groping for the key to the safe, the shiny serge was drawn tight across the ponderous buttocks of the corpse. He found the key in a fistful of loose change.

As he left the room, Garnett heard Pugh say, 'Oh, Mrs. Vallance this is Sergeant-Major Pugh. Your husband just rang me to say he wouldn't be home for lunch or supper...'

He gave Nash plenty of warning because Garnett knew that he was standing behind the door with the knife ready in his hand, and he didn't want to be sliced up like a piece of stewing steak.

He kicked the door and said, 'Come on out, there's been a change in plan.'

The door opened and Nash appeared. 'One thing about you, Garnett,' he said, 'no one gets into a rut with you around to organise things.'

'I'm glad you appreciate my qualities,' Garnett said drily. 'Now fetch Taylor and get him working on the safe. I want him to cut away the combination lock.'

'What with? He hasn't brought any oxyacetylene gas with him.' Nash laughed mockingly, 'He's been giving you a load of bullshit about using a torch, hasn't he?'

Garnett said, 'I want the safe opened quietly and without any fuss. I don't give a damn how Taylor does it.' He tossed the key to Nash. 'If he can get the combination lock off, this key will probably open the safe.'

Nash smiled sardonically. 'One thing about this team of yours,' he said, 'it's got a wealth of talent in it for making a balls up.'

And when he came to think about it, Garnett could see that, in a way, Nash was right. They were a discordant group, and he had to go back a long time to recall a similar situation. He had drifted into it in the first winter of the Soviet occupation some four months after he had assassinated Commissar Willie Vosper in the Market Place at Salisbury. Control had had the bright idea of appointing him as a tactical advisor to a new group which had just been formed in Kingston. It hadn't worked out because the group leader resented taking advice, especially from someone who had been a professional soldier, which in his view, meant that Garnett was automatically a failure. As they failed to agree on almost everything, the group had staggered from one disaster to another. Lacking a coherent policy, they had planted time bombs in phone boxes, left luggage offices, shopping precincts and crowded tube trains, and they did a great job in killing innocent by-standers. They were so bad, that Hanson the group leader was court-martialled and condemned to death. Garnett had opposed such an extreme measure, but in those times, there were enough influential people to quote precedents established by the I.R.A., Eoka and the Stern gang and they won the day.

Pugh stepped out into the corridor and said, 'Is it all right if I go home to lunch?'

'What?'

'It's nearly one-thirty, I usually go home for lunch at one.'

'You're worried about lunch at a time like this?' Garnett said incredulously.

'You don't understand,' said Pugh. 'I have to look out for my family. For years I have had a bolt-hole prepared for them against the day when I might be flushed from cover. I have to go home and tell my wife what to do.' He searched Garnett's stony face looking for a sign of under-standing. 'You can trust me,' he said intensely, 'I won't run out on you.'

'What are we going to do with Vallance?'

'We'll deal with him when I come back, okay? We can hide him in one of the empty detention cells downstairs.'

Garnett said, 'How long do you need?'

Pugh sighed with relief. 'About forty minutes.'

Garnett smiled. 'All right,' he said, 'and see if you can bring back a tin of something for us.' He turned away and went into Vallance's office to wait for Taylor.

The safe was a bastard to open because, for all his sup-posed expertise, Taylor hadn't come equipped for the job. They needed to take the combination and hinge bracket off without distorting the key-hole underneath it, and as Taylor pointed out, it would have been a simple enough job if they had had a cutting charge like Cortex. Blast and noise were the major problems, because if Taylor was ham-fisted enough to blow the windows out, there were enough policemen in the immediate area to settle the issue beyond doubt.

In his anxiety to muffle the noise of the explosion, Taylor

reduced the charge to the point where it was no longer fully effective. It took them three goes to remove the bracket, and even then they had to use an adjustable spanner to wrench it off. Taylor was right about one thing —after he had been at a safe there was no hiding the fact that it had been tampered with.

Apart from the scantlist, the safe held little of interest. There was a cash box and two dead files marked Confidential. One dealt with a drug ring amongst the militia conscripts at Normanton Barracks, and the other appeared to concern two prostitutes who had set up shop in the recreation centre in the same barracks. A few months back, Normanton must have been jumping, but Garnett failed to see why Vallance should be interested until he noticed that both files had been referred to him by the S.I.B. with a note saying, 'Are there any security implications?'

Taylor said, 'Some haul.'

'What?'

'The cash box contained eight pounds forty-seven pence.'

Garnett said, 'You've just earned five hundred pounds, what are you cribbing about?'

'Good. Pay me now and I'll be on my way.'

'Ah, well, Ernie, I don't know about that. I may still need your services for a bit longer.'

'Nothing doing. You pay me off.'

'How would you like to be paid off for good, Ernie?' Nash said quietly. 'There's a dead man and his dog in the cells downstairs, you could always join them.'

Taylor's jaw dropped. He looked from Nash to Garnett and said, 'What's he talking about?'

Garnett said, 'We killed a man who got in our way.'

Taylor sat down. He shook his head in disbelief. 'Jesus,' he said shakily, 'I could use a drink.' Nobody offered him one.

'This scantlist,' said Garnett, tapping the folder, 'shows ten separate nets.'

Pugh said, 'It's designed to cover every eventuality, but there will be only three nets working tonight—a forward command, a police rear link to the other constabularies, and a command guard net. The guard is on standby in case the command net is jammed. The police rear link will use alternative frequencies if there is any interference. You will find them in the scantlist too.'

'You will be doing the jamming.'

'I guessed as much.'

'So how do you propose to go about it?'

'I've got three sets and a J-Box on my vehicle. The J-Box will allow me to monitor two nets simultaneously and I can jam them alternately as the need arises. I'll put the third set on to the guard net because the way I see it, if I blot out the command net, the police rear link will be working in the dark, since they won't know what is going on.'

'Do you need any help?'

'Are you offering me Taylor?'

'Yes.'

'My sets have a working range of thirty-two kilometres which means I have to stay within that distance of the control stations to jam them—for how long?—half an hour, an hour, two hours?'

'As long as you can give me without cutting your own throat.'

'In that case,' said Pugh, 'I'll manage on my own.'

'Drive the Land-Rover and operate the sets?'

'It can be done.'

'And Ballentine?'

'What about him?'

'It's my guess you normally travel with Vallance, and I know Ballentine is his driver.'

'You leave me to worry about Ballentine,' Pugh said quietly.

Well, why not? thought Garnett. There are enough problems to solve as it is, beginning with Nash and how far I can trust him. He needed two other navigators and if he excluded Nash, Garnett was left with Keilly, Allen and Taylor. He came to the reluctant conclusion that he was saddled with Nash. Nash cleared his throat. 'For God's sake,' he said, 'how much longer are we going to be kept in the dark?'

Their faces showed that they expected Garnett to come up with the answer, and they needed to be reassured that they were in with a chance.

Garnett said, 'I want three small-scale maps covering the area between here and Dorset.'

A plan had begun to take shape in his mind. Provided they followed his instructions to the letter, they had at least a fifty-fifty chance of pulling it off, and in the circumstances no one could ask for more than that.

18

A WARM FRONT HAD moved in behind the cold, and the intermittent snow showers had given way to a fine persistent drizzle which was to their advantage. As they drove along the Mansfield Road they could see the pickets in the side streets. These small groups of infantrymen in soddened capes, who were clustered round their vehicles, heartened Garnett. Here and there he spotted the glow of a cigarette, and that too was a comfort because it was a sign that discipline was slack and the soldiers were fed up. There was nothing like a spot of rain to dull the wits of a sentry.

Nash said, 'I didn't expect them to deploy their pickets this early.'

'I'm glad they did,' said Garnett, 'it gives them more time in which to get thoroughly bored.'

'This is going to be a chancy business.'

Garnett glanced at Nash. 'We'll make it,' he said quietly.

'Vickers gave you the option of calling it off.'

'I don't recall him saying so.'

Nash lapsed into silence. He broke it as they turned into Upper Parliament Street. 'Maybe Dane won't be there,' he said desperately.

'She will.'

'You seem very sure all of a sudden.'

'I am. Vickers will see to it that she is. You know why?— because he will make sure that Dane knows she has a relative going on that train.' He smiled briefly. 'There are no flies on Vickers.' Garnett tapped Nash on the arm. 'Slow down and drop me off here,' he said.

Nash pulled into the kerb to let Garnett out. 'Have you got everything you need?' he asked.

Instinctively Garnett touched the flick knife in his hip pocket and then patted the black holster on his right hip and felt the reassuring presence of the Makarov automatic.

'You're making me jumpy,' he said. He closed the door of the Land-Rover and walked away.

The hotel looked dead. Heavy drapes covered the down-stairs windows, and he could see that the bar and dining room were closed because no lights were showing any-where. Garnett slipped past the entrance and made his way down to the basement garage.

It was too brightly lit for his liking, but the lights in the roof were out of his reach and he discovered that although there were two switches, it was a case of all on or all off. Edwards's Mini-van was parked in the far corner of the basement beside a Vauxhall Viva where, fortunately, it was partially in the shadow of one of the wide concrete pillars. Garnett crouched down behind the Viva.

A lot was going to depend on how good an actor he was. He had to put the fear of God into Edwards, make her believe that if necessary he would kill her in cold blood without a second thought, and that was something he knew he could never do.

At ten minutes to twelve, Edwards, wearing a green trench mac over her uniform, walked into the garage and made straight for the Mini. Garnett waited until she had started to unlock the car door and her back was turned to him. He came at her fast, and as he had anticipated, she whirled around to face him, her mouth opening. The scream never materialised because he landed a solid left jab in her stomach which winded her, and before she had a chance to recover, the flick knife was resting against her throat. The dark glasses which had concealed her black and swollen eye had been knocked off in the brief struggle and broken underfoot.

'Not a sound,' he whispered savagely, 'understand?' She nodded.

Garnett took a handkerchief out of his pocket and rolled it up into a wad. 'Open your mouth,' he said. 'Wider, I don't want you to choke.' Garnett pushed the gag into her mouth, and still holding the knife at her throat, removed his tie. 'Turn round,' he said curtly. 'Put your arms behind your back and lean forward over the bonnet.'

She hesitated long enough to convince him that she was working up her courage to do something stupid. A slight prick from the knife encouraged her to do as she was told. Garnett folded the flick knife and slipped it back into his hip pocket and then used his tie to lash both her arms above the elbow, drawing them together until her shoulder blades almost met.

Garnett opened the car door, forced Edwards inside and made her scramble across the driver's seat. He then raised the bonnet, checked the distributor and, satisfied, got inside the car.

'You're slipping,' he said, 'you used to remove the rotor arm.'

He reversed out of the parking slot in an L-turn and drove out of the garage. He covered the best part of two kilometres before he found a call box which was off the main thoroughfare.

Garnett said, 'I'm going to remove the gag, and God help you if you make trouble.' He fished the damp handkerchief out of her mouth.

Edwards almost choked on the saliva. 'You bastard,' she spluttered.

'I'm also vindictive,' he said softly, 'especially with people like you who get in my way, and I also believe in equality, so the fact that you're a woman won't help you. Now we are going to make a phone call to your office and you are going to do all the talking. You will tell the girl on duty that you are on your way to the station but have had a little ignition trouble which will take about ten minutes to fix, and then you will ask to speak to Littlewood. Can you remember all that?'

'I'm not stupid.'

'I hope you aren't, because when Littlewood comes on the line, you will tell him that Vallance is sending a special team down to the station to check it over, as Field Security

188

has been tipped off that a number of time bombs have been planted inside the main hall. You will also inform him that the N.C.O. in charge of the team is a Corporal Nash and that his sergeant will be arriving shortly with you. In the meantime Vallance requires Littlewood to give Nash every assistance. I want you to put it over to him word perfect.'

'Much good it will do you,' Edwards said scornfully.

'I shall be able to hear every word of the conversation, and if you try anything, I'll kill you.'

'I bet.'

'Don't,' he said icily, 'it's a stone cold certainty.' He rammed the point home by dragging her roughly out of the van and shoving her into the call box.

Garnett dialled the number, fed the money into the box, and held the phone out while she spoke into the mouthpiece. She didn't attempt any heroics, and apart from a certain tenseness in her voice, he couldn't have wished for a better performance. He hung up as soon as she had passed the message.

'You won't get away with it.'

'We'll see.'

Her eyes widened as she saw him cut off a length of telephone cable. 'What do you want with that?' she said anxiously.

'I want my tie back. Now turn round.' He laced her arms together and then removed his tie. 'Can't have Littlewood picking me up for being untidy,' he said cheerfully. He knotted the tie around his neck and then checked his wristwatch. 'We'll give it another five minutes.'

'I'm in no hurry.' Edwards moistened her lips. 'What's going to happen to me?'

'Nothing, as long as you're a good girl. You will be driving from now on, and we may be stopped by the militia pickets outside the station. I want you to realise that I have nothing to lose, and I don't intend to be taken prisoner. If the worst comes to the worst and the shooting starts, you will be in the way. I tell you this in case you should be tempted to call for help. Do I make myself clear?'

'Very. How do you expect me to drive with my arms tied behind my back?'

'Don't jump the gun, I haven't finished yet. When we arrive at the station, you will tell the girl on duty that she can leave. At all times you will stay close to me, for where I go, you go. You can refer to me as Sergeant Copping if names become necessary.'

'I see. Now will you tell me how I am expected to drive the Mini like this?'

'I'll release you in good time.' He checked his watch again. 'It's time to go,' he said.

It went better than he had any right to expect. The pickets were still getting into position around the station and they were much too busy sorting themselves out to bother with a stray military vehicle. As they swept into the station and parked in the covered yard, Garnett was relieved to see that Nash and the rest of the team were already there. There is an old adage which says that when in doubt run about and scream and shout. Nash was doing just that, and he had Littlewood's policemen running in circles. A stronger warrant officer wouldn't have stood for it, but Littlewood was a man who, all his life, had taken the easy way out, and he had no objection to a corporal in Field Security taking charge.

Martin, eyes blinking behind her thick glasses, hurried forward to meet them. Dull-witted, anxious to please, and above all scared to death of Edwards, she was the last person to suspect that anything was wrong.

'Gosh, I'm glad to see you Jo, I mean Sergeant,' she said. 'I was getting worried.'

Edwards tried her best. 'You had reason to be.'

The innuendo was lost on Martin. 'Shall I go now?' she said brightly. 'All the civilian staff have been sent home but it seems there is a bomb scare. Field Security is dealing with it.' She was halfway towards the exit and still moving. 'Is the Mini in the yard?' she said.

'It is,' Edwards said grimly. She watched Martin run towards the van and the anger showed in her face. 'The stupid cow,' she hissed, 'all she can think about is her bed and her belly.'

Garnett dug his nails into her wrist. 'Try anything like that again,' he whispered, 'and you won't have a brain left to do any thinking with.'

Keeping Edwards with him, Garnett went looking for Littlewood. He found him poking around inside the ticket collector's hut by the barrier, apparently engrossed in his self-appointed task.

Garnett said, 'How is everything going, Sergeant-Major?'

Littlewood turned to face him. Droopy lids half-concealed brown lacklustre eyes. 'Haven't found a thing yet.'

'How many of your men are helping with the search?'

'Four.'

'I understand all the station staff have already left?'

'Of course. Those were my orders.'

'Pity, we might want to question them.'

Littlewood grunted again. 'It's probably only a rumour. We haven't found anything.'

Garnett said, 'The tip came from the K.G.B. They don't think it's a rumour.'

'They can see a bomb under every bed in the country,' Littlewood said in disgust.

A voice from outside the station shouted something and a second or so later Keilly appeared in the archway gesticulating wildly to attract Nash's attention.

'I've found one,' he shouted.

'Where?' said Nash.

'In the taxi office. I forced the door and looked inside.'

Garnett smiled at Littlewood. 'I think we had better take a look,' he said.

The bomb, which Taylor had planted, was lying on the floor near the outside wall of the taxi office. Wrapped in brown paper, it resembled a parcel except that there was a pencil shaped object sticking out of one end.

Nash elbowed his way through the throng and knelt down beside it. He studied the parcel carefully and then looked up at Garnett. 'An acid time-pencil, Sergeant,' he said, 'looks like the work of an amateur. Shall I deal with it? I can't see any complications.'

'Are you sure of that?'

'There's no trembler wire attached to the pencil.'

'All right,' said Garnett, 'fix it, but get a move on. The special train is almost due and we don't want to alarm the Russians.' He turned to face Littlewood. 'I suggest you send your people off, we'll finish the search.' Littlewood seemed doubtful. 'Listen,' said Garnett, 'for all I know this could be a put-up job. The Soviets aren't too keen to take these political prisoners back to Russia. Our government has pressured them into it. We don't want to give them an excuse to call it off, and they may do so if they think things are going wrong.'

He spoke rapidly trying to convey a sense of urgency. A more alert man wouldn't have swallowed Garnett's story but Littlewood was slow on the uptake.

Littlewood said, 'I'll send my men away if you think it's for the best.'

'Good. Who's got the keys to the booking office?'

'I have.'

'Give them to me. We'll check it out.'

'It has already been looked over.'

'Then we will do it again,' Garnett said patiently.

Littlewood plainly didn't like it but he parted with the keys before ambling off to collect his men together.

Garnett waited until Littlewood was out of earshot and then said, 'As soon as the military police have cleared out, I want the kit in the Land-Rovers split between the R.T.O.'s hut and the booking office, and then Taylor and Allen can park the vehicles round the corner in Queen's Road.'

Nash said, 'Okay, but what about Dane? She's concealed in the back of Allen's vehicle.'

Garnett rubbed his chin. 'Wait until I have dealt with Littlewood,' he said, 'and then tell her to get inside the R.T.O.'s hut.'

Time was running against Garnett. The station clock showed 00: 30 hours and he could hear the noise of the diesel and the coaches clanking as the train crept into the platform. He grabbed Edwards and hustled her into the booking office and shouted to Littlewood to join them. Littlewood took his time. The expression on his face showed that, at long last, he had decided to put Garnett in his place. He wasn't going to have any jumped-up sergeant in Field Security ordering him around any longer, and he started to say as much as he came through the door, but he never finished his speech. Garnett clubbed him with the Makarov, cracking the barrel across his skull. Littlewood staggered towards Edwards, his arms outstretched trying to clutch on to her for support. Garnett hit him again, and as he went down, his hands pawed her breasts. Edwards cried out in disgust, stepped back out of his reach, dodged behind one of the large ticket machines and made a run for the door. Unfortunately for Edwards, Keilly and Nash were in the way.

Nash grabbed her. 'Stay around,' he said, 'the fun is only just beginning.'

Garnett put the Makarov back in its holster. 'Are we all set?' he said.

Nash said, 'We will be in another minute or two. Allen and Keilly will be with me in here, Dane and Taylor in the R.T.O.'s office. I've also given your Kalashnikov to Dane to look after.' Nash handed Garnett a mitre radio set. 'You will be needing this,' he said.

Garnett put the tiny set into his pocket. 'Look after Edwards, I want a quick word with Keilly outside.'

Keilly followed Garnett out of the office. 'What's the idea?' he said.

Garnett reached inside his breast pocket, pulled out a folded map and gave it to Keilly. 'You'll take the second car,' he said. 'Taylor and two of the prisoners will be going with you. You will make for 24, Westbury Road in Chard, and wait there until you get further instructions.'

'Are they expecting us?'

'They will be if Dinkmeyer has done his stuff. Now, if there are no more questions, let's get moving.'

Even as Keilly ducked back into the booking office, the first Russian soldier appeared at the top of the steps leading down to the platform.

It would have helped if Garnett had known the name of the Russian who was in command, but he didn't, and he wasn't going to ask Edwards because he felt there was a good chance that she would deliberately mislead him. He had never underestimated her intelligence but she had a lot more courage than he had bargained for.

The entrance hall was filled with milling infantrymen, but one man was attempting to bring some sort of order out of apparent chaos. The stars on his shoulder boards indicated that he was a lieutenant-colonel. He caught sight of Edwards and Garnett and a faint smile of recognition appeared on his face and died quickly to be replaced by a frown.

Out of the corner of his mouth, Garnett whispered, 'If the shooting starts you will get it first.'

He walked forward, saluted the Russian and said quickly, 'I'm representing Lieutenant Vallance, 464 F.S. Section, sir.'

The colonel looked at Edwards. 'Where is Sergeant-Major Littlewood?' he said.

'I'm afraid he's in trouble, sir,' Edwards said carefully.

'As a matter of fact,' said Garnett, 'he is under arrest, that's why I am here with Sergeant Edwards.'

'Arrest?'

'Yes, sir. We found a bomb had been planted in the station. The civilian staff and military police are being questioned now.'

'But not Sergeant Edwards?'

'No sir,' said Garnett, 'being a Field Security agent herself, she is above suspicion.'

'Naturally. I have your assurance that the station has been cleared of bombs, Sergeant?'

'Yes sir.'

'Good. And where can I find you if I should need you again?'

'Sergeant Edwards and I will be in the R.T.O.'s hut, sir.'

The Russian nodded, turned on his heel and walked away. Garnett let out his breath slowly, hardly daring to believe his luck. Gripping Edwards by the elbow, he steered her into the R.T.O.'s hut where Dane and Taylor were crouching out of sight under the office counter.

Garnett pushed Edwards into the corner and then sat down in a chair.

Glancing at Taylor, he said softly, 'Ernie, if this bitch opens her mouth you will turn your Kalashnikov on her.'

He checked his watch again. It showed 00:55 hours. The head of the convoy was due in another twenty minutes, and if things had gone well Rainbow's group should already be in position. Garnett wondered how they had made out.

Rainbow had crossed the railway below the bridge and, keeping to the shadow of the embankment, his group had worked its way towards the multi-storey car park. Including the drivers, they numbered fifteen and between them they carried two 84mm. Carl Gustavs, three 7.62mm. general purpose machine-guns, two 40mm. M79 grenade launchers, four self-loading rifles, one Sterling 9mm. sub-machine-gun and twenty Schermuly flares. The drivers were equipped with .38 police positives.

They had entered through one of the exit doors and had cautiously made their way up to the third deck keeping an eye out for the prowler guard. They hadn't met anyone but they had heard muffled voices coming from the deck above, and they had waited, taking cover behind the parked cars, and shortly afterwards, two men, carrying their rifles slung over their shoulders, had wandered past. They had discovered that there were only five men on the flat roof above the filling station and the two prowler guards to deal with when the time came, and Garnett had gone up in Rainbow's estimation. Any man who could figure the odds as accurately as Garnett had done obviously knew what he was doing.

Garnett saw the Russian look up at the station clock and then shake his head angrily. He knew how the colonel felt because he was just as impatient to see the convoy arrive. He watched the minute hand jerk forward on to 01:17, and as he resigned himself to another sixty long seconds, he heard the sound of vehicles on the move.

'They're on the way,' he whispered. Dane started to get up and he had to move quickly to stop her.

She was on edge like the rest and Garnett knew that they would perform like machines, killing without thought, because he had placed them in a situation where only the quick would survive. They were an oddly assorted group; Keilly, the model-railway enthusiast, Taylor the thief, Allen the former policeman whose wife had been raped before she was murdered, and Nash the enigma, but for all that they were a makeshift team they would take some stopping.

The first packet, wheels drumming on the tarmac, surged into the yard and noisily came to a halt. Air brakes hissed, doors banged, and then, to the accompaniment of raised, hectoring voices, the first batch of prisoners stumbled through the archway and passed between the double file of Russian soldiers who were drawn up to form a narrow path leading from the station entrance to the ticket barrier. With their hands tied in front of them, their thin boiler suits hanging from skinny frames, and their shaven heads downcast, the prisoners made a demoralising sight. They were an unending, sluggish stream of broken men and women.

There were thirty-two soldiers inside the hall standing an arm's width apart from each other, and Garnett couldn't see how they could fire on them without hitting some of the prisoners unless there was a gap in the stream, and then they could start at the front and work their way back, knocking the infantrymen off one at a time like so many skittles. And the longer they waited, the more confident Edwards seemed to become. There was a look of assurance on her face now, as though she sensed that any delay put them in even greater hazard.

'You've had it,' she hissed.

Garnett was prepared to concede that she had a point, especially when the colonel chose to approach the hut. She did her best to attract his attention with a bright eager smile but his eyes were on Garnett.

'Does this not make you feel ashamed?' he said.

Garnett said, 'Why should it, sir?'

'Because they are your people.'

'They are our enemies too.'

The Russian said, 'Of course, I was forgetting myself. Tell me, Sergeant, why does this country of yours have such a unique talent for making a hash of even the most simple task. This convoy, for instance, is running ten minutes late.'

'Perhaps the prisoners aren't moving quickly enough, sir?'

'Should we beat them with the butts of our rifles, Sergeant?'

'You must do as you think fit, sir,' Garnett said woodenly.

The Russian glanced at Edwards and then frowned. 'You have a black eye,' he said sharply, 'I did not notice it before. How did it happen?'

Garnett's right hand came to rest lightly on the

pistol holster and Taylor jabbed the muzzle of his Kalashnikov against her thigh.

Edwards cleared her throat and in a hesitant voice said,
'It was an accident, sir, I tripped over the carpet.'

The Russian turned his back on them. 'I see the flow has
stopped,' he said. He checked his watch yet again and then
walked away from them.

The last of the prisoners shuffled through the barrier
and disappeared from sight. The two lines of guards remained in the hall.

'Any minute now,' Garnett said quietly. 'When I give
the word, come up and start shooting from right to left,
okay?'

Dane said, 'Don't you want me to identify the prisoners
before we open fire?'

'Not with that bloody colonel looking our way.' He
heard the engine throb of the B.T.R. 6op, counted slowly
up to thirty and then shouted, 'Now.'

Dane came up fast, pulled the butt of the A.K. 47 into her
shoulder, and let go with one aimed shot after another as
she swept down the line of sentries. A split second later,
Keilly, Nash and Allen opened up from the opposite side
of the hall. Garnett grabbed the Kalashnikov, which was
standing in the corner of the hut where Dane had left it
for him, rushed out of the hut and came face to face with
three militiamen who appeared in the archway opposite
him. He threw himself flat, thumbed the catch on to full
automatic and let go with a long burst which caught all
three men with a spread of shot between the waist and
thigh. The super velocity rounds bored through their
frames shattering bone and sinew, and flung them bodily
through the air like chaff before the wind. Scrambling to
his feet, Garnett dashed to take cover behind the bookstall
from where he could enfilade the ticket barrier.

The sudden crash of gunfire in the confined space of
the R.T.O.'s hut had so unnerved Taylor that, without
meaning to, his finger had jerked on the trigger, and the
rifle which had been pointing upwards at an angle of forty-
five degrees had bucked in his hands as the round went off.
The bullet took Edwards in the abdomen, was deflected by
her spinal column and travelled upwards to burst out

197

behind her left shoulder blade. Thrown back against the wall under the impact, she then pitched forward on to her face and lay still. Taylor screamed, threw the rifle to one side and ran out of the hut. He pounded through the archway into the station yard and ran slap into the side of a B.T.R. 6op. In a blind panic, he turned to his left and raced towards Queen's Road presenting his back to the machine-gunner in the armoured personnel carrier. Like a man who has suddenly seen a hare popping up under his feet, the machine-gunner was slow to react. He got off a short burst, saw that the 12.7 M.G. was firing high and depressed it. The belt contained armour-piercing rounds designed to penetrate twenty millimetres of high tensiled steel. Three such rounds hitting Taylor virtually cut him in half.

Caught in a murderous crossfire by the concealed marksmen, and lacking any cover, those Russian infantrymen who survived the initial wave of fire, rushed through the archway and spilled out into the station yard. A trigger-happy militiaman, mistaking their identity, opened fire on them with his sub-machine-gun.

Garnett quickly edged his way round the bookstall until he had a clear view of the archway through which the prisoners had been driven into the main hall. Two figures dressed in dungarees and handcuffed together were lying in an untidy heap some ten metres from his position. Neither man showed any sign of life and it seemed to Garnett that they must have remained frozen in the entrance while the hail of fire crept towards them, and then finally cut them down. There was no sign of the remaining four V.I.P.s and it dawned on him that they were probably still inside the prison van.

Garnett was only partially right. All six men were already out of the van and in the process of entering the station when the firing broke out. The warder in charge of this small party was quick to react. Using his truncheon, he drove the four prisoners back into the van and was locking the rear doors just as Garnett crawled round the far side of the bookstall to get a better view. Garnett rolled over on to his right side, roughly aligned the A.K. 47 and squeezed off three single shots in rapid order. All three shots missed their mark and the warder ducked out of sight behind the van. Large slivers of wood were gouged out of the bookstall above Garnett's head as the 12.7 M.G. on the B.T.R. 60p halted in rear of the van opened up on him and sent him scrambling back to cover. Seconds later the small convoy began to pull out of the station yard. It wasn't destined to get very far.

Rainbow had spent an anxious hour and a quarter waiting for the shooting to start. The constant drizzle had encouraged the picket on the exposed parking area above the filling station to seek shelter, and at the same time it seemed that the prowler guard had suddenly become a popular duty. Before the first packet had arrived there were four men prowling the car park and the remaining three were standing in the lee of the office block where it was difficult to see them clearly. Had the prowler sentries been the least bit inquisitive the group would have been discovered, but instead, they had preferred to find a quiet spot where they could have a smoke without being seen.

When the time came to move in, Rainbow had to send four riflemen after the prowler sentries who were above and behind him, while the rest of his party went for the reduced picket on the open parking space. Engaged in a running fight, it took longer and cost him more men to secure the building than he had anticipated, but some eight minutes after the shooting started inside the station Rainbow was able to engage the militia picket at the junction of Queen's Road and Arkwright Street with machine-gun fire.

Wildly gyrating Schermuly flares whooshed up into the night sky and, bathing the front of the station in an eerie light, picked out the B.T.R. 60p which was nosing its way out of the yard. A quick accurate shot from an 84mm. Carl Gustav hit the armoured personnel carrier behind the driver's compartment and brought the eight-wheeled monster to a grinding halt, effectively blocking the exit.

Garnett heard the thunderclap of the 84mm. Carl Gustav striking the B.T.R. 60p above the sparodic rifle fire inside the station. He crawled forward and saw that the last armoured personnel carrier in the small convoy was right opposite the entrance. As soon as he showed his head, the riflemen in the back of the open-topped B.T.R. 60p opened fire, and once more he was forced to scuttle back to safety. It seemed that they had reached an impasse. The prison van was trapped inside the station yard but it was impossible to reach it. He saw Keilly's head and shoulders appear above the level of the window in the booking office and Garnett waved frantically to attract his attention. Keilly caught sight of him, pointed to the shambles inside the main hall and raised one hand expressively as if to say, what do we do now. Garnett mimed pulling the pin out before lobbing the grenade, and then held up three fingers and tapped his chest.

It took Keilly a minute or two to catch on to the fact that Garnett wanted him to pass three grenades across. Keilly momentarily disappeared from sight, then bobbed up again and, with a slicing motion like a man playing quoits, he sent the grenades flying across to Garnett. Two of the grenades fell close enough for Garnett to reach them without crawling out into the open. All he had to do now was to lob a grenade into the B.T.R. 60p in such a way that the occupants didn't have time enough to pick it up and throw it back at him. He pulled the pin out, allowed the safety lever to fly off, and with the 36 grenade fizzing in his hand, counted two before leaning round the corner of the book-stall and heaving the grenade in an underarm lob. The grenade struck the side of the armoured personnel carrier, bounced off it and exploded in the gutter. He tried again and this time the lob was perfect. In the confined space of the B.T.R. 60p the lethal effect of the grenade was devastating. As he ran out into the yard, Garnett signalled Keilly to follow him with more grenades.

Allen was conducting his own private war. As soon as the main hall had been cleared, he left the booking office and, carrying a full sandbag of 36 grenades, went through the left luggage department and took up a new position forward of the ticket barrier. He posted himself at an oblique angle to the steps leading down to the platform and methodically rolled one grenade after another down the staircase. It was an effective way of buying time, but he knew that it wouldn't be long before the Russians crossed the railway lines and forced their way up the other staircase at the far end of the concourse. He would have liked some help, but Nash was full of excuses why he shouldn't go with him.

The militiamen in the leading B.T.R. 6op who had not been killed or wounded by the Carl Gustav, lost no time in abandoning their dead vehicle. Unable to move forward because of the withering machine-gun fire coming from the multi-storey car park, they had run backwards towards the police van, and in so doing they had to cross the open space commanded by the R.T.O.'s hut. Dane saw them out of the corner of her eye, and turning, shot them down one by one like so many clay pigeons.

There was one B.T.R. 6op between Garnett and the prison van. With Keilly keeping their heads down with short bursts from his A.K. 47, Garnett managed to get close enough to drop a grenade into the armoured personnel carrier. Moving down on either side of the police van, Garnett and Keilly now tried to execute a pincer movement on the driver and guard up front. A split second before Garnett shot the guard, the driver saw Keilly in his wing mirror and, holding the .38 Lee Enfield in his left hand, he pointed the pistol over his right shoulder and squeezed the trigger. The bullet entered Keilly's mouth. The driver turned in triumph to face his companion and the flash from Garnett's rifle burnt his face and then his head blew apart.

Garnett dragged the guard's body out on to the pavement and rolled it over. He found the keys on a chain attached by a leather thong to a button on the waistband of the trousers, and snapping it off, he ran to the back of the van, unlocked the door and yelled to the prisoners to come out. He took the mitre radio set out of his pocket, erected the aerial and told Rainbow to come and get them.

Rainbow tore across the flat open roof and vaulted the barrier into the third deck of the multi-storey car park where the three drivers were sitting behind the wheels of their Zephyrs with engines idling.

He waved his arms wildly and shouted, 'Go, go, go.'

Engines snarling, the cars pulled out one after the other and corkscrewed down to the entrance. The leading car smashed through the barrier doing thirty k.p.h. It was doing sixty when it hit the main road.

And on Garnett's signal they came running—Dane and Nash but not Allen. Allen wasn't looking in the right direction and he was too preoccupied to hear Garnett yelling and cursing at him. When it dawned on him that the others had pulled out, he had left it too late. He was halfway across the main hall when the first Russian got to the top of the stairs. He was a bare five metres from the archway and freedom when a burst of fire cut the legs from under him.

And now they were out in the open running hard for the cars, and they could hear the grenade launchers popping away at the bridge, and the sky was criss-crossed with red tracer bullets arching into the town centre and the flares were turning it into a Brock's Benefit.

Garnett sent Nash and two prisoners away in the first car, waved the second car out of it, and left Dane to put the remaining two V.I.P.s into the last car while he looked round for Allen. He hung on for one agonising minute, and then giving Allen up for lost, he leapt in beside the driver.

'Melton Mowbray,' he shouted, 'I'll guide you from there.' The driver banged the gear lever into first, gunned the engine and let in the clutch. The tyres spun and then bit. They made ninety k.p.h. down Arkwright Street and held that speed all the way to Trent Bridge. The man drove the Zephyr hard, and giving nothing away at the curving intersection, he lost control as they came into the final bend. He hit the brakes savagely, slammed the gear stick into third and yelled out to hang on. They did their best but they were still doing thirty when they hit the kerb and mounted the pavement, and they were flung about like so much washing in a machine. They travelled along the pavement for about twenty metres and then bounced back into the road. The driver played it cool as though nothing had happened. He moved back into top, pressed the pedal flat and the speedometer began to climb up to 160 k.p.h.

They were out of Nottingham now and moving along the A606, and the first hurdle was behind them because Pugh had denied the security forces the information they needed to be able to deploy road blocks close in. Garnett wondered how much longer Pugh could give them.

Pugh gave them all the breathing space they needed. He had slipped away from the Mansfield Road and tucked himself deep in the woods below Bestwood Lodge where it was unlikely that any of the mobile patrols would think of looking for him. He allowed both nets to function normally until he heard the first contact report from the troops ambushed at the station. He then kept his pressel switch on transmit and blotted out every other station on the net. He repeated this procedure on the rear link and on the guard net as soon as that came into use, and as a result, the security forces were forced to rely on the civil telephone network which made rapid redeployment virtually impossible. He kept up this jamming until 02:30, when he went off the air, abandoned his vehicle and struck out on his own. He had to make the safe house in Derby, where his wife and children were waiting for him, before daylight. If he failed, he knew a place where he could lie up until the following night.

They were south of the M1 now and were moving down the B4036 to Banbury and their chances were getting better all the time. They had made a detour around every town of consequence in order to minimise the possibility of being seen by routine police patrols and this precaution paid off. Denied any information about their movements, the security forces were faced with the task of mounting a nation-wide blocking operation and that took time to set up. They hit the freezing fog after they had by-passed Devizes and they were forced to crawl the rest of the way to Seend. Garnett didn't give a damn. He knew they were going to make it.

19

BLACKWELL AND SCHONFIELD WERE bickering again and there was nothing unusual about that. Whoever had handcuffed them together had had a wry sense of humour. Their political beliefs and interests were so far apart that they couldn't even agree on what time of day it was without going to arbitration. There was nothing like a confined subterranean existence for highlighting the flaws in a man's character, and after living in close proximity with them for over five weeks, Garnett was beginning to think that springing Blackwell and Schonfield hadn't been worth the sacrifice and effort.

He sat there on a camp stool beneath the air vent looking up at the empty fireplace above his head anxiously watching the daylight fading and wondering why Dane was late. They had planned that she was to spend the night in London after meeting Dinkmeyer at the Palladium and then catch a train back to Westbury first thing in the morning. Garnett had expected her home by three o'clock at the latest. He had never been reduced to biting his fingernails before but he had caught the habit now.

He told himself that the first part of the plan had gone off without a hitch. After all, the theatre tickets had arrived addressed to the Reverend Cadbury, which meant that Dinkmeyer was still operating freely, because if he had been taken, and under questioning had betrayed the contact arrangements, Special Branch would have simply swooped on the hide. There would have been little point in doing anything else once they had Dinkmeyer and knew where to find the rest.

The trouble was that Garnett had no clear idea of what was really going on in the world outside the hide. His sources of information were the press and the radio, and both of these media were censored. Outwardly, nothing had changed. The same faces were still in the Cabinet as far as he knew. The Nottingham business had been played down and distorted so that anyone who didn't know the inside story, might be forgiven for thinking that the security forces had won a significant victory. There was no mention of the attempted take-over of the nuclear ammunition depot at Clumber, nor of any other major anti-government demonstrations which Vickers had hinted at. There was just one crumb of comfort—Jane Powell, social worker, was no longer being featured in the *Daily Express*.

It was possible that Dane had been roped in by a snap check on Paddington Station. It had happened to her once before and it could happen again if the security forces were being stirred up by the Russians or the puppet government or by a combination of both. They had waited five weeks before making a move, and yesterday morning it had seemed safe enough, but now it came home to Garnett that he had gambled with Dane's life on the strength of an editor spiking a cartoon strip. His stomach took a nose dive, and suddenly he couldn't stand being cooped up in the hide a moment longer. Standing on the camp chair, he pushed the grate forward and heaved himself up and over the lip of the flagstone into the lounge.

Schonfield said reprovingly, 'I thought you said we had to stay underground, or don't the rules apply to you?'

'With him,' said Blackwell, 'it's a case of don't do as I do, do as I say. He's just a bloody fascist.'

Blackwell looked to Papworth for support, but the man from Nottingham merely lay on his camp bed looking up at the earthen roof and ignored him. Five weeks of Blackwell and Schonfield for company was more than enough for any man. Ten years of hacking a cab had made Papworth a good judge of character and he thought that both men were largely wind and piss.

Blackwell said, 'Haven't you got anything to say for yourself?'

Papworth raised his head. 'Yes,' he said, 'why don't you shut up?'

Blackwell's jaw dropped. 'I was merely pointing out that Garnett is taking an unnecessary risk.'

'It didn't sound like that to me.' Papworth rolled over on to his right side turning his back on them.

The snub got through to Blackwell. He threw up his hands in disgust, sat down on his bed, and picking up a greasy pack of cards, started playing patience. The protest movement fizzled out.

The shadows were beginning to creep across the room now, and there was a thin belt of mist over the fields beyond the kitchen garden which hung in the air like cigarette smoke in a crowded room. Garnett turned away from the window and sat down in an armchair. He needed something to occupy his mind but the shelves on either side of the fireplace didn't hold any light reading, and he wasn't in the mood to delve into any profound theological work.

A sudden rattle brought him to his feet hoping that it was Dane, and then he realised that it was only the boy from the newsagent pushing the *Western Evening Mail* through the letter box. He listened for Cadbury's footsteps in the hall, but the house was silent, and then he remembered that Cadbury wouldn't be at home because Thursday was Mothers' Union and Choir Practice day, the one following on the heels of the other. He went out into the hall and picked up the paper from the mat.

The headlines announced a government re-shuffle. The country had got itself a new Minister of Internal Security. According to the caption under the photograph his name was Troughton, but Garnett knew him better as Moxham. There was no hint of a post for Seagrave but Warner had been eased into the job of Inspector-General of Police. It was the beginning, not the end—the game of musical chairs had only just started, and he wondered if Vickers was playing the piano in the background. He wandered back into the lounge, flopped into a chair and lit a cigarette. Moxham had come from nowhere, a member of the Resistance one minute, a Cabinet Minister the next. That was some deal and not what Garnett had been led to believe. He had expected a faceless nominee who could be manipulated.

A key slipped into the lock, a knee banged against a sticking door, heels clattered in the hall and then the door to the lounge opened and Dane came into the room.

'Oh, hullo,' she said gaily, 'I thought you would be in the hole with the others.'

The long anxious hours waiting on her return and worrying about her had frayed his nerves, and the casual, almost flippant greeting didn't go down well. Seeing her standing there with a shopping bag and overnight suitcase and looking as if she had just returned from a shopping spree was the final straw.

'What the hell kept you?' he snapped.

'I waited for the right train,' she said coolly.

'What do you mean, the right train? Were the others too dirty for you?'

Dane slipped out of her coat and draped it over the back of a chair. 'I deliberately caught the four-thirty from Paddington because it is always crowded and I feel safer in a crowd. I thought you would approve.'

She sat down in the armchair facing him and crossed one silken leg over the other. As always, her legs were a great distraction.

Garnett stubbed out his cigarette. 'I was worried about you,' he said, 'I didn't mean to bite your head off.'

'Do you like my dress?'

'What?'

'Harrods—I treated myself to it.'

'You look marvellous.'

She smiled. 'You didn't even notice.'

'No,' he said slowly, 'I didn't.'

'Dinkmeyer sends his regards.'

'And what else?'

'He said to tell you that everything is going smoothly. He's buying a guest house in Charmouth.'

'Where's that?'

'A small place on the coast between Bridport and Lyme

Regis. The purchase should be completed in three weeks, and then he plans to collect us just before Easter.'

'How?'

'In a fifteen-seater coach. He's putting it around that his first guests of the season are a party of physically handicapped people. There will be a couple of Red Cross workers to make it look right. I shall be one of them.'

'Who's the other?'

'Some girl he's recruited. He will pick up Nash's party first and then call for us. He also said he didn't want you to bring an arsenal with you. Those were his words, not mine.'

'Three weeks you said?'

'To complete purchase. We actually move from here three weeks this coming Monday.' She stood up and started to move past him. 'Ah, well,' she said, 'I suppose I had better change into something more suitable if we are going back into that hole again.' He reached out, caught her by the hand and pulled her down on to his lap. He tilted her head and kissed her on the mouth.

'What am I going to do about you, Katy Forbes-Windsor?' he said.

'You're fishing again,' she murmured. 'Forget Katy, she never existed.'

'There is a man called Schonfield who says she did.'

She brushed her lips against his. 'Why worry what he says, he's not important.'

'Why won't you tell me?'

'Because there's nothing to tell, and because I prefer to be Valerie Dane.' She started to get up. 'Now I really will have to change.'

'There's no hurry.'

'No?'

'No.'

She ran a finger down his nose. 'You've got a wicked look in your eyes, David.'

'I've got a wicked thought too.'

'I know,' she said. Garnett moved his hand from her thigh.

'It's all right,' she said, 'I'm not complaining.'

20

GARNETT SAT IN THE bay window of their bedroom where
he had a commanding view of the wooden bridge which
spanned the mouth of the river before it spilled out into
the sea. It was hard to tell where the overgrown and
neglected garden ended and the river began, for the rushes
on its marshy banks had forced their way through the rotten
wooden fence. He searched the landscape carefully from
left to right through foreground, middle distance and background, noting the caravan site which he could just see to
his left, the open field dotted with bracken which led up to
the hill overlooking Chideock in the centre, and, on his
extreme right, the narrow lane which petered out when it
reached the shore. The sea and sky were a matching grey,
and on that cold afternoon, only a boy and his dog were out
walking along the shore.

They had come a long way for this view and the cost of
the journey had not been cheap. He had lost three men
and gained two in Papworth and Brading, the other driver
from Nottingham. Measured against what they had
achieved he supposed it was a fair exchange, but he wished
Keilly had made it. Over the years he had developed a
sixth sense for picking out the survivors, and right from
the start he had known that Nash would come through
without a scratch. He had an uneasy feeling that, for reasons

of his own, Nash was about to pull the carpet out from under their feet.

Dane said, 'God, this room is cold.'

'Try putting the electric fire on.'

'It already is. The house is damp.' She burrowed into her coat and shivered. 'Did you see what happened when Dinkmeyer lit the fire in the lounge? There was more smoke in the room than went up the chimney.'

'Look on the bright side,' said Garnett, 'providing the weather doesn't get any worse, you won't have to sleep the night here. A rough sea could be nasty for an inflatable dinghy—they might have trouble making the correct landfall.'

'I would have thought that the weather was the least of our problems.'

Garnett turned to face her. 'Something on your mind, love?' he said.

'Nash.'

'Oh?'

'I don't trust him, David.'

'Neither do I, and I don't intend to let him out of our sight once it gets dark.'

'Perhaps he has already contacted the police?'

'I doubt it. He had no idea where he was going when Dinkmeyer collected him, and I didn't notice anyone following the coach.'

'I wish I shared your optimism.'

'Look, when it gets dark, Dinkmeyer and I will go down to the beach and put the marker lights out. We'll have Papworth watching the lane in case Nash manages to slip past you and tries to make contact with the local police.'

'I'm not armed and Nash is.'

Garnett took the Makarov 9mm. automatic out of his hip pocket and handed it to her butt first. 'You are now,' he said. Dane frowned. 'It's all right, it's not loaded.'

'I've heard that one before.'

She took the automatic, removed the magazine from the butt, eased the slide back to make sure the chamber was empty, and then replaced the magazine, fed a round up into the breech and put the catch on safe.

'It's not like you to ignore safety regulations,' she said.

'I'm slipping.'

'I hope not. I think enough mistakes have been made already.'

'We're here, aren't we?'

'Oh yes. Did you ever stop to think why?'

'That's obvious, isn't it? We are here to ensure that Blackwell, Schonfield, Newman and Gordon make it to the other side.'

'To form a government in exile, if I remember correctly?'

'You do,' said Garnett.

'And do you really believe that those four pathetic creatures will make much of an impression on the Americans, I mean, apart from arousing their natural sympathy? Do you see them being able to influence the United States government to do anything which isn't in their interest?'

Garnett said, 'After six years in a prison camp, I don't think I would win a personality contest either. What do you expect, Moses fresh from the Mount? They are the best we've got.'

'Who says so?'

'Vickers.'

'Think again.'

'All right, Moxham.' Garnett sat down on the bed. 'You think that Moxham has used us for his own ends?'

Dane said, 'I don't know, but he has come out of it rather well, and I can't say I have noticed any significant change in government policy as a result.'

'Vickers would never sell us short.'

'No?'

'No. Whatever else he may be, Vickers isn't bent, and if he didn't like the way this new government eventually runs the country, he would do something about it.'

'Would you?'

'We're talking about Vickers,' said Garnett. 'You and I are taking a trip on that boat.'

'You seem very sure.'

'You can bet your life on it.'

Dane shivered. 'I wish you hadn't said that,' she said quietly.

'You're getting superstitious, love.'

'Perhaps I am.' She got up from the bed and walked to the door.

'Going somewhere?' he asked.

'I'm going to make a pot of tea.' She looked back and smiled at him. 'I need to do something,' she said.

The door closed behind her and he resumed his vigil on the shore. Grey sea and grey sky merged into one as the light failed. The beach was deserted. He hoped it would stay that way.

The weather was being kind to them. An overcast hid the prying moon, the wind had moderated, and the sea, although choppy, was less hostile. Garnett and Dinkmeyer were lying up in a natural hollow at the foot of the cliffs within twenty metres of the beach. The saplings, which struggled for survival in the sludge formed by the landslip, offered them little protection against the fine drizzle, but at least they screened the landing markers from either flank. They calculated that the red and green marker lamps were high enough up the landslip to be seen by the dinghy when it was within 300 metres of the beach, and they proposed to use a medium-range transistorised U.H.F. set to guide the boat to within visual distance of the lamps. The signal from the U.H.F. set would register as a pointer on the display panel of the dinghy's Nav-Aid and would enable the helmsman to correct the drift and heading of the craft. This guidance system was simple and reliable but was vulnerable to intercept and jamming if there was a coastal patrol boat in the immediate area. The traffic on the ship to shore waveband suggested that the coastguard was inactive. Garnett drew close to Dinkmeyer. 'How much longer?' he whispered.

'We'll start transmitting in another five minutes.'

'Good.'

Dinkmeyer smiled. 'Nervous?'

'Yes, I don't like this bay. It's too close to Lyme Regis and Bridport.'

'So it's not ideal. I had to find a place which wasn't too isolated where we would have stood out like a sore thumb, nor one so populated that we would have had a hard time trying to avoid everybody. This was the best I could find.'

'I suppose so.'

Dinkmeyer said, 'Listen, we'll make it if our security remains tight.'

'And that,' thought Garnett, 'brings us round to Nash.' He hoped Dane was keeping a watchful eye on him.

The fire in the lounge had long since died, and they sat there in the dark huddled close to one another, for the warmth was beginning to go out of the room. Dane had elected to sit by the door because it was the best vantage point for keeping a tight rein on Nash. Short of diving head first through the window, he would have to come past her to get out of the room. Schonfield and Blackwell were arguing in low key and someone was snoring, and although she couldn't be certain, Dane had an idea it was Brading, the other driver, who was lying on the floor next to Nash. Nash, she sensed, was wide awake and watching her like a hawk, and instinctively her fingers curled round the butt of the Makarov in her coat pocket.

A slight scuffing alerted her, but after a few seconds she relaxed because the noise had stopped, and she assumed it was merely someone trying to get into a more comfortable position on the hard floor. And then a floorboard creaked and a tall figure loomed over her. She scrambled to her feet and saw that it was Nash.

'Where do you think you are going?' she hissed.

Nash said quietly, 'To the lavatory. Any objection?'

'I'll come with you.'

'I'm a big boy now.'

'I'll still come with you.'

'All right,' he said affably, 'maybe it will give you a thrill.'

He stepped out into the hall and Dane followed him and put on the light.

'Leave the lavatory door open,' she said coldly.

'Why don't you come inside and hold it for me?'

Dane took the Makarov out of her coat pocket and pointed it at him. 'Don't make a big thing out of it,' she said softly.

Nash shrugged his shoulders. 'Why should I care if you and your boy friend can't trust me?'

He left the door ajar and she could see him standing

there, and presently she heard him urinating. He zipped up his flies and then, as he flushed the toilet, he slammed the door and tripped the latch with his free hand.

Caught off guard, Dane squeezed the trigger with the safety catch still on. That split second made all the difference. She heard Nash jump up on to the lavatory seat, and shielded now by the dividing wall, he was out of the line of fire and she knew it would not take him any time at all to open the window and slip out. She ran back to the lounge, kicked the door open and snapped on the lights.

'Everybody up,' she shouted. They were slow to come to life.

'For God's sake, Brading,' she snapped, 'get these people down to the beach. Nash is loose.' She didn't wait to see what happened.

Dane thought Nash would avoid using the lane which Papworth was watching, and would try instead to work his way round to the town by the river at the back of the house. She ran into the kitchen, unlocked the door and started after him. Hurdling had never been her strong point. She took the fence at the bottom of the garden awkwardly, and the tip of her right foot failed to clear it. She went face first into the rushes and, falling on her chest, winded herself. She lost another few precious seconds picking herself up again.

There was no sign of Nash, but Dane was convinced that she was on his track, and although her first instinct was to run on blindly, she stood there listening intently, and in doing so, heard his footfalls in the distance and got a bearing on him. Dane could beat most men over eight hundred metres and Nash was no exception. She felt sure she was closing the gap between them with every stride, and when she heard him break through the hedge surrounding the caravan site, she knew that whatever time Nash had gained when she had fallen, had now been lost in the effort of forcing his way through the privet. She followed the path he had made through the hedge and caught her first glimpse of him. She was about thirty metres away when Nash turned and fired a snap shot. In the dark, out of breath and at that range, the average shot would have stood an even chance of missing a barn door.

and Nash was only an average shot with a pistol. Dane swerved to her left and, jinking every few paces, made a dash to get behind the nearest caravan. Nash took potshots at her all the way. He made a lot of noise and splintered the woodwork, and then suddenly he didn't have a target to shoot at any more, and he figured that Dane was going to work her way down the line of caravans, and they were parked so close together that his chances of hitting her when she appeared in the gaps between the trailers were about zero.

Nash didn't hesitate, he turned and ran for the site entrance one hundred and fifty metres away. He ran as he had never run before, head thrown back, legs pumping, arms flailing and he was damn glad they had turned off the street lights at midnight because otherwise he would have been a sitting duck. And the dark, friendly street was only thirty metres away now, and then she started shooting, and he knew from the flash that she was nearly level with him and he wasn't going to make it.

Nash changed direction abruptly and ducked behind the end caravan on his right. He was out of condition and breathing heavily, and it was some minutes before he got his second wind. He peered round the side of the trailer and fired three shots in quick succession. He was shooting blind but it didn't matter.

At the top of his voice, he shouted, 'It's a stand off. You hear me, whore? It's a stand off, you'll have to show yourself if you want to nail me.'

He fired again and the pistol shots boomed like a cannon. Nash was no fool. He sought to make as much noise as he could because he was relying on disturbing the neighbourhood in the hope that someone, somewhere, would telephone the police.

The faint popping sound reached Garnett's ears and the hairs stood up on his neck.

He gripped Dinkmeyer's shoulder, 'What the hell was that?'

Dinkmeyer said, 'I don't know, maybe it's the outboard on the dinghy misfiring.' He stood up. 'It must be that,' he said excitedly, 'I can see it, I can see it.'

'You're wrong, nobody would be fool enough to use an outboard as close in as this.'

Dinkmeyer said, 'For Christ's sake, are you blind? Look, it's there. Jesus, it's there.'

There were other sounds now. The pattering of urgent feet driving towards them and a breathless voice shouting, 'Garnett, Garnett, where the fuck are you?'

Garnett walked towards them. 'I'm here,' he said quietly, 'and so is the dinghy.'

And then they were milling round him while Dinkmeyer was running forward to meet the landing party, and in the sea of faces, Garnett couldn't find Dane, and he took Brading by the shoulders and shook him like a rag doll.

'Where's Dane?' he shouted. 'Where the hell is Dane?'

Brading caught his breath. 'She went after Nash,' he said. 'Where?'

'Towards the caravan site, I think.'

'You think?' Garnett echoed hoarsely. 'Can't you do better than that?' His hands were around Brading's throat and he wanted to choke the life out of him. 'You bastard,' he hissed, 'you let her go alone.'

A thick arm went around Garnett's neck and a knee was planted in the small of his back and he felt himself being drawn like a bow and he lost his grip on Brading's throat. Dinkmeyer threw him sideways, and falling, he buried his face in the wet sand.

Dinkmeyer said harshly, 'All right, cool it.' He turned to face the others. 'You people can get into the dinghy, and don't rush it, there's no need to panic.'

They filed away unhurriedly with the exception of Sue Dinkmeyer who remained at her stepfather's side.

Garnett scrambled to his feet. 'I've got to find Dane,' he said desperately.

'Sure you have, I'll give you five minutes.' Dinkmeyer reached inside his jacket pocket and brought out a .45 Remington Rand automatic. 'You'll be needing this,' he said.

Garnett snatched the weapon out of his hand and started running. He was not alone. Papworth too was running, past rows of silent, dark houses, guided by the distant sound of voices punctuated by gunfire. As he approached the

T-junction ahead, he heard the bleep of a police siren and instinctively he slowed to a jog trot.

Nash heard the siren and knew for certain that the car was coming in his direction.

'You hear that, whore,' he shouted, 'they are coming for you. Did you think we'd let you slip away to be a thorn in our flesh for ever? We used you, Dane, we used you and Garnett and that madman Vickers.'

Dane stood there watching the headlights drawing closer, and then the car stopped and the lights went out. She heard the doors open and presently a spot came on and a long finger of light probed the darkness, and a metallic voice through an amplifier said, 'Come on out.'

The light fastened on her and the glare blinded her eyes.

She put up her left hand to shield her face. 'Not me,' she shouted, 'the man you want is over to your left.'

Nash screamed, 'Don't listen to the bitch.'

The spot swung away from Dane and turned in his direction and the side glare of the light picked out the three policemen. Dane raised her right arm, gripped the wrist with her left hand to steady it, and taking a deliberate aim, pumped out shot after shot, emptying the magazine as she traversed from left to right. The drumbeat of each explosion merged with the next to make a continuous roll. The three figures danced like animated puppets and then collapsed. The spotlight was now pointing up at the sky.

Garnett crashed through the hedge and raced up the path between the two lines of caravans. He could see Dane standing in the open and he tried to shout a warning but Nash got in first, and the impact of the bullet spun Dane round like a top before she fell on to her face. Nash turned to face Garnett, took aim and confidently squeezed the trigger. The hammer went forward but there was nothing in the chamber, and he stared disbelievingly at the useless gun in his hand, and when he looked up, Garnett was only ten paces from him. He raised his arms in surrender but the gesture was meaningless. A giant hammer struck him in the chest and slammed his body against the caravan, and as he pitched forward, the same hammer struck him again, and even as the sound of cannon reached his ears, the blood gushed out of his mouth. Garnett, his eyes fixed on Dane, ran past him without a second glance.

Garnett flung himself down beside Dane, and dropping the automatic, gently turned her over on to her back. The bullet had gone in under her left shoulder and he could see no sign of an exit wound. Her face looked pinched and drawn and the breath rasped in her throat, and Garnett thought, 'Christ, I hope it's not in her lung.'

A voice said, 'Is she badly hurt?'

Garnett looked up and saw Papworth standing over him. He swallowed, and with difficulty said, 'She needs a doctor.'

'They'll have a surgeon on the boat.'

'Yes,' he said dully, 'they are bound to have one on a Hunter class sub.'

Garnett picked up the automatic and stuffed it into his coat pocket and then gathered Dane in his arms. He carried her gently, trying not to jolt her, but the ground was uneven and sometimes he couldn't help stumbling.

Papworth said, 'Let me help.'

Garnett caught his breath and said, 'No, you run on and tell Dinkmeyer to wait for us.'

And with each step his legs felt as though they were turning to jelly, and he longed to stop and rest. He kept to the river bank, and it seemed to him that the shore was an agonising light year away, and the blood was pounding in his head, and his eyes were swimming, and then he felt his feet sinking into the wet sand and he said, 'Not much farther, love.'

And Dane whispered, 'Don't worry about me, I won't die on you.' And then Dinkmeyer came to meet them.

They laid her carefully in the dinghy beside Sue, and Garnett was barely conscious of the cold sea lapping around his legs because the naval officer was saying to Dinkmeyer, 'I told you there wasn't enough room for everyone. Now that we have a wounded girl on our hands, two of you will have to stay behind.'

Papworth said, 'I'll stay with Garnett. I was never keen to be a sailor anyway.'

And someone said, 'We'll come back for you.'

And in a daze, Garnett found himself helping Papworth to shove the dinghy out to sea, and then the water was up round his waist, and as the naval officer started the outboard engine, he thought he heard Dane say, 'For God's sake, don't leave me, David,' but he couldn't be sure.

And they stood there staring after the dinghy until it was out of sight, and they both knew that it would never return to pick them up.

Garnett said dully, 'She will be all right, won't she?'

'Of course she will. That girl has a will of iron.' Papworth looked up and down the beach. 'We'd better get out of here,' he said.

'What?'

'You want to see that girl of yours again, don't you?'

'Of course I do.'

Papworth said, 'You won't if we hang around here much longer.'

21

GARNETT CAUGHT A GLIMPSE of his reflection in the mirror, and the face staring back at him was lined and drawn, and for a moment he thought he was looking at a stranger, and depressed by what he saw, he turned away quickly. The view from the bedroom window, which looked out over the park, was more cheerful. In the distance, two girls in white tennis skirts and blouses were playing on one of the hard courts; a man in shirtsleeves was weeding his allotment by the railway line; and five small boys appeared to be disputing the umpire's decision that one of their number had been run out. A couple, arm in arm, strolled slowly round the park with a mongrel dog trotting at their heels. On that warm, lazy, June evening, it was easy to believe that peace had come to stay.

Garnett drew the curtains, switched on the portable television set and sat down on the bed. He felt inside his jacket pocket and brought out a tin of tobacco and a slim packet of filter papers and began to roll a cigarette. The fingers which held the filter paper were ingrained with oil and the nails were black with grease. He struck a match and lit the cigarette and the filter paper burned quickly until it reached the tobacco. He had not yet mastered the technique of rolling his own cigarettes.

Moxham's face appeared on the tiny screen, and he was plumper than when Garnett had last seen him. He was nursing a pipe in his hands and this had become part of his image. During the few months in which he had been in office, Moxham had managed to project himself as the trusted father figure, and he had borrowed Roosevelt's gimmick of regular fireside talks with some success. It was part of his programme of keeping the nation informed, and to make sure that his message had got across, he invariably repeated the major points in the final minutes of his address. He had got to the point where he was summing up the theme of his talk.

'And what does this non-aggression pact with Russia mean to us?' Moxham said. 'It means that, in exchange for a guarantee that our island will not be used as a military base for future operations against the continent of Europe, the Russians have agreed to withdraw all—and I repeat all —of their military personnel who were stationed in Great Britain as a result of the armistice which terminated hostilities between our two countries seven long years ago. In addition, we, and the Russians, have agreed to station a number of observer teams on the continent of Europe to ensure that France, the Low Countries and Western Germany observe the conditions of strict neutrality which will lead to the Russians withdrawing all their forces behind a line east of the River Elbe. I think you will agree that this has been a remarkable achievement on the part of your government.' A serious expression replaced the faint smile on Moxham's face. 'And yet,' he said sternly, 'there are some people in this great country of ours who believe that this non-aggression pact is a betrayal of everything we stand for. These misguided people argue that we should take advantage of the conflict between the USSR and the Chinese Peoples republic to re-unite the continent of Europe, and by that they mean the re-unification of Germany.'

Moxham paused to let the spectre of a re-united Germany sink in. 'These same people have branded your government as a malevolent, evil dictatorship. Those are their words, not mine, nor, I believe, yours. Where now, they shout, is your promise of free elections?' Moxham smiled and shook his head sadly. 'The promise is there in our manifesto, and perhaps, since they still seem to be in some doubt, I had better repeat what I said three months ago when I became

Prime Minister. I said then, this is a caretaker government, a government whose mandate has not been obtained through the ballot box. We are a divided nation, facing a complete breakdown of law and order. For nearly seven years, our people have been intimidated and, in some cases, murdered. Those who were killed were not all traitors, or fifth columnists or sympathisers—many of them were decent people like you and I, intent on minding their own business. This climate of senseless violence serves no purpose and has no place in our way of life, and until it is curbed, an election held in such circumstances would not be free. Your government, with your support, will take whatever measures are considered necessary to bring these evil forces under control, and when fear no longer walks our streets, we shall not hesitate to seek a fresh mandate from the country.'

The faint smile was replaced by a look of concern. 'As a first step to restoring law and order, we offered an amnesty to members of the former Resistance movement. We asked nothing more than that they hand in their arms at the nearest police station. I must confess that the response to this gesture was very disappointing. Far from accepting that we had achieved our aim, these dangerous men have continued to harry the forces of law and order, and regrettably the Privy Council has therefore been forced to adopt sterner measures to deal with this threat. These measures, which I must emphasise, will not in any way affect the lives of ordinary citizens, include the detention of subversive elements under Section 18b of the Defence of the Realm Act. No one regrets taking this step more than I do, but it is an essential prerequisite to holding the free elections which all of us desire.'

The picture faded out and Garnett switched off the set. He noticed that the cigarette between his fingers had burnt out and he dropped the stub into the ashtray on the bedside table. It was, Garnett thought, pretty much where he had come in. Moxham would hold his so-called free elections all right, but only when he was convinced he would win.

He stood up and drew back the curtains and the evening sun filled the room. 'Moxham,' he said aloud, 'our Lord Protector, our new Cromwell.' He supposed he should feel bitter because there was very little to show for all the years of hardship and danger—one repressive regime had been replaced by another of a slightly different persuasion—but, in fact, he no longer cared. His hopes were pinned on a money belt round his waist, an American passport under the floorboards, and a plan.

And the plan was simple. One morning, very soon now, he would walk out of the house, go to the tailor's shop in the High Street, pick up the suit he had ordered and then find a quiet place in which to change his clothes. On that morning he would buy a suitcase, because a suitcase gave one an air of respectability, and then he would take the tube to Knightsbridge, walk down Cromwell Road, enter the West London Air Terminal and get a return ticket to Belfast. He wouldn't be using the return half, for he intended to slip across the border and make for Dublin, where he planned to stay at the Gresham until he judged the time was ripe to show his American passport to the reception staff before asking them to book him on the next Pan Am flight to New York. After that, finding Dane wouldn't be too difficult.

Garnett looked at his cheap wristwatch and swore. Time had a habit of running away from him, and time was money, and he needed every penny he could lay his hands on, and that meant working day and night. By day, work was a factory in Acton; by night, it was helping out behind the bar in the Working Men's Club. He slipped out of his old jacket, unbuttoned his shirt and pulled it off over his head.

The front doorbell started to ring insistently, and when it stopped, he heard muffled voices in the hall, and that was unusual because few people called at the house at that hour. He tiptoed across the room and opened the door carefully. A man's voice said, 'Are you sure you can't recognise this man, madam?'

And his landlady said, 'Well, I'm not really sure, but it could be our Mr. Grainger.'

Garnett closed the door and ran to the window, and there in the park below he saw two uniformed policemen looking up at the house. He ducked out of sight but he needn't have bothered. He knew that, even if he managed to give them the slip, there was no safe place he could run to and no Vickers to bail him out because they had lost touch with one another.

And now everything was an automatic reflex. He bent down, flipped the lino to one side and raised the loose floorboard under the bed. Groping in the cavity, he pushed aside the useless passport which had cost him so much, and found instead the oilskin packet. He whipped it out and unwrapped it with shaking hands. Racing against time, he fed five rounds into the magazine and slapped it home into the butt. He pulled back the slide and a soft-nosed .45 bullet slid up into the chamber of the Remington Rand.

He crouched there in the room, listening for the heavy tread of feet on the staircase, watching and waiting for the door knob to turn, and for a long time he had had a premonition it would end like this, in a small back room, without Dane and alone.